ROGUE

HAND

Juwon Abiola

Dad, this one is for you. Hope I made you proud.

Chapter One: A Cold Hand

Rogue Hand Syndrome, Grey Harrow mused. *That's what they called it.*

Sitting on his chair by the hearth in his barricaded apartment—cigarette in-between his right fingers, smoke blowing out of his mouth and nostril—with nothing on except a pair of Calvin Klein black-button boxer shorts, he watched the flames dance and crackle and pop. To his left was his window, it was dark outside, and he could now see the condensation crawling down the glass like long fingernails. Winter was here; ready to make its home in London for the next three months, smothering everything with a metallic sheen and frost. He glanced to his right, eyeing his front door, checking to make sure the metallic bolts were still firmly locked in place. They were. He was alone and safe, just the way he wanted.

Rogue Hand Syndrome.

He shook his head. Who would've thought that the "Rogue" part of those words would be befitting of his current predicament?

Grey stared down at his left arm; it was all black with golden screws and mechanical parts and wirings. He was fully machine from the fingers up until his shoulder blade on that arm. His right arm, on the other hand, was fully organic and human, although, it was tattooed to the brim, just like all his other body parts, including his face, which had a small sign of the cross etched on his left cheekbone. He was a rogue, all right, a good-for-nothing, freak of nature to the rest of the city, but he didn't care. That arm might have made him an alien, but it had also saved his life.

Grey vaguely remembered the biomedical engineers and neuroscientists telling him that, as well as losing his left arm in the accident, he had also suffered a severe brain injury, which required surgery, and quite possibly led to the likely diagnosis of the condition itself. He'd also been told that the attachment of the mechanical arm had helped to stop severe blood loss and made it possible to send electrical impulses throughout his body to keep him alive during the surgery, and after, while comatose.

Still staring down at his mechanical left arm, Grey clenched and unclenched the fingers . . . nothing, all feeling in that hand had gone cold.

They did this to you, a voice whispered. Grey's eyes searched the room. *They took everything away from you, robbed you of an arm, and left you for dead.* That voice again, alluding to Grey's former gang. They were known as the Foxhound Syndicate. They ruled over most of London City's criminal underworld, ruling with power and fear and extorting many.

Grey scrunched his face to try and block out the voice. Ever since the accident and the attachment of the mechanical arm, it's like there were now two people living inside his head, like the dual nature of his arm—one organic and one machine.

He stood up from his chair, holding his right hand against his head as he shouted, 'Shut up, get out of my head . . . it was an accident.' His left hand began to take on a life of its own; it wrapped its cold, mechanical fingers around his throat, squeezing his windpipe. Grey's cigarette dropped out from his fingers, onto the dark-oak, hardwood floor, and he gasped for air.

You fool. They did this to you, can't you see it? The voice kept coming. *Why are you so blind? Those you called friends did this to you, made you into this freak that you see before you. Are you just going to sit back and let them get away with it?*

The machine fingers unclenched from around Grey's neck, he dropped to the ground, onto all fours, drawing in deep breaths, his eyes burned in their sockets, his vision now hazy and, as he slowly wiped his forehead with the back of his right hand, he felt his dark skin moistened with cold sweat.

You and I are one, Grey. I am the rational part of your mind, I compel you to see and comprehend, to do things you otherwise wouldn't. Like what happened to you six months ago. I am here to help you, to guide you, on your path for vengeance. Let's work together, what do you say?

Grey, still panting on the ground, reluctantly nodded his head. What was he supposed to do? The voice was coming from his own mind, his dual mind, and it had just attacked him. Grey was its hostage and he had to abide.

Gathering his bearings, Grey slowly stood back to his feet. 'So . . . so what do we intend to do?' he found himself asking out loud. Had he gone crazy?

First, you should head back to the facility that worked on you and gave you this arm, the voice said. *You should find out who exactly ordered the operation. The procedure must've cost a fortune. Someone wanted you alive for a reason.*

Grey headed for his bedroom trying to process the things his mind was telling him. Can it be true? Can it be that those he once considered his close friends—his brotherhood clan—had tried to kill him? Could the accident have really been a façade? Or was this just paranoia? He tried to shake the thought off, and just as he did, there was a loud *knock* and then a *bang* at his front door. His heart quickened. *Who could it be?* He'd never had any visitors in his apartment since being discharged following the operation. No one knew about this place, not even his so-called syndicate.

He heard his metallic door slamming wide open with a booming thud; its bolts crashing down with a jingle. Not wanting to wait around like a sitting duck, to see who or what might happen, Grey jolted up and fled into his bedroom, shutting the door behind him. He put his ear against the door, hearing footsteps and then murmurings. He turned, his heart thumping in his chest, picked up his black cargo pants that lay on the ground and thrust his legs into them. He yanked up his grey T-shirt—also sprawled on the ground—shoving his arms through it. With trembling fingers he finished off his attire by tying his grey scarf around his neck, shrugging on his black overcoat, and then stepping into his black converse trainers. He made sure to grab his holo-phone from his top shelf, and, of course, his last pack of cigarettes from his nightstand. He took out one from the pack, putting it behind his right ear and the rest in his overcoat pocket. He then lifted his bed, pulled out a 9mm semi-auto pistol, detached the magazine slightly to check if it was still loaded—it was—and then slapped it back in, setting the safety on and holstering the gun behind his back on his waist. He then turned to his window, and as he pulled it opened, a cold breeze hit his skin, sending chills down his spine. He breathed deeply, white puffy mist emanating out from his mouth in the cold, night air.

He jumped out of his five-storey building window just as they burst through into his bedroom, his mechanical left hand reaching for the side of the building as he fell.

Chapter Two: A Warm Heart

Grey landed with a thud, crouched, feet first, on the concrete streets of the Kings Cross apartment blocks, his converses kicking up small dust from the soft impact. His mechanical left hand clinging to the side of the building, like sharp claws, had cushioned his fall from his five-storey window.

Standing to his full height and looking back over his shoulder, up at his bedroom window, Grey saw four men wearing balaclavas, dressed in black suits and white shirts, one of them pointing at him, another one readying a weapon of some sort. Grey thought it looked like a rocket launcher, but in hindsight, he thought not. They wouldn't risk causing a commotion, drawing unwanted attention to them, killing innocent people in the process. Or would they? That was one question he wasn't waiting around to get an answer to.

He bolted, running full speed ahead toward an alleyway, breaking their line of sight. He continued on, occasionally glancing over his shoulder to see if they were following him, his heart racing, his breathing coming out in haggard, short bursts.

Finally, after running for what seemed like an eternity, Grey made it to Kings Cross station. Neon coloured lights filled the streets; holograms of half-naked whores filled the top of buildings and skies. He looked around; it was still busy despite it being really late in the night. That's Kings Cross for you, wouldn't expect anything less from a revived Red-light district. The nightlife was one of the highlights. The smell was another. The street stank of alcohol, weed, and urine. *Typical,* he thought. People were coming and going all around him; it made him paranoid as if one of those four men in balaclavas would appear out of nowhere and grab him.

He walked to the front of the station and watched as men and women came out of a Nightclub just opposite the station: drunk, kissing, and caressing one and other.

He needed a place to lay low for the night, to evade his pursuers, and to refocus his mind. There was only one place he knew where he could do that. And that was Bethany Rose's place.

She was working late that night. Well, speaking of Red-light districts, she worked late most nights. Bethany Rose worked as a bartender and occasionally as an escort, and that's how Grey and her first met. The two met at a point in time in Grey's life where he felt vulnerable and alone. He was just getting ready to get his life back on track and to leave the life of crime and the Foxhound Syndicate behind him. One day he felt the need to let off some steam and so he had called a local escort agency in the city asking for one of their best girls—this girl so happened to be the girl he'd end up sweeping off her feet and would later fall head over heels for. They dined together that night, both of them instantly feeling the spark and liking each other's vibe. One thing led to another, and Bethany ended up in Grey's bed. Not once, not twice, but many more times. The first time involved payment as would be expected, her agent would demand their fees from the initial hook-up, but soon after they were seeing each other on a more regular mutual basis. They were basically dating—and not counting Bethany's part-time job—they were dating exclusively, seeing only each other, although neither would admit nor say out loud that they were actually in a relationship now.

He took out his holo-phone and dialled her number over the holographic keyboard, putting the phone to his ear as he began to cross the street. Her phone rang, but no answer as wheel-less hovering cars with neon lights emitting from their base zoomed and zipped past him—about 30 miles an hour—from both directions. His eyes were still shifting every which way, cautious of the four men that had broken into his apartment as he made his way safely to the front of the Nightclub where Bethany worked.

She's probably busy, he thought.

He put his holo-phone back into his overcoat pocket and leaned against the wall to the side of the Nightclub just by the entrance. Two colossal bouncers; one Black and one Asian stood by the entrance. Grey was a tall man himself, roughly six foot one, but these two bouncers towered over him. He guessed they were about six foot four/five—give or take. Grey continued to survey his surroundings outside the Nightclub, the name above the Nightclub read: STARLIGHT, as men and women hung around aimlessly; some of them— chatting, some of them—snorting something white that resembled cocaine round the side of the building, and some of them downing alcohol like there was no tomorrow, and those that couldn't handle their drinks ended up vomiting whatever content they'd had for dinner out on to the ground, some even passing out and lying in it.

Grey shook his head, half-disgusted, half-grinning to himself. He remembered the days he'd been like that. His younger years in the Foxhound Syndicate were filled with many unproductive nights. But who could blame them? They were young, and they still had time.

One of the main reasons he cut back on his alcohol and drug habits was due to his Rogue Hand Syndrome. Use of those substances aggravated his symptoms further and made it even harder for him to be in control of his left hand.

He reached for the cigarette behind his ear, House music blasted out from the Starlight Nightclub. He reached into his pocket and fumbled around, realising he had no lighter to light his cigarette. He walked toward a mismatched couple—a pencil-thin of a man and a brute of a woman—who seemed to be besotted with one and other, they gave him a lighter and he lit his cigarette, returning back to post up on the wall of the Starlight Nightclub. As he took a drag on his cigarette, throwing back his head and blowing out smoke high into the air, Grey noticed the four men in balaclavas in the distance now, loitering by the station across the road from him. He thought to call the feds, but then he decided not to. Involving the police in their disputes was the one thing members of the Foxhound Syndicate never did. Even though he was no longer part of the Syndicate, Grey knew it could all blow up in his face if he did. After all, in their eyes, a black man like him—especially one with a mechanical limb—was a criminal, and he'd had his fair share of run-ins with them in the past. He had to handle this on his own, but he needed help.

He threw his cigarette to the ground, stepping on it with the toe of his converse trainer to put it out, and then made his way to the entrance of the Starlight Nightclub. When he got there, the Asian bouncer stretched forth a hand and stopped him. 'Hold it there, mate. We're closed for the night. No more allowed in.'

'I'm just here to see someone,' Grey said. 'Bethany Rose. She works here. I won't be long.' He looked back over his shoulder, anxiously.

'Still, I'm sorry, mate. I can't let you in.' The Asian Bouncer said.

Grey turned back to face the Asian bouncer. He noticed the bouncer wasn't looking him in the eye or really paying him any attention when he had said that. Frustrated, Grey tried to barge his way through, but both bouncers grabbed him by the arms and threw him backward, Grey collapsed to the ground, grimacing.

His peripheral vision filled with onlookers and Grey felt a slight humiliation eat at his pride. Without hesitation, he stood back to his feet, dusted himself off, and clenched his mechanical hand into a fist as he approached the two bouncers. Grey saw them glance down at his left hand, though he wore an overcoat, from the wrist down they could see a black and gold mechanism of a hand. They instantly recoiled, putting up their palms. 'Hey, hey, no offence man, we were just doing our job, we didn't mean to disrespect you.' The Asian bouncer said, turning to look at the black bouncer next to him. 'Isn't that right, Joe?' Joe nodded, his head moving up and down in quick succession.

Grey couldn't care less, raising his mechanical hand, he saw the fear in their eyes, and relishing that moment, his Rogue Hand came to life and grabbed the Asian bouncer by the throat, squeezing his windpipe. The bouncer choked and gurgled. The other bouncer—Joe—watched in shock and seemed paralysed by fear. Some of the crowd of people (mostly females) outside the Starlight Nightclub started screaming, and Grey, wary of the four men still in pursuit of him, just across the road, at the station, raised his voice.

'I didn't want any trouble,' he said through gritted teeth, 'Just wanted to go in peacefully, wasn't planning on staying long either; just wanted to see Bethany and come right back out, that was it, but you wouldn't let me, would you?' The Asian bouncer struggled for air, his hands tapping away at Grey's mechanical arm, trying to break his grip, but to no avail.

'Hey, hey, buddy, let's calm down,' Joe said, 'you can go in, okay? Just let him go, you hear me?'

He heard him, all right, but his temper—the one thing that has plagued him since his Foxhound days—was getting the better of him, clouding his judgement. And though his Rogue Hand had taken the initiative, in that moment of frustration they were in total agreement. But now in his mind, he'd had enough, but the Rogue Hand didn't want to relent. He used his other hand, placing it on the Rogue Hand, trying his best to restrain it. *Enough. Stop this. Stop this now. Now is not the time to draw attention to ourselves.* The Rogue Hand didn't budge, it continued to squeeze the throat of the Asian bouncer; his eyes bulging out of their sockets, his teeth clenched and protruding out of his mouth, his hands flailing, as his life was slowly draining away.

'GREY!' a distinctive voice that Grey knew shouted. The Rogue Hand immediately released the Asian bouncer from its grasp, the colossal bouncer falling to the ground with a thunderous thud, Joe—the other bouncer—dropping to his knees to tend to him.

Grey didn't know whether he was still alive or not, but seeing Bethany Rose, calmed his soul. She was a sight for sore eyes. Her delicate fair skin was glowing, her cheeks, rosy, her beautiful, crystal, blue eyes glistening in the star covered night skies, and her luscious, brown hair flowing past her shoulders, reaching down to her bosom. She looked as gorgeous as Grey had last seen her.

A true English Rose.

Looking at her now, then up just behind her, he caught a glimpse of the four men in balaclavas about to cross the street toward them, their special guns—drawn and pointed. The crowd of people gathered outside the Starlight Nightclub who had already been screaming due to Grey's earlier attack on the bouncer, panicked further when they saw the four men. The crowd promptly dispersed in a reckless fashion, pushing and shoving one and other, scared for their lives, as police sirens slowly echoed in the distance. Using the crowd as cover, Grey quickly took Bethany by the hand and brushed past them, trying his best to avoid the sightline of the four men, all the while Joe—the black bouncer—continued to attend to his Asian colleague on the ground by the entrance of the Starlight Nightclub.

Grey turned west with Bethany, both of them picking up speed with their walk.

'What the fuck is going on, Grey?' she asked, glancing over her shoulder, the wind blowing her hair across her face. 'Who are those men, and why the hell were you choking our security guard?'

'Not now, Beth,' he breathed, looking straight ahead. 'Not now.' They were jogging now, hover cars blaring past them.

'Where are we going?'

'Your place.'

                                        ***

'Now,' Bethany asked. 'Will you tell me what the entire ruckus was about?' Bethany asked.

They were now in her apartment, a few minutes' walk from King's Cross, in Euston. She was undressing from her work clothes as she spoke, Grey helping her to unzip her black skirt from the back, pulling down on the zip; she removed her legs from the skirt and slowly took off her white shirt. She was now in her black Victoria's Secret underwear as Grey blindly threw the skirt onto the king-size bed behind them. He stared at her underwear and chuckled in his mind. They were the ones he had bought her. She drew her hair back from her face and tied it into a ponytail with a small green band, and as she slowly turned around to look him in the eye, he gently pressed his lips against her faintly freckled shoulder.

'It was nothing, Beth. Honestly. Just some lowlifes, you know—the usual late-night antics.' He lied. He didn't want her to worry.

'Yeah, but what *you* were doing didn't look like nothing, Grey. You were choking the life out of Tanwar. Let's hope you didn't injure him, he's a really good bouncer, as is Joe.'

'I'm sure he'll be fine.' He hoped so, given the amount of force he used with his mechanical arm. 'It's kind of funny when you think about it: for a six-foot-four giant, he sure didn't put up much of a fight.' Grey chuckled. Bethany gave him a stern look of disapproval and smacked him on the arm. Grey winced playfully and then pulled her close by the waist, staring at her full, rosy, pink lips. They were so kissable, so plump and sweet like ripe cherries—or strawberries—and Grey couldn't wait to taste them.

She looked at him a long while, silent. 'I've missed you,' she whispered. Then she frowned; her eyes and hand lingering on his mechanical arm for a while, her fingers sketching invisible words. She had been one of the only few people that stuck around and was there for him after his accident. This he knew very well and seeing him part man and part machine seemed to worry her.

'You've got to look after yourself better,' she said. 'You've got to stop getting yourself into this sort of situation.'

Grey's jaw tightened, staring down at the ground. 'I know. I will.'

Bethany slapped his shoulder and started for her kitchen, Grey loving the view from here and adoring how good she looked in those Victoria's Secret. God. She was a dream. 'Come on. I'll make us something to eat. You must be starving. I know I am.'

'What're we having?' he shouted and followed after her.

'What do you think?'

'I don't know.'

'Guess,' she said as he entered the kitchen behind her. 'It's your favourite.'

'You?'

She laughed, and Grey thought it was the purest sound he'd ever heard.

'Chinese, silly.'

So Bethany whipped up a nice meal of special fried rice and chicken, and they ate and inhaled each other's company for a long while.

Afterward, they took it in turns to head into the shower—Grey doing the honour of going in first.

By the time he'd got dressed again and Bethany strode out the bathroom with a white towel wrapped around her body, Grey was reaching for his 9mm semi-auto pistol that was tucked in the belt of his cargo pants. He took it out and placed it on her writing desk. Bethany saw but wasn't startled. Grey knew she understood the type of life he had been living, previously. And he knew that she knew he was trying to change his ways. After all, he had left the Foxhound Syndicate, even though his last job—which was supposed to have set him up for retirement—left him in a coma (and with only one good arm to boot) instead.

Bethany ambled over, hips swaying between that soft towel, slowly reached over and took Grey's clothes off again: She tugged his overcoat, pulled his grey T-shirt, and then yanked his cargo pants like a wild animal, his infinite tattoos coming into full view.

'You're not going anywhere tonight,' she said. 'You're staying put, and that's that.'

15

Grey nodded. He wasn't arguing with that: a beautiful woman and a warm setting? Hell, yes. Besides, that was what he genuinely wanted . . . and needed right now.

She softly ran her thumb across his left cheekbone.

'I love all your tattoos,' she said, her eyes lighting up. 'But I *love* this one the most.'

'Which one is that?'

'The sign of the cross on your left cheekbone. Makes me feel safe knowing Christ is watching over us.'

Grey smiled and she lightly squeezed his face, then, as she leaned in, Grey felt time stop, electricity coursing through his veins as their lips met for the first time that night. Oh, how he'd missed the taste of those sultry lips . . .

He traced his fingers up her back, unfurled her towel, and her bare breasts swelled and dangled out like water inside a balloon. With her bare body now exposed; he embraced her slim figure tightly. Their bodies were so close; he could feel the touch of her breath on his chest. Hot warm breath on his skin as he stared down at the skin-on-skin contact he shared with her.

Grey felt a trickle of cool saliva on his shoulder, where her lips had been a moment ago, and he pulled away from her momentarily, studying and admiring her figure.

He liked her body. She'd worked on it every so often at the gym, and it paid off, her curvy physique and peachy bum vouching for that.

His eyes and hands darted around her pale flesh. He liked it—flushed, creamy, covered in a smattering of freckles, and soft. And then he felt the heat between her legs. Entering her, the sensation was magnetic, pulling him inward, swallowing him whole. The contrast of her ivory slipping and sliding and beating wet against his ebony was a work of art in its own right—a masterpiece—one that only the truly gifted artist could paint. And with each stroke, she groaned, louder and louder, the smell of her breath so intoxicating, and Grey felt their bodies colliding, dissolving into each other, becoming one, becoming whole, and leaving nothing of them behind. Like forbidden fruit, they were tempted, and they ate each other.

But most of all, Grey liked her heart.

It was warm, charitable, un-judgemental, forgiving, and Grey felt no condemnation whenever he was around her.

With Bethany now lying in his arms, curled against his chest with her eyes closed— fast asleep—it was blissful.

And basking in the tranquillity of her silence, he waited the night out, hidden from those who were out there in the shadowy night, plotting to get him.

Chapter Three: An Elusive Man

Jasper Barnes was working late in his office in Knightsbridge when he received an anonymous call about an attack on a bouncer at the Starlight Nightclub in Kings Cross by an individual who seemed to possess a robotic hand.

'Is this Agent Jasper Barnes?' the caller asked.

'Speaking,' Jasper said. 'Who's this?'

'Never mind who this is. There's been a crime here in Kings Cross by the Starlight Nightclub. A bouncer was attacked and is in critical condition. You should get down here as soon as possible.'

'Why? Can't the police deal with it? What makes *this* incident my problem?'

'Military-grade Robotics was spotted being used.'

'Wait, what? By whom?'

'I wouldn't be calling you if I knew,' the anonymous caller said. 'Just get down here and investigate.'

'How did you get my number—' the person hung up.

Jasper stared at his holo-phone a while, confused by it all, and then shoved it in his pocket. He pushed off the edge of his mahogany desk with his hands and stood, his chair scraping and then tumbling to the marble ground behind him with a *clang* as he quickly sifted through the mountains of holo-documents that hovered over his desk, like ghosts, trying to organise them well into holo-folders, as best he could so that when he returned tomorrow morning it wouldn't be so excruciating for him to resume proceedings. His hands moved swiftly, fingers swiping at floating holo-screens before him. He ended it off by typing on the holo-keyboards that felt as if he were touching empty air and nothing at all.

The future. That was what this was. Everything advanced. Everything digital now. It has been this way for almost twenty years now. And it was only ever going to evolve. Jasper liked it that way. Technology was the future, but only in the right hands, he thought. Not everyone should have the privilege. In the hands of the wrong person, it could be detrimental.

When he was done, he stifled a yawned with his fist, pausing to look down at his holo-watch. It was 11:15 pm. What was he still doing here rummaging through heaps and piles of holo-work when he could be home with his wife and son?

That's right; he was putting in overtime—hard work he hoped would pay off for him and his family in the long run. He had been part of the top-secret Robotics Enforcement Administration (REA) for three years now, starting off as a Rookie Agent fresh out of University when he was just twenty-three years of age. And now, he'd earned the title *Agent* (without the *Rookie* attached to it anymore). He figured if he kept at it, he could one day reach *Special Agent* or *Intelligence Analyst*.

Still, being an *Agent* had given him more autonomy to do as he pleased; he along with his partner—Martin Silas—have helped the REA work—in secret—to clamp down on the illegal use of dangerous Robotics around London and the surrounding cities ever since it was outlawed. Dangerous meaning: Military-grade Robotics. The kind that can do some serious damage to a military force.

Jasper walked over to his office window, a mere two feet away, his office the size of a restroom in an airplane. He stared out of it, looking at the soft, star-covered, night skies, the bustling nightlife of West London, the hovering cars shooting past at illegal, breakneck speed, and he wondered whether this city could ever truly be free of Robotics—especially when you have criminal organisations scheming and vying for their illicit use.

He took it all in for a few seconds, then proceeded to exit his office, manoeuvring and squeezing his broad frame through the tiny room, reaching the door; he grabbed his overcoat on the hook behind it, put it on, and turned the knob. *It's only for a little while longer,* he told himself. *Soon I'll be out of this hamster cage and into a bigger office.*

When he got out of his office, he headed straight for Martin Silas's office; he too had been working late. They worked as a team, and whenever one worked late, the other did also. Not that it was compulsory for either of them to, but it was more out of loyalty to one and other than anything else. Jasper was Martin's right hand, and Martin his. They were a team, a team that had been together since they first joined the Administration. They had been lodged collectively by their bosses, forced to work as partners. They initially didn't do well, but the two quickly built a strong bond and before you knew it, wherever Jasper was, Martin was there also, always looking out for each other and dismantling illegal Robotic operations.

He knocked on Martin's office door, and after hearing shuffling and then footsteps from behind the door, it opened.

'Hey, Jasper, what's happening?' Martin said, his hand leaning against the door frame.

'We've got to go, Martin,' Jasper said, his eyes wandering over Martin's shoulder to inside his office. It was slightly bigger than Jasper's, but even that seemed like an exaggeration. Maybe it was because Martin was much smaller and much more compact than Jasper that it made his office look bigger?

He looked back at Martin. 'I just got an anonymous call about illegal use of Military-grade Robotics in the Kings Cross Red-light district area by the Starlight Nightclub.'

'Right, I see,' Martin said, scratching the crown of his close-cropped, ginger hair. 'Let me just get my jacket, excuse me.' Jasper took a step back and Martin shut the door slightly so he could reach for his jacket behind the door. He put the jacket on and then pulled the door back, sliding out the room, shutting the door behind him.

They made their way down the REA building. It was quiet tonight, no one else around, the proximity sensitivity lights coming on briefly as Jasper and Martin walked through on to the outside.

'You got your protection, yeah?' Martin said to Jasper as they made their way to the parking lot.

Jasper patted the side of his overcoat by his hip. 'Of course. No protection—no action for me. Sorry not sorry, if you know what I mean.' Jasper winked at Martin.

Martin shook his head, smiling. He reached inside his jacket pocket, pulled out a set of hover car keys, and threw it Jasper. 'You're driving.'

***

When they reached Kings Cross Red-light district area, it was in complete disarray.

Jasper and Martin stepped out of the hover car and people immediately swarmed them, running in all directions as police chased and arrested half-naked people: butts and breasts galore, body parts hanging out as if they were inside a brothel. Then an unholy stench immediately hit Jasper; it attacked his sinuses, seared his throat, and caused him to have an instant headache. He scrunched his face and looked to his left, toward a darkened, neon-lit alleyway, to where the odour emanated from. There a man stood, urinating, against a wall near where they had parked—a man that looked as if he hadn't washed for decades, his hair was a mess and his clothes had many incisions on it, small blood was smeared on his clothes also, which clearly wasn't his, and Jasper wondered where he could have got it from.

He then felt a hand on his shoulder, turning he saw Martin, 'Let's go,' he pointed toward the Starlight Nightclub. 'Over there.'

Jasper gave the smelly alleyway and the man in the vicinity one last suspicious glance as they made their way over to the nightclub. They brushed past many people along the way, it was busy, almost 12:00 am and people were still out in full force, partying the night away, it wasn't even a weekend. Jasper held on to the side of his coat as they moved through the crowd, closer to the nightclub, protecting the only protection that lay on the inside of his coat by his waist. He wouldn't want it getting into the wrong hands now.

They reached the front of the nightclub; the City of London Police (CLP) surrounded the area. An ambulance was present, and both Jasper and Martin saw someone being stretched off into the back of it. The person—an Asian man, looked about six foot three, or four. Jasper and Martin tried to move closer but were halted by a CLP fed with a close-cropped, brown hair and a cheeky grin plastered on his chubby, clean-shaven face near the front of the entrance. He raised his palm to them. 'Don't move any closer, scene of a crime here; I can't let you go any further.'

Martin rolled his eyes at the CLP fed and pulled out his REA badge, shoving it right in the CLP fed's face, so close that the front of the badge nearly touched the fed's nose. 'Robotics Enforcement Agents,' he said smugly. 'We believe robotics was used here today to commit the crime.'

The CLP fed's smirk instantly disappeared, as if by a switch, and he frowned at Martin, giving him an icy, cold stare, clearly affronted by the remark. He gently waved Martin's badge away from his face, turned to look at Jasper. 'You too? You're REA?'

Jasper smiled, nodded, reached inside his overcoat, and brought out his own badge, flashing it at the CLP fed. Both he and Martin seemed to be feeling themselves tonight. And Jasper didn't know why in the hell that was. They were never usually this arrogant. But maybe it had something to do with that cocky, self-assured look the fed had in his eyes.

'Alright, both of you can go through. Talk with that bouncer over there if you want the low down regarding what went down here tonight.' He gestured to the tall black man standing by the side of the ambulance.

Jasper and Martin strode over to him. When they got to him, they both had to strain their neck just to look up to him. He was a giant, all right. Built like a tank, too.

Martin coughed, getting the attention of the giant bouncer, prompting him to turn around to them.

'REA Agent Martin Silas,' he said, and then gestured to his right, 'This is REA Agent Jasper Barnes. What's your name?'

The bouncer remained silent, looked at them both. Jasper could read scepticism in his eyes as they darted back and forth between him and Martin.

'We are with the REA,' Jasper tried to reassure him. 'We are here to help you, catch whoever did this to your friend.'

After a few more sceptical look from the bouncer, and after a few more minutes of silence, he finally relented. 'My name is Joe Black,' he said, in a typical hardboiled voice you would associate with a brute like him. Nothing new there then.

'Joe, we heard robotics was used here today, is that so?' Martin asked.

'Yes, a man, with a mechanical-looking hand, or perhaps arm? I don't know. He had worn a black overcoat that covered most of his arm and only his hand from the wrist down were visible. And it was clearly not human.' The bouncer said.

'Can you be a bit more specific?' Jasper queried. 'What did the person and the hand look like?'

The bouncer glanced over to the ambulance; it seemed like it was getting ready to leave for the hospital. He glanced back at Jasper and Martin. 'He had a small tattoo of the cross on his left cheekbone and he was here looking for Bethany Rose. She is a bartender that works here, and when we didn't let him in, he became violent and that's when Tanwar—the guy in this ambulance—and I noticed his mechanical hand. It was black and gold with all kinds of machinery parts and wirings and screws and wheels.' He hesitated, looking over at the ambulance; they were waving him to come if he was going with them. 'Listen, I got to go, that's all I know.'

'It's okay, go on ahead, I think we have all we need here, for now, get going, we'll pay you and—' Martin trailed off.

'Tanwar,' the bouncer finished for him.

'—Tanwar, a visit at the hospital tomorrow. Just a routine follow up.'

The bouncer nodded and sprinted into the back of the ambulance, the hover truck took off, gliding above the ground as if floating, and blowing hot air from the exhaust back toward where Jasper and Martin stood. It was rather soothing to Jasper, apart from the petrol smell, warming them up in the freezing night.

Jasper and Martin exchanged looks.

'I think we've found our elusive man,' Martin said.

'I don't think so,' Jasper said, turning his gaze away from Martin and looking into the distance, into the Red-light district still hectic nightlife, to the neon coloured streets, and then to the half-naked whores' holographs that illuminated the top of the buildings. 'Joe said he had a small tattoo on his left cheekbone and a black and gold mechanism of a hand or arm, but our guy doesn't have a tattoo in said area, and has a black and *silver* mechanism, remember?'

'Oh, yeah, that's right.'

'There seems to be a new guy here in play, maybe he's also working with our guy, either way . . . once we get them for sure, this time, surely, no more holo-work and late nights for us.'

Chapter Four: A Tale of Two Partners

Once Jasper and Martin were done for the night with their investigation outside the Starlight Nightclub they stopped by a bar for a couple of drinks.

Martin was always one for a strong glass of vodka after a long day's work, wanting nothing more than to drown out the noise of the rough day, as well as the ones still looming ahead of them, no doubt. Jasper, on the other hand, was more of a cold bottle of beer kind-of-guy. He loved how it tasted. The foamy, dry, alcoholic, malt flavour of beer on his tongue made him feel just about the right kind of tipsy, but not too far gone that he could no longer function as a civilised human. As he had learned over the years, at any given time, duty may call, and he had better be ready and of sober mind.

Martin, on the other hand, didn't care as much. He'd always told Jasper; no matter how much he drank, he was able to keep a sober mind and his judgements very much intact.

That wasn't the case tonight, though (and many other nights for that matter). After about six rounds and three shots of vodka, they were ready to leave. Jasper saw his friend try to stand on shaky legs, wobbling, trying his best to keep his balance, but to no avail, and he tumbled toward the hard ground. There was a thumping sound as Martin's right temple connected with the side of the bar as he fell, Jasper instantly feeling and sharing in his pain with a grimace.

They exited the bar; stumbling out onto the streets, Martin's left arm was swung around Jasper's shoulder as he carried his pal toward their hover car. Jasper noted Martin's forehead now—bruised, purple, and swollen.

Once they reached the hover car, Jasper eased Martin's small but compact frame inside the passenger side of the hover car, cupping his legs and arms and setting him on the seat. Whilst he applied the seat belt, his friend stared up at him with glazed-over, unsteady eyes. 'Jasp . . .' he said softly, his voice barely a whisper, his breath ricocheting with vodka, the whiff hitting Jasper in the face like a strong right hook, causing him to momentarily shudder. 'Is that you, brother?' he trailed off, tried to reach for Jasper with his hands, but couldn't, they fell inches past Jasper, and he passed out.

Jasper continued to strap him in safely, finally hearing the *click* of the secured belt. 'Yeah, buddy,' he said softly. 'It's me, I got you, let's get you home, alright?'

Jasper wasn't expecting a response; his friend had passed out and fallen into a deep sleep. And as per usual, whenever they went out drinking, Jasper knew, he wouldn't wake for another six or so hours. Martin was a deep sleeper like that. Not even a tornado could wake him from his drunken slumber.

Jasper eased his frame out of the passenger side and shut the door. He headed for the other side and got in, swiping the key over the holo-touchscreen by the dashboard, then touching the start face-button on the holo-touchscreen and then roaring off into the night.

On his way to Martin's house, in Brixton, he decided that tomorrow, he'd have to pick up Martin on his way to work in the morning as they'd taken Martin's car for their mission tonight and his was back at the precinct. No worries, he wasn't exactly going to allow Martin to drive in his condition, anyway.

As he drove, the hover car humming silently, outside, it was a cold, winter night, and the moon still hung in the sky like a ghost of itself. He looked over at Martin; his friend was still fast asleep, his head tilted to the side toward the window, his mouth slightly opened. Jasper pressed on the holo-button beside him to the bottom right and the window slid down a little bit, letting in small, fresh air. The air was cold but smelled so clean, Jasper wished he could put it on a plate and eat it.

He turned back to the road; the cold winter weather had given everything the look of metal that had been rubbed with steel wool. The wind blew and leaves scuttled across pavements. It was quiet, a little too quiet; the roads were clear, with no pedestrians, and no other hover cars around. Even if it was for only a short while, he felt tranquil at that moment, felt as if he and Martin were the only two people left in the world.

When they finally reached Martin's, Jasper got out, hoisted one of Martin's arms around his shoulders and carried his friend to his front door. Martin's wife opened the door— a beautiful blonde of a babe with bright, hazel eyes that hypnotised you, making you go weak in the knees. She was wearing a light pink dressing gown that exposed long, slender, naked legs. And when a small cold breeze hit, she tightened up, pulling hard on the robe, revealing the small whites of her breasts and the fact that she had nothing on underneath. Jasper swallowed, doing his best not to let his imagination run wild.

'Again?' she said, her face the picture of disappointment. 'Drunk again? When will he learn, this needs to stop. Jasper, why do you let him do this to himself?'

Jasper, why did you? He didn't know why or what to say. He'd always just let his friend do as he pleased. But perhaps he shouldn't. Perhaps he should put his foot down; after all, he's got a beautiful wife to come home to every night. What could be so bad that he has to drown out his sorrows inside bottles of vodka rather than come home to his wife and drown in her instead?

'Teresa,' he said finally. 'I'm sorry—consider this the last time I bring him home in this state.'

'Better be, Jasper,' she said as she moved to one side of the door, giving Jasper space to carry Martin inside. 'Take him upstairs, bedroom's first room on the right.'

Jasper eased Martin through the door and up the stairs. 'I know, Teresa.' He grinned at her. He had done this one too many times before to count like he was Martin's chauffeur and bodyguard and servant—all rolled up into one.

He reached the bedroom and laid his friend on the bed, helping to undress the small hulk of a man, starting with his shoes, then his coat—which housed Martin's REA issued firearm as Jasper could feel the shape of it in the pocket it resided in—followed by his top and trousers. Martin lay there in his boxes. Jasper looked around the room, looking for his nightwear.

'That's okay,' Teresa said from behind him from the doorway, 'Leave him in his boxes, I'll turn on the heater, and he likes to sleep in them anyway.'

Jasper turned around to face her. He smiled, then stood, and then turned back to stare at his friend for a while. His once strong-willed friend, who never took shit from anyone, the brute of the two, now lay here, vulnerable, naked, and Jasper realised he was the one doing all the protecting now, not the other way around—the way it had always been: Martin always putting him first and having his back.

'I'll be back for him in the morning.' Jasper said to her.

Jasper left the Silas's resident, but not before kissing his pal goodnight on the forehead and hugging Teresa, catching a faint whiff of the perfume she had been wearing—it smelled of roses and a hint of orange—and feeling all that soft flesh of hers underneath that nightgown. His trousers had bulged a little and he hoped she hadn't notice, he couldn't help himself, and he'd felt embarrassed, but who could blame him?

Women were his weakness, still, even though Teresa was the wife of his best friend, and even though he had a wife and a kid waiting for him back at home.

He made his way downstairs and back to the hover car and drove home. Home was in the vibrant area of Victoria.

When he got in, being as quiet as a mouse, he made his way to Zack's room; the young boy of six was fast asleep as the faintest of moonlight slid in through his room window casting him in a soft, pale glow. Toys filled the floor of his room as Jasper made his way toward his bed; he kissed the boy on the forehead and gently rubbed the same forehead with his thumb as he slept. Jasper could have sworn he saw Zack smile, faintly. Zack was his pride and joy, everything he was doing, he did for him, for him to have a better future, for him to have a peaceful city to live in, one where he could grow up in, where he wouldn't have to worry about getting attack or killed before his time. One that is safe from the illegal use of Military-grade Robotics, and from the criminals that use them.

He slowly made his way out of Zack's room, trying his best to avoid the sprawling mess of toys on the ground.

He entered his darkened bedroom, slipping off his clothes, along with the baggage of the day, hanging them both to one side in his wardrobe. He removed his firearm belt with his REA issued Chrome .357 Magnum Revolver holstered in it from around his waist, gently placing it on the nightstand near the wardrobe—the faintest of knock echoing in the silent house—then sliding onto one side of bed and under the covers, his wife, Sarai, lay beside on the other side; he slid his arms around her and pressed his lips against her shiny, dark-brown cheek from behind. She smiled, dimples exposed—the smile of heaven on earth—and she gripped and pulled his arms tighter around her, snuggling closer to him as they spooned.

'I've been waiting for you,' she said. 'I tried calling you. I was worried sick, thinking something happened—'

He placed his index finger on her lips. 'Shush. I'm home now, aren't I?' he said softly into her ear. It tickled her and she flinched, tittering like a school girl. 'I've missed you.'

Chapter Five: A Rude Awakening

Grey awoke to what sounded like a gunshot from the hallways of Bethany's apartment. He sat bolt upright, and after using his right hand to quickly rub his face and clear his blurred vision, he noticed Bethany wasn't lying beside him. He shouted, 'Beth!'

'Yes!' She responded from the bathroom. 'What is it? I'm taking a shower!'

'Nothing babe, it's all good!'

He stood to his feet, wearing nothing but his Calvin Klein black-button boxer shorts; he reached for the balcony window curtains, drawing them back. It was morning, but the skies were grey (as usual in London during this time of season), and the tall trees—with what little yellow and orange and brown colours of autumn leaves that had not yet fallen off—blew and rustled from side-to-side in the cold morning breeze. Though Grey was in a warm setting due to Bethany's apartment heaters, he could literally feel the cold outside just by staring out of her five-storey balcony window. He looked down at the city below: Euston was filled with people on their holo-phones, rushing to work, hover-trains arriving and leaving the station, hover-cars stuck in rush hour traffic, and the odd guy and gal doing the walk of shame.

Grey started to the bathroom, no doubt to join Bethany in the shower. A mischievous thought filled his mind.

That thought was cut short, though, when bullets flew in through Bethany's front door, just nearly missing him, and then when the front door was kicked wide open after.

The apartment was relatively small; there was only one floor, with the bedroom, living room, and kitchen all in close proximity, the bathroom the only one on its own, to the side on the left.

Grey dived and ducked beside the king-size bed, his back against the bed and at an angle as the unwelcomed guests came thudding in with what Grey thought sounded like pairs of workman boots. Grey slowly peeked up from below the bed and saw that the intruders were, in fact, the same four men in balaclavas that had broken into his apartment last night, their guns readied and pointed in every direction of Bethany's apartment as they slowly started. In the distance, on her writing table, where the men were positioned, he could see his 9mm semi-auto pistol. Grey ducked his head back down. *Shit,* he thought. *I'm a sitting duck here.* He looked down, clenching his left fist and flexing his mechanical arm.

Trust me, the voice said. *We've got this.*

'No, we don't,' Grey found himself whispering. 'There's four of them and only one of me.'

'What's with all the noise, Grey?' Bethany said as she came out of the shower, eyes closed, a towel wrapped around her body, another one on her head, as she dried her hair with it, ruffling it with her hand.

'No! Get down! Beth!' Grey roared as he stretched to try and reach for her.

Grey watched as she slowly halted in ruffling her hair with the towel, opening her eyes to see the four men, their guns were pointed toward her; they were just as startled as she was, and one of them opened fire.

The bullet pierced through her left shoulder, her mouth opened in shock as blood spewed out in front of Grey. He rolled forward to catch her as she fell and then quickly ducked back beside the bed, away from the men's view. Bethany bled out in his arms as he heard the sound of the men's boots slowly approaching again.

'Listen, babe, hang in there, you're going to be okay, you hear, you're going to be okay.'

'I . . . I . . . I'm sorry, Grey . . .' she said, her voice hoarse.

'You've got nothing to be sorry about. Hold on to your shoulder,' Grey grabbed one of the towels, put it on the wound, and then put her hand over it. 'Keep pressure on it. I'm coming back.'

'Where are you going—?'

Grey barely remembered what happened next, but felt his left hand instantly tightened into a fist, and he leaped up from behind the bed, almost acrobatically, rolling over the bed as the four men drew their guns to him. He quickly grabbed the closest one to him—using him as a shield—as the other three opened fire. They filled their comrade with bullets, riddled him with holes upon holes, which caused them to halt in their firing, and Grey took full advantage of this.

He threw the bullet-ridden body toward the other three, knocking two of them down, and then punching the last one standing with a thunderous left hook with his mechanical left fist. Grey felt bones *crack,* and half the mask and the skin on the man's face peeled back from the strong impact, blood smearing. His face spun to the side as if trying, purposefully, to avoid eye contact, his neck *snapped*, and he fell to the ground in a heap, unmoving.

Grey figured he was dead—no one was surviving that—and quickly picked up the now-deceased man's weapon—a carbine assault rifle—turned, and fired at the remaining two who were almost to their feet again, readying to fire at him. Grey's bullets penetrated both in rapid succession; blood splattered everywhere, marring the beautiful interior of Bethany's apartment with red.

Grey, covered in a smattering of blood, his heart racing, his breathing deepening, frowning, approached one of the men on the ground. Miraculously, he was still alive, the other not so lucky.

Grey hovered over him, and then dropped to one knee, yanking off the balaclava. Grey couldn't believe his eyes, his throat clogged up, and his heart broke. It was Hector Foreman. Hector was one of his closest brothers in the Foxhound Syndicate. Could the voice in his head have been right, after all? Did they try to kill him before, in the supposed accident? Grey wouldn't have dreamt in his wildest dreams that he—Hector; his Foxhound brother—would do what he just did here today.

Perhaps because, Grey, deep down, was a loyal soul—and betrayal was never in his vocabulary.

'Hector . . .' Grey said softly. 'Why?' Grey wrinkled his brow.

Hector coughed up blood. 'Why do you think?' he tried to steady his breathing. 'You arrogant son-of-a-bitch, thinking you could just up and leave the Syndicate, saying you're done with that life. After all the Syndicate has done for you, after all you've done and seen, you think they were just going to let you leave? Think again, that's not how Foxhound works. If you're in this, you're in this for life.' He paused, spitting blood on the ground beside him, 'I didn't have a choice either, Grey. David came to me, he told me the order had come from up above, that I had to do it without batting an eyelid. I didn't want to but, friend or no friend, it was either you or me, it's nothing personal, it's just business.'

'Who from up above ordered the hit?' Grey asked.

Hector laughed and wiped his mouth with the back of his hand, blood smearing around his chin. 'The man in the back of the cart need never see the horse's face. Even if I knew, you know I can't say, but all I know is someone at the very top really wanted you six feet under. The initial plan was to take you out six months ago, apparently, that night, in the spring, after our neurons and gun errand, but you survived, somehow, I don't know how, but I see you're now sporting a fancy new mechanical arm to boot. Impressive.'

'How did you know I was still alive and how did you find me?' Grey queried again.

'People talk, Grey, you should know that. There's nothing that goes on in London City that the Foxhound Syndicate doesn't know about. Word of your survival had spread like wildfire.'

'You know I can't let you go,' Grey's voice was still soft. 'You know that, right?'

'Killing me won't change a thing, Grey, once they know we're missing, they'll come for you again. You're still a dead man, Harrow!' he spat on Grey's face and Grey could feel phlegm mixed with blood sliding down his cheek, like tears.

Grey did not flinch one bit, but gently wiped the spit off with the palm of his right hand, then slowly wrapped his mechanical left fingers around Hector's neck, his fingers like talons, gripped tight his windpipe as Hector tried to gasp in air. Turning his head to the side, he didn't want to see his friend suffer, despite every reason to want to. He heard Hector struggle, felt his throat throb, his body quiver—like he had just been shocked by a jolt of electricity—and then one final jerk as his body slowly gave up the fight. Nothing. No more movement coming from him. Grey turned back to him, Hector's glazed over chestnut eyes were wide open, staring into space, lifeless, and Grey used his two fingers—index and middle—to slide Hector's eyelid close, letting out a deep sigh.

He stood back to his feet, saw that Bethany's door was still wide opened, he glanced out to the hallways, his head looking to the left then to the right—empty—but still not wanting anyone to be privy to the carnage that took place in her apartment; he shut the door, then started to her.

When he reached her she was still on the floor, holding her shoulder in a tight grip, silent, blood seeping through the towel she had used to hold the wound. She was still alive, and that's all that had mattered to Grey. He quickly grabbed and cradled her in his arms, then reached for her holo-phone on her desk and dialled 911. The phone rang and a woman picked up.

'Hello, I need an ambulance, there's been an incident. My . . .' Grey trailed off, looking down at her, in a world of pain. They had never once made it clear whether they were official or not, what with her escorting and the causality of their relationship, but he carried on. 'My girlfriend has been shot. Please get here as soon as possible.'

Grey didn't give them her address, but the name of the road outside. He didn't want them to see the state of the apartment and the police catching wind of what had happened here. And the fact that no one came to help, he thought it had meant no one had heard the ruckus, and the fact he was awoken to gunshot earlier, only serves to corroborate his theory that people around here were used to this kind of thing happening on a daily basis, and wouldn't be suspicious at all. Grey felt this was an isolated incident, and that he would do the clean-up himself. Just like the old days.

He packed a bag full of clothes and wrapped Bethany in her pink robe, applying pressure to the wound and listening to her breathing as they waited beside the bed for the ambulance, the corpses of the three men and Hector, lying all around them, bloodied.

Chapter Six: A Five-Day Deadline

Jasper was on his way to Brixton to pick up Martin so they could head to work. He wondered if Martin was feeling up to his usual self today. Whether he was good for the day ahead or whether he would rather call in sick.

Yesterday he'd succumb once again to his alcoholic tendencies, and this time, he'd wounded himself, cracking his forehead off the curved part of the bar table, his head bouncing off the table like a tennis ball. But knowing Martin, a little headache and a hangover was not going to keep him down; he would make it in even if it killed him. Today, they will catch their man, and all the hard work will finally pay off.

Jasper gazed on out from the comfort of his hover car, the faintest of sunlight sipping through, its presence only for show, doing nothing to warm up the cold morning. The front windscreen started to fog up, and Jasper reached down to the floating, holo-dashboard, turning on the heater, low setting.

Next, he flicked on the radio; a news talk-show came on. Yesterday's antics by the Starlight Nightclub were one of the talking points. They also spoke of masked gunmen in suits, wielding some kind of robotic guns, frightening civilians around the Kings Cross Area.

'First, a crazy man with what looked like a military-grade robotic limb is seen being aggressive, and then witnesses are saying they saw a group of four men with balaclavas, wielding special weaponry, in public, in a very busy area and time, pointing their guns at civilians for no apparent reason.' A woman on the radio said. 'Where were the police? And better yet, where were the so-called REAs? Why are there still people roaming the streets with illegal robotics? They are supposed to keep this from happening! What are they getting paid to do? Just sit on their asses all day and eat doughnuts and drink coffee? Slobs, the lot of them.'

Jasper frowned and pursed his lips. He reached out at the holo-dashboard and turned off the radio, irritated. He pushed down on the gas, the hover car picking up speed to roughly thirty-eight miles per hour. With his left hand, he reached down to the gearstick, feet now on the clutch, and switched to third gear. In a time when everyone was using automatic hover cars, both Jasper and Martin preferred the old fashion way of driving—even with the short-range anti-gravity of it all.

When he finally reached Martin's home, he looked out the driver's window, saw that Martin was sitting and waiting by his doorstep, dressed in his usual white shirt—with his bulletproof vest over it (the way jasper wore his also), black tie, black trousers, and his brown overcoat. There was a cigarette in Martin's right hand, a yellow lighter in his left, and he blew out smoke into the open air, though, Jasper wondered whether it was actually smoke from his cigarette, or just mist from the freezing cold air, he couldn't tell.

'Finally,' Martin said, as he stood to his feet and started toward the hover car's passenger side. 'What took you so bloody long?'

Jasper chuckled. 'I came as fast I could, you Muppet, just get in. Come now, we've got a long day ahead of us.'

'Yeah, yeah, whatever,' Martin opened the passenger side door and hopped in. 'Let's go.'

Jasper turned the hover car around and they sped off to the precinct in Knightsbridge.

When they got into the office, the first thing they had to do was turn in their reports of yesterday's incident to their boss—Walter Marshal. Walter was a round, bald-headed, hot head. He ran the REA in this part of the country, and though he had never been out in the field since the Administration started five years ago, he had previously been part of the military, and in his own very words: "he was a hard knock."

He had been given the power by those higher up in the headquarters abroad. With all that power, came responsibility; he was responsible for seeing this part of the country free from the illegal use of military-grade robotics. He didn't take shit from anyone and always told everyone in the REA how he really felt at any given time, no sugar coating.

'Still no luck in finding our man?' The boss asked, scanning the holo-document Jasper had sent him earlier. His hands moved swiftly through the air, flicking and swiping the translucent projection.

Jasper and Martin both shook their heads, 'Not yet, sir,' they said in chorus.

'Well, get to it then. You two better have something concrete for me by the end of this week.'

'We will,' Martin started, 'it's just . . . there has been a new development in our search.'

'New development?' Walter closed the holo-screen between them with the flick of his wrist. 'Well, speak.'

Martin hesitated. 'There's . . . there seems to be a new robotic user that was spotted by the Starlight Nightclub yesterday. Apparently, he was asking for a bartender named Bethany Rose, and when the security didn't let him in, he proceeded to use a robotic arm. We think he might be connected—'

'Listen, Martin . . . ' Walter said softly, cutting him off, then he trailed off, looking as if he'd lost his train of thought, but then he turned and pressed down on the holo-touchscreen beside his table and leaned in. 'Toby, get me a cup of coffee, would you, thanks.' He turned back and resumed. 'Listen, Martin . . . Ezra Hawthorne, that's your target, that's your mission, we need him brought in.'

'But, sir—'

'I can assign someone else onto this new guy—'

'With all due respect, Sir,' Jasper interrupted. 'I think Martin and I can handle both cases, we can close it and have them off the streets by the weekend.' Martin turned to glare at Jasper, his eyes wide as though he couldn't believe what Jasper had just said.

Walter tapped his hands on his desk, swaying side to side on his chair, his eyes never leaving Jasper's or Martin's. 'You do know it's Tuesday, today . . . that leaves you with five days.'

Jasper nodded. 'Yes, sir.'

Martin's mouth opened slightly, his face—a picture of disbelieve. He scrunched his face and turned away.

'Fair enough, but you do know this your area of jurisdiction, anything goes wrong involving robotics here, and it's your head. Our agency works in top secret, let's keep it that way.'

Toby, Walter's assistant, knocked and then entered, setting down a ceramic mug filled with coffee down on the table. Walter thanked him and he left.

Walter reached down, grabbed the mug and drank, slowly. 'Alright, don't just stand there, get going, you have until Sunday. It would be a shame to see you guys go.' He paused, gave them a forced smile, his cheeks wrinkling, his eyes disappearing slightly in the process. 'Get it done.'

Jasper and Martin turned and left Walter's office.

Once they reached outside, shutting the door behind, Martin turned and smacked Jasper on the arm, hard. 'What the hell? What the hell do you think you're doing? Five days? Who said you could speak for both of us, huh, Jasp?'

'Relax,' Jasper said. 'We can close this case by then, trust me—'

'Trust you? Are you serious? Jasp, I've got a family, a wife, bills, I need that promotion, and better yet I can't lose this job.'

Jasper remained silent. He studied his friend's face. Martin was a hard worker, no doubt, but he was always one for safety, only doing what he thought was in his comfort zone, what he knew he couldn't fail at, but what kind of life was that? Life was for risk-taking, without it life would have no meaning, and one would never know what one could truly be.

'Erm, hello, sir!' one of the young admin by the front desk raised her hands and gestured to them to come over.

They walked over. 'What is it?' Martin asked.

'I went through your holo-report of last night, and I just received some rather useful information, hopefully, regarding the suspect.' The young Admin said.

'Yes go on,' Martin gestured with his hands, wanting the young admin to hurry up and get to the point.

'Bethany Rose has just been reported to have been a casualty of a shooting in the early hours of this morning in Euston. She's been taken to Royal Free Hospital in Hampstead.'

'Really?' Jasper said. 'Good job . . .' he trailed off, squinting at her, trying to figure out her name, he felt bad, she had worked here for how long? And she had just given them a boost on their assignment—which was make or break for them at this point—and he didn't even know her name. How bad of him, he thought.

'Mary.' She said finally, decoding his thoughts.

'Good job, Mary.' He reached over and gave her a gentle pat on the arm.

'Thanks, kid,' Martin injected with a less than an enthusiastic nod.

She beamed, feeling proud of herself. 'You're welcome, sir.'

'Let's go, Martin.' Jasper turned and tapped him on the chest, and then started for the exit; Martin, seemingly reluctant, trailed after him behind.

Chapter Seven: A Mutual Trouble

Grey held on to Bethany's hand as they wheeled her in the stretcher through the corridors of the Accident and Emergency (A&E) at Royal Free Hospital in Hampstead—the nearest hospital the ambulance had taken them to. Grey stood by her right side, while a grey-haired doctor—whose name badge read "Smith"—stood on her left and a nurse—whose name badge read "Sarah"—at her front.

'Breathe, Beth, breathe,' Grey said to her, 'Everything's going to be okay.'

She gripped his right hand tighter, but didn't say a word; she just stared at him through tired, swollen, red eyes. Grey stared back at her, he hated seeing her like this, all vulnerable and in discomfort. He wished he could take her pain away, make her feel at peace again. He didn't have to imagine what she was going through, he only had to recollect his previous experiences of being shot at, the burning sensation of the bullet that had penetrated her left shoulder, now lodge in-between her flesh as the wound heals around it. It was a gruesome experience, no doubt. Thinking of it made him angrier. But now was not the time for him to be, he realised. Now was the time for him to just be there for her.

Push-doors slapped opened and close as they continued to wheel Bethany through the corridors. Grey took in the scenery: left, right, and straight-ahead, patients all around the hospital were being attended to by doctors and nurses, young and old, wearing their hospital gowns, some standing, some sitting, and some lying down. When they finally reached a ward, more doctors and nurses came to their aid. Grey released his grip from Bethany's hand, and her hand fell down, lifeless, like a loose string, and they propped Bethany on a bed and immediately started to go to work on her. Holo-screens popped up all around the ward; wires were being connected to her to monitor her vitals.

'I'm sorry, but we need room to work on her now,' Doctor Smith said turning to Grey. 'Please wait for her outside in the waiting area.' Grey didn't want to. He didn't want to leave her side. But after a long stare from the doctor, he reluctantly stood back, and the nurses drew the blue ward curtains all around the bed.

Grey started to the waiting area; he slung the bag full of Bethany clothes over one of his shoulders. He was in his usual grey T-shirt, black cargo pants, and black overcoat. He also now wore a pair of cotton-soft gloves, covering his mechanical left hand—which he should've done last night, he realised—so as to not draw attention to himself. It was the one thing he knew he didn't want right now.

As he walked out of the ward, Grey glanced to his right, squinted, and saw two distinctive men walking —with bravado—side by side, toward him. They both wore black trousers and a white shirt with a bulletproof vest over it, their REA badges—a picture of a robot head with a giant X across it—hanging out from their necks all the way down to their bellies from small metallic chains, dangling, for the whole world to see.

Grey squinted again, then his eyes widened, reality hitting him. They're going to want to know what happened to Bethany. They must've heard about the incident last night, and know that robotics was present in the attack. The truth was not an option, no. He couldn't tell them what had really happened, not until he got to the bottom of it, and he was going to need to get back to Bethany's apartment soon and clean up that bloody mess that was left behind.

He ambled on over, acting oblivious to their presence, and sat on one of the waiting area chairs, beside an old couple. They looked at him, smiling, and Grey forced himself to smile back at them. His face hurt. He wasn't one that smiled a lot. He turned his gaze back down the corridor and toward the ward. There they were again—like they were tied to the hips—side by side, the two REA Agents. They stood by the entrance to the ward, looking in, and Grey couldn't but wonder what they were thinking. One of them turned around and glared toward Grey's direction. He had a square jaw, with stubbles, and short brown hair.

Grey was not expecting that and so he promptly averted his gaze back toward the old couple. They were still smiling.

Grey turned back his gaze, hoping the two Agents had disappeared, but the square jaw officer was now walking over to him, bravado still in his stride. The cocky fool. He kept his gaze on Grey, and Grey did the same this time, unwavering in his stare.

'Hi, I'm Barnes,' he extended his right hand to Grey. 'Jasper Barnes.'

Grey, hesitated, but then moved to clasp Jasper's right hand in his. He didn't know why he did. 'Grey Harrow.'

'That's Martin Silas over there,' Jasper said, pointing behind him toward the other Agent. 'We are with the Robotics Enforcement Administration. We're just here to investigate an incident we were told about. Say, do you know a Bethany Rose?' He took out a pack of chewing gum from his pocket and threw three tablet size into his mouth, crunching away rather loud.

'Yeah . . . I do.' Again, Grey didn't know why he told him that.

'So you're the guy that found her with a gunshot wound? Her boyfriend?'

Grey ran his hand through his buzz cut, scratching. 'That's right, it was me.'

'Did you see the men that did it? Did you get a good look at them?'

'I didn't see anything; I only arrived after they had done the deed.'

Jasper placed his right hand on his chin, stroking his 5'oclock shadow and glaring at Grey with steely eyes. 'That's odd, why would someone want to shoot an unarmed woman?'

'I don't know. You tell me. Isn't that your job to find out?' Grey was getting agitated, and Jasper's convicting steely eyes were penetrating straight into his soul.

The other Agent, Martin, a ginger-haired, clean-shaven man, walked over and Jasper laid a hand on his shoulder, 'Hey, Martin, get a load of this,' he said, pointing at Grey, while his mouth still moved at hundred miles an hour due to the gum he was chewing. 'Grey over here is the boyfriend of that Bethany girl.'

'Really?' Martin asked. 'Have you told him about the other the guy—the bouncer—in one of the other wards,' he paused turning his gaze to Grey, 'the injured bouncer's friend—I believe his name was Joe—said a black man, about six foot, roughly mid to late 20s, with a buzz cut and a small tattoo on his left cheekbone—similar to the tattoo you've got on yours here, mind you—was looking for a young bartender lady named Bethany at the Starlight Nightclub yesterday, and when he didn't get in, the attacker grabbed his friend by the throat . . .' he trailed off, glancing down at Grey's now gloved and hidden left hand. His brow furrowed, eyes narrowed, and he continued. 'Choking him with what looked like a Robotic hand.' He looked back up at Grey, his eyes narrowing further, filled with scepticisms and hatred for some reason. 'So, there was no fingerprint evidence left behind that we could go by. Do you think these two incidents were connected?'

Grey took a second to compose himself from the questions Jasper and Martin were throwing at him. All the questions and evidence were pointing toward his involvement in both incidents and he knew that as experience Agents, Jasper and Martin were only just beginning. They were not going to stop until they get to the bottom of both cases. Furthermore, it seemed Tanwar had survived last night altercation at the Starlight Nightclub and will live to tell the tale. A relief for Bethany—one of her favourite security guards lives––but a headache for Grey, he couldn't care less whether the arsehole had lived or not, but now that he had, he could very much make life that much difficult for Grey.

'Like I told Mr. Barnes here, I know as much as you two.' Grey paused, turning to the ward entrance; a doctor was coming out, and then he turned back quickly to the two Agents, 'When you find them, please let me know. I, too, have a bone to pick with them.' He stood up brushed past the two Agents, feeling their eyes burning like beams at the back of his head as he went to meet with the doctor.

'Ah, there you are,' Doctor Smith said. 'She wants to see you. You can see her now.'

'Cheers,' Grey said as he made his way into the ward. He pulled back the blue curtains slightly, eased his body in, sitting on a chair beside the bed. The holo-screen was disabled currently, but she was looking a lot better, her shoulder wrapped in bandages. He gently lay his hand on her, she groaned quietly, twisting her body ever so slightly so that she met Grey's gaze.

'Grey . . .' she said softly. Her voice was hoarse and so tired, which was understandable since they'd said she had been put under a sedative while they worked on her and removed the bullet.

'It's me, Beth,' he said as he brushed strands of hair from her face and smiled down at her.

'Water,' she said in a low voice.

Grey reached for the plastic cup filled with water on the table beside the bed. He picked it up, pulling closer to her; he put the cup to her lips and slowly tipped the cup so she drank and swallowed, like a baby learning all over again.

'I'm sorry,' Grey said.

Bethany set the cup down beside her. 'For what?'

'All of it. I never meant to make my trouble your trouble.'

Bethany reached forward with a hand and touched the side of Grey's face, her hands felt warm and soft.

'I'm pretty sure your trouble *is* my trouble now.' She said as she winced from the discomfort and pain. 'It's not your fault, I don't blame you.'

Grey couldn't understand it. It was his fault he got involved with the wrong people, and it was his fault she was laying in this bed, having just had a bullet removed from her shoulder, yet she still doesn't blame him? It made Grey feel some type of way. Made him want to punish those who did this to her. Punish those who did this to his beautiful angel. He wanted to punish the Foxhound Syndicate.

And then it happened, the voice in his head started to whisper again its malicious plans.

Tick-tock, Grey, tick-tock. Time to go . . . time to head back to that facility . . . time to head back to where it all began . . . so we can end this . . . once and for all.

Grey scrunched his face, placing a hand on his head, he felt his mechanical hand—by a will of its own—clenched into a fist within the glove. Bethany reached out for him, touching his left shoulder, and he relaxed again.

'Grey, what's wrong?' she said. 'Tell me.'

'There's nothing wrong, Beth.' Grey stood to his feet. 'Get some rest; I've got to go somewhere. I'll be right back, I promise. Also, if two REA Agents come by and talk to you— don't speak to them, don't tell them anything, okay? You didn't see the attackers, everything happened so fast, okay?'

She nodded, meekly. 'Okay, where are you going?'

'To make everything right again.'

Chapter Eight: A Café Nearby

Jasper and Martin arrived at Royal Free Hospital. They strode through the hospital, brushing passed patients, nurses, and doctors alike. They headed for a particular ward, and when they reached it, there lay the bouncer from the attack the night before, his name—Tanwar, Jasper remembered.

Jasper and Martin, stood, watching him as he lay there, unconscious, receiving intravenous therapy. He was in no condition to talk at all. Jasper narrowed his eyes, squinting, he could see red marks from the corner of each side of his neck—whoever did that wasn't relenting, and they were squeezing to kill. That was definitely not done by a human hand. His prying was cut short, though, when the doctors spotted them and ordered them to exit the room. They showed him their badges, but they were told Tanwar was in no condition to talk right now. And so they left, left the ward and walked down the hall, toward their second lead—Bethany Rose—who, apparently, had been shot in the earlier hours of the morning.

When they reached the A&E front desk, Jasper spoke to one of the female receptionists, 'Where can I find a Bethany Rose?' he asked. 'She was rushed in here earlier.'

After she squinted and gave Jasper a sceptical—up and down—look, she turned and gave Martin the same look, 'And who might you guys be?'

'We—'

Martin stepped forward and grabbed Jasper's forearm, 'We are relatives—cousins— and we've come to see that she's okay.'

Jasper tilted his head at Martin, wondering why he would make up such a lie. Was there any reason to?

The receptionist's eyes darted back and forth between the two of them, scepticism still lingered in the air as her feathered, long lashes fluttered and swept past her light eyes. She raised a finger to them. 'One moment, let me check what room she was taken to . . .' she lowered her head and tapped away on her holographic screen, and after a few minutes, she raised her head up again and pointed to her right, 'Just down the hall this way, gentlemen. Room four, Ward seven.'

'Thank you,' Jasper nodded.

When they started down the hall, Jasper turned to Martin, 'What was that for? Why didn't you just tell her we're with the REA?

Martin smiled softly. 'My friend, that would be the easy thing to do,'

'Easy? Of course.'

'We need to start taking more care, Jasp. We don't want to start alerting every robotics criminal to our whereabouts, now, do we?'

'Robotics criminal? She was a receptionist for crying out loud, Martin.'

'Even so, we need to move stealthy, hide in plain sight, no more shouting from the rooftops that we are REA Agents. Well, not until we're done with this mission, that is, not until we apprehend this Hawthorne fella.'

'Fair enough'

They stopped when they reached outside room four. They turned to look inside. Jasper scanned the room with his eyes; landing on ward seven, the curtains were drawn closed around it.

'Besides,' Martin said. 'Ezra is not the only one we're after now, remember? Yesterday's attack on the bouncer and today's shooting regarding this Bethany Rose girl are somehow connected, I know it, and it seems we now have a new player in the game. Ezra wouldn't be so sloppy, not like this, not with his entire military prowess.'

They continued to stare into the room from the outside, the doctors and nurses were all busy attending to patients: the wards were all occupied, Jasper hearing screams, shouts, and the clattering of hospital equipment onto the floor reverberating out from behind each and every curtain-covered ward. The room smelled of sweat and medicine and for some reason, burning plastic. Jasper couldn't quite figure out where the latter smell was coming from. Strange.

He glanced to his side, peering down toward the waiting area; a few people were waiting there, mostly old folks, each one of them probably waiting for a loved one here in this room, no doubt. But then he narrowed his eyes to the last seat on the end. Seated upon it was a black man with a buzz cut. Jasper could only see the back of his head, but he knew it was a black man, he could tell. The man had broad shoulders and what looked like tattoos covering the whole of his neck.

Jasper waited, staring at the man, waiting for him to turn around so he could get a good look at him. From the corner of his eye, he could still see Martin was engrossed with whatever was still taking place inside the wards, oblivious to what had taken Jasper's attention.

The man turned around and his eyes met Jasper's. They exchanged a long intense stare. Finally, the man turned away and engaged with the old couple beside him.
Jasper couldn't quite put his finger on it, but his intuition was telling him that the man there was somehow there for Bethany Rose.

He started toward him, Martin didn't follow, and when he reached the man, the man was already staring at him. Jasper stretched fort his hand and greeted the man. The man said his name was Grey Harrow and that he was waiting for his girlfriend Bethany Rose, and after Martin came over to join them in the conversation, they spoke about the bouncer from yesterday's attack, which seemed to make Grey Harrow uncomfortable. He got up, brushed past them, and went into the wards.

'He's a strange one, isn't he?' Martin said.

'Yeah, he is, very strange.'

'You don't think?—

'I don't know . . .' Jasper trailed off and scratched his chin.

'He does fit the description, though, the tattoo on his left cheekbone, the gloved hands . . .'

'He does, we'll keep a close eye on him.'

After a while, Grey Harrow came out of the ward, and with not even as much as a glance at them, he left the hospital. Jasper and Martin went into the ward after Grey Harrow had left to talk with Bethany Rose. The girl was as stubborn as a hardened dried-up leftover food stain on a plate. She wasn't budging, and Jasper didn't know what this Grey Harrow had said to her to make her so resolute in her stance. Jasper reached into his jacket pocket and pulled out a card and gave it to her. 'Call me, whenever you're ready to talk.'

Jasper and Martin left the hospital not too long after, strolling down the street of Hampstead and into a café nearby. They entered and were greeted by the smell of fresh coffee bean and by a smiling young lady with a brown apron that had an image of a white coffee mug with three white streaks leading off it, which represented hot steam, Jasper decided. She led them to a table for two, they took off their jackets, hanging it around their chairs, sat, and then the waitress asked them what they would like.

'One large coffee—black,' Martin said, then he gestured with his chin at Jasper, 'the same for him—'

'But with milk, please . . . thank you.' Jasper added.

She nodded and went about her business.

Martin glanced over at Jasper, his lips pursed and twisting. 'Jasp . . . our lead has gone cold, and the only person that could help us is not talking, what are we going to do? We only have till Sunday . . . Monday morning latest.'

Jasper looked over at one of the other tables, three young ladies and a man were seated talking, they seemed like they were having the time of their life. The man said something and the three ladies laughed, hysterically. On the next table, a waiter came over and cleared four plastic cups from it, spraying the table with sanitizer and wiping it down afterward.

Jasper looked back at Martin, who looked stressed out. 'Listen, don't worry, Martin. I promise we'll be done by Friday—'

'Really, Jasp?'

'Really.'

'You cocky son of b—'

The waitress came back and set two plastic cups full to the brim with coffee in front of them—one black as night, the other white as snow. She gestured at the holographic receipt hanging in the centre of the round table. They both nodded and smiled at her and she let them be, heading back behind the holo-tills.

'This is on you, Jasp, if we lose our jobs or better yet if we die, it's on you, my family, my wife, my bills, everything, it's on you!'

Jasper smiled warmly at his friend, shaking his head. 'Sure,' he didn't think that Martin's wife being on him was so bad after all. He thought back to last night, her on that front porch standing there as he carried an intoxicated Martin inside the house, of her plumped white breasts, her bare legs propped up—revealing her nakedness—her long throat, his big hands wrapped around it, but then he thought of his wife and banished the adulterous image as quickly as it came. *You bloody sinner, you*, he rebuked himself. *Shame on you. What would your grandfather say?*

Martin's phone vibrated in his pocket and he took it out, raising it to his ear. He nodded once . . . twice . . . mumbled something, then nodded one more time and then hung up. He glared at Jasper. 'We got to go,' he reached for his jacket behind his chair.

Jasper said, 'But what about our coffee? We just got them . . .'

Martin was already heading for the exit. 'Bring them with you,' he yelled back.

Jasper grabbed his jacket from the chair, shoved the two plastic cups with coffee in-between his left arm, and on his way out, he slapped his right hand down on a biometric scanner by the till. The machine lit up, blue line swarmed around his fingers, registering its client. After a few seconds, JASPER BARNES popped up in bold letterings on the holo-screen, to the waitress delight. She reached out her hand and touch his arm softly, 'Thank you, Mr. Jasper Barnes,' she said and she winked at him, her eyes sparkling, her teeth gleaming. Damn. She was beautiful. Damn. Why do they all keep falling for him? Don't they know that he's a married man? Can't they see the wedding ring on his finger? Or was he just way in over his own head—

'Jasper!' Martin called from the entrance.

He broke away from her grasp, turned. 'I'm coming!'

Chapter Nine: A Royal Star Corporation

Grey stepped onto the platform at Camden Town Station. The hover-train behind him, suspended just above the ground by magnetic waves, slammed its sliding door shut, his overcoat billowing out behind him from the cool breeze.

He made his way out of the station, placing his right hand on a biometric scanner before exiting, the machine beeped and his name popped up on the screen. The scanner uses the fingerprints of the person's hand to confirm their identity. He remembered when the scanners were first introduced in London, five years ago. The government had introduced it to make buying, selling, tracking, and travelling, faster, easier, and more efficient.

Cyberhands—that's what Grey dubbed it, access to your personal information and digital bank account(s) all in the palm of your hands—literally. But with great accessibility comes great exploiters. The ease of the machine led to many miss-use of the system, many tweaking it to their benefits. The Foxhound Syndicate were one of those people. The criminal underworld skyrocketed; many unsuspecting civilians became victims, they were tracked, their personal information became like stocks, hands were decapitated, and sold to the highest bidder. Nothing like that happens anymore though, the CLP have clamped down on it, and criminal organisations have moved on up to bigger exploits.

He stood by the entrance; the faintest of sunlight was seeping through the grey skies of London and shining in his eyes. He squinted, looking out at the building opposite him, it had a large holographic clock on the top of it, and it was 12:30 hrs—peak-time for everyone out and about. Camden Town was normally busy, but during this time, it's at its most crowded, as people were mostly on their breaks from work, out and about trying to find a place to eat.

Speaking of eating, Grey felt his belly rumble and he decided to get something to eat before heading to the Facility. He started, making his way through the large crowd of people.

He felt slightly hot despite the cold weather, and he could smell meat. Turning to his right, he saw a fast-food restaurant; he looked at the sign, it said: BURGER COURT. Grey made his way in, the smell of meat getting stronger, but he liked it.

When he reached the counter, a blonde woman, with a diamond-shaped face, wearing a yellow and red uniform with a red baseball cap asked, 'Hi, welcome to Burger Court, what can I get you, sir?'

Grey surveyed the transparent hologram images of the food dashboard above him, it was sticking out toward him like he had been wearing 3D glasses—he could almost touch it, almost taste it.

'I'll have a King Burger and Fries to go . . .' he glanced down at the blonde woman that was serving him, then at her name badge, '. . . Rebecca. Thanks.'

'Anything to drink, Sir?' Rebecca asked.

'Diet Coke'

'Anything else?'

'No, that's all.' Grey watched her punch in details into a transparent holographic touchscreen just below her, each holographic press let out a beeping sound.

'That's £5.59, sir,' Rebecca said as she pulled and then extended a biometric scanner toward Grey. He placed his right palm on the machine, letting it linger for a while until he heard a beeping sound, then removed his hand again.

'Thank you, *Grey Harrow*.' Rebecca said with a smile. She had a set of perfect milk-white teeth, which Grey thought rivalled even that of Bethany's ones. She turned and went to the back, coming back a minute or so later with his order. He grabbed the paper bag it was placed in and left the restaurant.

Grey munched on his burger and fries as he walked through the streets, his hunger not letting him eat with proper etiquette. He dashed the remains of the food in a bin he had walked by, then cracking open his diet coke, he titled his head back, and drank, feeling the cold fizz tickling and pouring down his throat. When he was done he dashed the can in the bin, reached into his pocket and pulled out a cigarette, placing it behind his right ear, at the ready.

He paused, looking north ahead of himself. In the distance, he could see a building that was surrounded by large trees and nothing else. That was the facility he needed to get to, where he was operated upon. The building looked high tech, the type that stuck out like a sore thumb amongst other buildings, and Grey figured that's why it was placed where it was— —between large trees—so as to not be so easily identifiable, given the drama surrounding military-grade robotics at present.

Grey waited by a pedestrian crossing, turning to his left, he saw a market stall run by a bearded man. He surveyed the stall: things ranging from mobile phones to batteries were on sale.

Grey saw a lighter, and remembering he needed one, grabbed it as the bearded man yelled, 'Hey.' Grey quickly placed his right hand on the biometric scanner on the stall, and hearing the beep, the bearded man's face relaxed and he smiled. Grey then crossed the street, the Hovering cars from both directions coming to a halt, letting the pedestrians cross the road. He quickened his steps as he made the way to the facility.

When Grey reached the facility, he paused and stood still for a while. He looked around, not a lot of people were in this vicinity. He reached for his cigarette on his ear and lit it with his newly purchased lighter. Smoke blew from his mouth. He looked up at the building, it had a sign: ROYAL STAR CORPORATION.

So this is what they were called? He had remembered he'd left in such a hurry, after waking up from the coma. He just wanted to be alone, and he didn't even manage to get the name of the organisation . . . until now. After all, they had saved his life, why didn't he ask?

He didn't even know who had ordered the operation. So many questions and the only place he was going to find answers was here.

He dabbed his cigarette bud on the side of the wall and then flicked it into a dumpster, then started to the facility.

He pressed on the holo-screen by the door; it asked for a passcode, but before he could try a few attempts to guessing the passcode, out the corner of his eyes, and to his surprise; the door had been left open. He pulled on it and eased himself through the door, and as he shut the door behind him, he was swallowed up in darkness. It was pitch black. He could barely see anything. But more than anything, what got to him the most, was the silence. It was quiet. A little too quiet, almost eerie.

He adjusted his eyes, trying his best to see as he made his way through the corridors, a hand touching the cold walls to guide him. Grey reached a door, pushed it through, and entered an area that was slightly brighter than where he had come from. He saw that a faint light was coming from somewhere up ahead and tried to trace it, making his way through another corridor. He crashed into a table, knocking over some equipment, and hurting his knee in the process. 'Shit,' he squirmed but carried on.

As he edged closer toward the room with the light, he heard chatter between two people,

'I won't say it again, where are the neurons?' one voice asked.

'I . . . I . . . I don't know. We don't have anymore. We gave everything away. Please don't hurt me.' A different voice said.

'You're lying!' the first voice said.

'I'm not.'

'Well then, you are of no use.'

'Please, don't . . . Ahhh,' the second voice screamed, and then there was silence. Seconds later, a thud.

Grey didn't know what was going on, but he quickened his steps. When he reached the room with the light, he hid behind a container and peeked out the corner. He saw a person on the floor, covered in blood. He figured he was one of the neuroscientists here, due to the lab coat he was wearing. Standing over him was a man—who looked to be of mixed ethnicity—with long black hair tied back into a ponytail, wearing a sort of khaki, mercenary-style, bulletproof clothing with a carbine assault rifle slung over his shoulders. Further behind him were two men dressed exactly like him, but wearing helmets. And opposite them were about a dozen men and women in lab coats—neuroscientist and doctors, no doubt.

'Bring up the next one,' the man with the ponytail said as one of the other in the helmets went to grab a female in the lab coat and placed her on her knees before the man in a ponytail. Any other time, particularly in his days in the Foxhound Syndicate, he wouldn't care much or do anything. Wouldn't bat an eyelid. It didn't concern him. It was none of his business.

But right now, at this exact moment, Grey knew he couldn't just stand back and do nothing. He knew the decent human thing to do was to help and he also knew if he was going to get answers for his questions he needed them alive.

'Where are the neurons!? You're just prolonging the inevitable!' the ponytailed man screamed in the face of the female in the lab coat, he slung off his rifle and pointed it in her face.

'I don't know! We don't have anymore!' she cried.

Grey had no weapon on him; he had left his 9mm semi-auto pistol back in Bethany's apartment on her writing desk, and in his haste to get her to the hospital he forgot to take it with him. He glanced down at his mechanical arm, the hand covered with a glove. All he had now was this. And even though he had taken out four members of the Foxhound Syndicate with it—back at Bethany's apartment—he reckoned he'd just been lucky, and lightning doesn't always strike twice.

As the man continued to yell, he felt his frustration of the whole situation give rise to his anger, his blood boiling.

He tensed his mechanical arm, his mind trying to whisper something he couldn't for the life of him make out, and gladly so, it would have only distracted him at this present time.

He stepped out into the light from behind the container and shadows.

'As the lady said, they don't have anymore . . .' he found himself saying like some kind of dumb hero.

Chapter Ten: A Song of Death

'Are you sure this is the place?'

Japer asked when he and Martin arrived at the abandoned warehouse in Charing Cross. "Abandoned" because there seemed to be no one around and it was quiet. The building itself was situated near a block of run-down apartments—the type that large corporations or the government could give two shit about these days, and the type Jasper knew housed the odd criminal, either dealing in military-grade robotics or other petty crimes.

Jasper eased his large frame through a narrow metallic electronic entrance situated at the back of the abandoned warehouse and glanced over his shoulder at Martin. He waved him forward, gesturing with his hands that the coast was clear. As Martin tried to ease his small frame through the door, he noticed that the narrow entrance itself looked very old and worn out. He was surprised they could get in at all, the electrical circuit that controls the door had been compromised, lying broken on the floor beside the door. Jasper grabbed one side of the metallic door and gently pulled it back, allowing Martin to enter the warehouse alongside him. But after he did, and Jasper let go, the door snapped and slammed shut, randomly and automatically, hard and loud, with a *clank*, cutting them off from the outside world and its many hover-cars that had drifted on by behind them.

Dust assimilated from the sudden clasp. Martin turned to look, his eyes wide. 'Well, that was close,' he stooped down and patted off the dust that had clung to his black trousers. It had turned half of it grey as if he'd just finished running through the Sahara desert. 'Guess we're going to have to go through the front door . . . if we ever want to leave this dump, that is.'

Jasper grimaced and then turned around. He reached inside his overcoat, to his firearm belt, slid out his Chrome .357 Magnum Revolver, flicking open the revolving cylinder chamber, spinning it with his fingers, then slapping it close, before readying it out in front of himself as he started forward in the silent warehouse. Martin drew and readied his weapon also—the REA issued .44 Magnum Desert Eagle—and followed suit to Jasper's left. They moved quickly but silently through the warehouse, almost tiptoeing.

Martin reached out a hand and laid it on Jasper's shoulder. 'This is the place, I'm certain. My informant over the phone, he was very sure of it.'

Jasper didn't blink or halt in his movement; he just continued to look straight ahead. 'Let's hope so.'

Everything, all around them, as they walked, was empty, no equipment, no crates, no boxes, not even a single robotic. Whoever was supposed to have been here must've cleared out before they'd arrived, Jasper decided.

They continued on up ahead, going in and out of rooms, going through shipment containers by containers, and still, nothing, just emptiness.

When they got to the final room that was situated near the front entrance of the warehouse, they saw two shipment containers: one to their left (the closest one to them) and one to their right (the furthest one away and the nearest to front entrance).

Jasper halted and turned to Martin. 'You sure your informant gave you the right address?' he turned his gaze back to the warehouse, slowly, surveying what was left. 'It doesn't look like there's anything here.'

'There is,' Martin said as he too looked around, slowly. He walked up to one of the last shipment container—the one closest to them——and touched the side, 'There has to be—' Jasper wrapped his hand around his friend's mouth, covering his lips and stopping his speech in its tracks. Martin grimaced and tugged and struggled, but Jasper dragged him behind the other side of the closest shipment container as a dozen or so men in khaki uniform matched out from a hover truck that had just pulled into the front of the warehouse, their numerous boots thudding the ground, echoing in the acoustic building.

'There,' one of the men in khaki said, pointing at a metallic door on the opposite side of the last and furthest shipment containment. 'Open it and bring out everything in there.'

'Yes, sir,' another replied.

Jasper slowly let his hand go from around Martin's mouth, red marks positioned themselves where his fingers were previously held, and the two of them peeked out from behind the container to watch on. The men entered through the metallic door and into the room beyond, two or three at a time, and then a few seconds later reappeared with military-grade robotic parts—armoured metallic body parts, slicked with all kinds of weaponry imaginable: hand cannons, sharp, sword-like knife fists, and even jet packs—in their hands, loading them on into the hover-truck with meticulous, careful grace—no doubt trying to limit damage, so they can fetch the highest price possible, Jasper decided.

Jasper was certain this was Ezra Hawthorne's own doing, and he decided that he and Martin, here, today, we're finally going to get their man, one way or another.

'Hmm . . . that's . . .' Martin said as his eyes never left the men and the robotic gifts they held in their hands.

Jasper nodded. 'Yes. We've got them now—'

'Freeze, Arseholes!' Martin popped out from behind the cover of the container, out into the open, his Desert Eagle leading and pointing in the men's direction. 'Robotics Enforcement Agency! Put the robotics down and your hands up, now!'

Jasper's eyes widened, and then he sighed. Shock horror. What happened to "going under the radar"? Gone out the window that is. He palmed his forehead in frustration and then he peeked out from the corner of the container, glanced over at the men, most of them had stopped what they were doing and were now looking blankly at Martin and his one-man army—his Desert Eagle.

Jasper's eyes darted back to Martin; he was still out in the open. 'I'm sure there was a better way you could have gone about this, don't you think, Martin? What happened to not alerting every robotic dealer in London's underworld to our whereabouts, you know stealthy and all that?'

Martin shrugged, his gun still directed toward the men.

'Get back in cover, you idiot.' Jasper rasped.

Martin glanced over to Jasper for a split second, 'Who—'

The sound of firearms went off, bullets from some sort of advance machine gun came screaming in their direction, and Martin was struck right in the chest and in the stomach as Jasper drew back his head behind the protection of the container, squeezing his eyelids shut as bullets flew by. He heard Martin drop to the ground. He opened eyes again. Glanced over, saw his friend lay there on the ground, motionless. He felt the bullets ricocheted off the container behind him, the container playing its own tune, the last verse of the song of death, the end music:

Ti Ta Top Thurm Blop rak rah ta ta ta ta. Ti Ta Top Thurm Blop rak rah ta ta ta ta. Ti Ta Top Thurm Blop rak rah ta ta ta ta. Ti Ta Top Thurm Blop rak rah ta ta ta ta.

And now, in the ensuing echoes, all he could think of—as he watched his friend slowly succumb to his inevitable fate, to his losing battle with life, as death comes calling for him—was Martin's wife.

Poor Teresa . . . what was he going to tell her?

Chapter Eleven: A World Gone Black

Grey knew he had fucked up when bullets cracked and sizzled and pinged and came raining down on him from behind what had looked like large supply metal crates. He'd guessed they were filled with some type of lab or science equipment, techs, and fixtures. He'd hoped so; given this was his only protection between him and the lead bullets. Both of his hands were over his head and ears in a vain attempt to protect himself. If the bullets had somehow penetrated those crates, he'd have had more holes in him than a cheese grater.

He didn't know why but he had half expected the three mercenaries to first engage him in oral conversation after he had revealed himself to them from out of the shadows. Instead, they began conversing with him right off the bat with bullets from their carbine assault rifles. He'd dived back into the shadows and pressed his back up against the crates, his rear on the ground, his knees up toward his chest and his elbows on them, his hands on his head and ears. The bullets popped like firecrackers and ricocheted off the crates, some chipping off bits of the crates as the Royal Star Corporation was set alight in a firework display.

Damn it! he thought to himself, his hands still over his head and ears, elbows still on knees, and knees still to chest. *I'm a sitting duck out here.* A few seconds later the bullets had stopped raining down on him, and as he removed his hands from over his head, peering out from out of the corner of the crates, he saw all three mercenaries reloading, one of them smacking a screaming neuroscientist woman over the head with the butt of their gun, knocking her out cold.

'Finally, some peace and quiet, stupid bitch,' the ponytailed man said as his finished reloading. 'You two head over there and flush out that guy.' He gestured to the other two men in the helmets. They started to where Grey was last sighted—behind the crates—and tentatively approached, carbine assault rifle at the ready, fingers on the triggers.

Grey stopped peeking out and slid back into cover. He breathed in deeply as he contemplated what he should do. Two men were approaching him from either side of the crates with assault rifles, and mechanical arm or not, he was a sitting duck and prey for those animals. He figured if he stayed in the shadows long enough, waiting to the final moment of their approach, he could at least catch one of them by surprise, taking his gun and—hopefully if not gunned down from behind by the other—use it on the other two remaining men. It was wishful thinking but one he had to entertain if he was to survive this ordeal.

Grey waited, his back against the crates in the darkness, he heard their footsteps approaching: one from his left, the other from his right. He ran his hand down his mouth, rubbing his stubble chin, briskly. He breathed deeply again, moving closer to his right. He saw the mouth of the gun of the man on the right peeking out toward him from behind the side of the crate—he was in the shadows, the man couldn't see him—and Grey popped out and quickly grabbed the mouth of the gun, using the strength of his mechanical arm to yank it down, so that the butt of the gun smashed into the man face, hard. The man staggered, Grey grabbed his gun, instantly turning it round to shoot the man at point-blank range—right in his chest, toward the left side, where his heart would be. The man didn't flinch but regained his balance and grinned. Grey should have known better, the man was wearing a bulletproof vest. The bullet laid there on his vest like a bottle cap. Grey then directed the gun to the man's face, the bullet pinging off the helmet, the man still smiling malevolently. Grey then tried to unleash the full load of the gun on every other part of the man, but it was a little too late as the man tackled him to the ground before he could, unleashing a fury of punches on Grey as the other mercenary with the helmet came in from the left.

Grey could see him approach from his peripheral, and trying his best to block the barrage of punches with his arms from the first man. He balled his mechanical hand into a fist and he swung for the man raining down on top him. His mechanical fist smashed into the side of the man's helmet hard, like a boulder to hover-car. It dented without breaking, but the inside of it erupted in a crimson mess: his head exploded, slamming against the crates, blood gushed out and filled the helmet.

Grey could still hear gasping and crying coming from the neuroscientists and doctors, pleading for their lives.

He heard the ponytailed man shouting. 'What was taking you guys so long? Finish off that insignificant troll, so we can get out of here. Come on!'

Grey shoved the first man off from on top of him. Standing back to his feet, he picked up the assault rifle of the dead man, turned, and started toward the other mercenary that was approaching from the left. As Grey came out of the shadows, he unleashed a hail of bullet storm on the other man, his arms shuddering from the burst, the gun loud in his ears. He aimed for the parts that weren't bulletproof protected: the legs, arms, shoulders, and neck. He figured this would get the job done. The man convulsed as the bullets penetrated his many body parts, spraying blood out. His helmet filled with steam from his breath and blood poured out of his mouth also, casting him in a red cloudy glow. The man slumped to the ground.

'I hear gunshots! I hope he's dead now.' Grey heard the ponytailed man shout out again, and then heard him continue with his harassment of the neuroscientists and doctors.

Grey had just taken out his men and he was oblivious to it. Grey wanted to use this to his advantage, approach him from behind and take him out quietly.

Grey, tired, stumbled onward. Saw the last man—the ponytailed man in the distance, along with the remaining nine neuroscientists and doctors. Grey approached from the right side of the room, using the crates and lighting as cover. Step by step, as quiet as he could be, he approached. He was gasping, though, feeling his breathing coming out in short bursts.

When he reached the area where the ponytailed man stood, the man had his back to Grey. The doctors and neuroscientists kneeled facing him, and Grey pursed his lips at them, putting a finger to his mouth, signalling for them to not make the ponytailed man aware of his silent approach.

Grey slowly edged closer, and then raised the assault rifle to the back of the head of the unaware ponytailed man.

'Freeze, motherfucker . . .' he whispered. 'One false move and I'll blow your brains out all over this beautiful marble floor. Now raise your hands in the air.'

'Is that so . . .' the ponytailed man said softly, seemingly unperturbed, but he started to raise his hands. 'How many rounds does that rifle hold?'

'What?'

'How many single rounds does that rifle hold?'

'I don't know . . . thirty . . . why the hell does that matter? I only need one to do the fucking job.'

'Fair enough, go ahead and pull the trigger. I think you'll be pleasantly surprised.'

'Shut up.'

The ponytailed man started to turn around and Grey pulled the trigger, nothing. He looked down at the gun confused as if he had been betrayed by it. When he glanced back up, staring back at him now with an evil smirk was the ponytailed man.

'Told you,' he said. 'I counted the number of bullets that had been sprayed back there when my men came to find you. I'm guessing you killed them. Impressive—but this is the end of the line for you. Let me introduce myself. I'm Ezra Hawthorne.'

Before Grey could say or do anything, Ezra pulled down and ripped both of his sleeves, revealing two mechanical arms just like his. Grey's eyes widened in shock and he froze, rooted to the spot. *There were others just like me*, he thought. He couldn't believe it. He had always thought he was alone, the only one of his kind. Not anymore. Was Ezra only the beginning? Were there more?

But then again to think he was the only one who'd been mechanically enhanced was quite naive. Of course, if it could be done to him, it was quite possible that it had also been done on someone else. But what's the Ponytailed man's story?

As he stood there, his mind still trying to process things, Ezra stretched fort his mechanical right hand, open-palmed, placing it gently on Grey's chest. Seconds later, after a bright white light emanated from the tiny space between his chest and Ezra's right palm, Grey was sent sprawling backward, viciously, crashing violently into some metal crates, large debris from the surrounding concrete and wooden fixtures crumbling on top him upon impact as he laid there, not moving.

As Ezra approached him, he tried to move but couldn't—not even an inch—his eyes shut instead, and his whole world turned to black.

Chapter Twelve: A Mechanically Enhanced Man

Jasper's heart pounded in his chest. *Thump. Thump. Thump.* Fear had overtaken his entire body. Sweat had filled the inside of his clothing. His head moved from left to right as if by magnets. He did his best to cover all angles from his perspective behind the large shipment container. It was only a matter of seconds before those men in khakis came around and finished him off, he decided. Though he wasn't exactly a rookie REA agent, he was still all alone now, and he was scared to death. He didn't want to die. He wanted to be able to go home after all this and see his wife and son.

Maybe they didn't see me? He thought to himself. *Maybe they only spotted Martin? After all, he was the only one who popped out into their view . . .* He glanced over again to his left. Martin still lay there, not moving, but, strangely enough, Jasper could not see any blood on him or in the area around him. That was strange. He witnessed the bullet penetrate through his chest and stomach.

Then it hit him.

Bulletproof Vest . . . Of course. How stupid of him. He had forgotten Martin wore one, just like himself. Martin was still alive, he was sure of it. He was just playing dead.

Feigning death so the men in Khaki will halt in their firing and by us time, he thought. *Martin you brilliant son of a b—*

He heard boots thudding the ground, approaching their area. Fear rose up again like a volcanic eruption. He couldn't quite make out how many were coming toward them, but he knew it was more than two from what he could hear. The footsteps echoed closer and closer. Jasper stood up behind the shipment container, his back spread against it as he slowing edged to the corner of it. He peaked out, slightly, half an eye sticking out the corner. Four men in khaki uniform approached him. One of them was pointing in the direction of Martin's body.

Jasper knew he had to do something. He squinted, saw Martin's body twitch. That was confirmation.

Jasper took a deep breath, sucked in air, exhaled. He raised his Chrome .357 Magnum Revolver to his chest, the mouth pointing upward toward his chin. His fingers lodged next to the trigger. And as he closed his eyes, images of his wife and son flashed before his very eyes: Sarai's heavenly face, her dimples, her glistening skin, her soft flesh, and her warm touch. Zack's innocent and naive nature, his warmth, and the way his eyes lit up when he sees his dad come home from work.

He shook his head as a single tear left his eye and dropped down his cheek and then to the ground, dissolving and disappearing without a sound.

The next thing he knew, he was diving out of the corner of the shipment container, almost acrobatically. He led with his shoulder, sideways, finger still on the trigger. He pulled back the trigger and let loose. The revolving cylinder chamber span in his grasp in quick succession as the bullets left the chambers, one by one, making its way toward the four men in khakis. Six bullets in total left Jasper's gun but only three bullets struck three of the men. One bullet struck a man in the throat. The man raised his hand up to try and stop the blood from gushing out, but he stumbled and fell to the ground holding his throat as a wet gurgle could be heard emitting out from him. Another one was struck in the eye, instant kill; he fell lifeless onto his back, the impact kicking up dust from the abandoned warehouse dusty ground. The last bullet penetrated the knee of a third man, causing his ligament to come apart at the joint, and he fell to the ground, walling there, grabbing on to his leg. Hellish groans could be heard coming from all around. Yet one of the four stood, unharmed, finding the nearest wall to take cover behind as Jasper witness the other men by the hover truck ready themselves for a battle, arming themselves with large weapons.

Jasper landed on his side with a thud. His elbow smacked off the ground and he let out a suppressed howl. It was painful. His arm trembled. His body arched. But he stumbled over, now in a prone position, toward Martin's body; he grabbed hold of him and pulled him into cover behind one of the many walls in the abandoned warehouse. There he took a position, surveying his surroundings.

'There's another one!' he heard one of them blurt out. 'There are two of them!'

'Goddamnit,' another one said. 'Flush them out. Kill them.'

Jasper looked down at Martin, who was now situated on his lap. His eyes were closed, but he was still breathing, Jasper could tell by the movement of his diaphragm. He quickly pulled apart his shirt. And there he saw the bullet lodge inside his bulletproof vest. A weak smile came upon Jasper's face. But then his eyes moved down to Martin's leg, it had a bullet lodge in there and was bleeding out. He frowned and used his hand to press down on Martin's wounded leg. 'Martin . . .' he said softly, 'It's going to be okay, buddy.' Jasper reached to the ground beside them and picked up his friend's Desert Eagle and wielded it in his other hand. 'Shoot anything that moves.' He whispered to himself.

Jasper eased the unconscious Martin from him, setting him to the ground. Jasper then moved and sat upright and pressed his back against the wall.

Jasper let out a small gasp.

Shots came ringing in his direction.

He returned fire and a gun battle ensued.

Jasper leaned back in and reloaded. *I'm going to run out of bullets soon.*

He fired a couple more shots, hitting one of the men in the thigh, sending him tumbling to the ground in agony. 'Gotcha,' he said to himself.

The shooting warfare went on for a few more minutes, as Jasper's bullets slowly diminished.

Then another truck arrived at the front. A mechanically enhanced man stepped out. His arms and body were all kinds of metallic and robotic, like a cyborg.

Jasper couldn't make out who he was, but he spoke to one of the men in the khaki uniform and the khaki uniformed man quickly grabbed the rest of the robotics that the rest of the uniformed khaki men had dropped on the ground and loaded it onto the hover truck.

As they continued to fire back, Jasper noticed the mechanical enhanced man come closer to the action, and his ponytail became evident.

It was Ezra Hawthorne.

He raised his mechanical arms up in the air. 'ENOUGH!' he shouted, his voice loud like the sea during a storm. His men, Jasper decided they were, stopped in their firing, took cover and looked at him. Jasper had stopped firing also, which was all good for him as he'd reached his last set of ammo. 'Get in the truck, all of you; your job here is done.' The remaining men jolted up to their feet, boots thudding the ground again as they all made their way back into the hover truck. Ezra stared all around him, and all around him was filled with dead bodies of his fallen comrades. His jaws clenched, hard, the bones stuck out like sharp objects. His head lifted up toward where Jasper and Martin hid, behind the wall, and Jasper could've sworn he saw a vein the size of a mountain protrude out of his temple.

'Start the truck up and get going,' Ezra said to his comrades. 'I won't be long. Deliver the goods and we'll meet up at the base.' One of the men in Khaki nodded and entered the front of the hover-truck. The hover-truck started and then it was gone.

Only the ponytailed cyborg now remained. 'Come out and face me. Let me see the faces of the people that this to my men.' He said, pointing at the dead bodies beside him.

Jasper glanced down at the unconscious Martin and remained where he was. Oh, how he wished Martin had been in a better condition, they could've taken him down, together, maybe.

They'd finally got to the man they had been searching for. He was right in front of them. If they could manage to apprehend him, it would solve all their problems. But yet, he didn't know how to go about it, alone. He needed Martin, but his friend was out cold and bleeding. Ezra was a dangerous man, one with dangerous military-grade robotic enhancements. One that he wasn't afraid to use against anyone who crossed his path, Jasper knew this very well from past experience with Ezra.

'Fine then,' Ezra Hawthorne said. 'If you won't come out, ill flush you out myself. This place needs a bit of rejuvenation anyway.' He lifted his hand to the ceiling; a hum-like sound echoed and Jasper saw a soft faint orange glow permeated his mechanical hand. He looked back down at Martin, he friend wasn't in a good state to be moved, and he knew if he let Ezra continue on with his rejuvenation plans, Martin will never ever be in any kind of state to move again.

Jasper lifted his head and stepped out from behind the wall and sprinted toward Ezra. He wasn't thinking. He wasn't thinking at all. He just put one foot after the other and ran. Fast as he could, toward Ezra. His brow was furrowed, his mouth opened and extended in rage. Teeth gritted. His Chrome .357 Magnum Revolver drawn in one hand, Martin's .44 Magnum Desert Eagle drawn in the other, both stretched out before him. Fingers caressed on both triggers.

He pulled back both triggers, simultaneously.

Nothing. . .

He had fired blanks.

The chambers were empty. He'd run out of ammo.

Ezra saw Jasper out the corner of his eye, and he slowly lowered his hand, the hum-like sound and the faint glow in his palm receded. He caught Jasper by the throat, mid-stride, raising him up into the air, smiling thinly. 'Well, well, if it isn't Jasper Barnes . . . long-time no see, buddy.'

Jasper choked, gasping for air, the Magnum Revolver and the Desert Eagle fell from his grasp as he struggled to break free from Ezra's mechanical grip.

His legs dangled there in the empty air, desperately searching for perch.

Chapter Thirteen: A Developer of Robotics

Grey awoke—his world slowly returning back to colour, bright white lights shone over him. He strained his eyes as he looked around; he was atop a bed of some sort, not a comfortable one at that, but a thin one that barely accommodated his whole body.

Attached to his mechanical arm were wirings of all sorts, wires of different colours: red, blue, yellow, green, black, and white. He softly jolted his arm back and forth, the wires swayed, and he wondered what in the hell had happened to him. He furrowed his brow and scrunched his face, trying to jog his memory. Prior to this, he recalled going toe-to-toe with a dual mechanical arm wielder and his gang of mercenaries at the Royal Star Corporation, but the last thing he vividly remembered was himself being sent sprawling into metal crates and crumbling under large concrete and wooden debris as the ponytailed man (and dual mechanical arm wielder)—Ezra Hawthorne—approached him. After that, he had blacked out from the pain that had swarmed all around his body.

As he slowly sat upright, his body ached, the bones in his spine crackled, and he saw two people approach him from his right. One was a male in a white Lab coat, he had broad shoulders, was clean-shaven with a square jaw, and he had blond hair that had been immaculately cut—not one strand of hair was out of place, he looked like someone straight out of the 1920's prohibition era. The other was a female, in a similar white Lab coat; her brown hair was drawn away from her face into a ponytail, making her striking features more prominent: An oval-shaped face, pale skin that was like milk, and dark eyes that commanded attention.

Grey realised then, that he was still at the Royal Star Corporation.

'Ah, Grey Harrow, you are awake.' The man in the white Lab coat said, extending his hand and placing it gently on Grey's shoulder. Grey looked down at the hand on his shoulder then back up at the blond man as if to say: *What do you think you are doing, touching me like*

that, do I know you?

As if he could hear Grey's thoughts, the man immediately withdrew his hand from

Grey's shoulder.

'Apologies,' he said. 'I'm Adam Cardon,' then gestured with his hand to the female

beside him, 'and this is Clare Barnes, my assistant. We are two of the many Doctors, well,

Neurosurgeons actually, here in this facility.'

Barnes. The name was familiar to Grey. Where had he heard it before? *That's right,*

back at the hospital, I was questioned by two REA agents, and one of them was a Jasper

Barnes . . .

'Are you related to an REA agent called Jasper Barnes, by any chance?' he asked

Clare.

'Yes,' she said with a warm smile. 'He's my brother.'

Grey was surprised, members of the same family working for the opposing team. He

wondered what she was doing here helping to create killing military-grade robotics,

machinery, and weaponry, while her brother was out there trying to stop said illegal robotics.

'Where am I?' Grey finally asked. 'What happened to that man?'

'Ezra Hawthorne?' Adam said. 'Don't worry about him, he's gone. You're safe now.'

'But . . . but he wanted something,' Grey said. 'He said he wasn't going to leave until

he got it.'

'And he got it,' Adam started walking around the bed Grey was situated upon. He

fiddled with some equipment next to the multi-coloured wirings and then checked a holo-

screen beside him, pressing some on-screen holo-buttons. 'We gave him what he wanted and

he left us alone.'

'What?' Grey said. 'Just like that?'

'Yes,' Clare inputted. 'He was about to kill you and so we had to give him what he wanted. We gave him the Neurons.'

Grey paused for a while, thinking back to when he heard Ezra kill one of the doctors, and then seeing the corpse lying there. Even for one for their own, they didn't budge, but for *him,* they had given Ezra what he'd come for. Why? Was his life more valuable than that dead doctor or neuroscientist? Grey tried to fathom the whole situation.

He looked over at Adam as he typed into the holo-screen; he felt a tingling sensation in his mechanical arm, which he attributed to what Adam had been pushing on the holo-screen. 'What are you doing?' he asked.

'Fixing you,' Adam responded. 'You just took a battering, remember?'

Yes, he remembered, frowning. 'What do those Neurons actually do?' he asked. 'And that man—Ezra Hawthrone—had a mechanical arm also; in fact, he had two, what's his story? Do you know?'

Adam raised an eyebrow and then gave Clare a look.

'I'll explain, shall I . . . ?' Clare said, Adam nodded and resumed his work upon the holo-screen, Grey still feeling a tingly sensation coming from those wires attached to him as Adam pressed the screen, the feeling now spreading to other parts of his body, his feet, his chest, his neck.

Grey tried not to think too much of the sensations, turning his gaze to Clare as she began to speak.

'So, where do I start?' she said. 'Royal Star Corporation (or RSCorp) is a developer of Robotics. It was founded in the United States fifteen years ago. We specialise in creating robotics for private militaries and those who can afford it. We had three branches situated in London including this one, and there were other branches all over the world in the US, Europe, and Africa.'

She paused, walking over to a table beside Grey; she poured some water from a filter into a cup and gave it to Grey. He took it with his other hand and drank. She watched him drink and she continued. 'But the thing is Robotics was banned in the UK seven years ago and is now illegal. One in fifty people would develop a strange case of Rogue Hand Syndrome Virus (RHS Virus) when augmented with Robotics and would go on a crazy rampage, so the government deemed it too dangerous for private militaries or even for it to land in the hands of civilians, so they shut it down. But as you know, Robotics was already out there in the open, and many people already have them, and not just augmentations, but powerful weapons and armours, too.

'The RHS virus was not even our fault; it's just life, just as in biology and science. Anyone is susceptible to catching a disease, cancer, or even the common flu. And not everyone with cybernetic transplant gets the virus. I'd even go as far as to say that you are the only one, Grey, in the last five years to come up RHS virus, and that might've been due to the stress and trauma from your accident.'

She paused staring into space, giving Grey time to ponder on her words. He decided she had to be one of the neurosurgeons that must've worked on him, told him about his Rogue Hand Syndrome, but that he just couldn't remember. He also now knew after the rude awakening back at Bethany's place that the so-called "accident" was no longer an accident, and he was determined to get to the bottom of it, but first, he would let her finish.

'Most of the operations all around the world were closed down,' she said, still staring into space, 'but some of the branches survived the closure, going deep underground to hide their robotics.' She turned back to face him, 'This facility is one of them. Though what we have left is deprecating and will run out soon, we have managed to find buyers in the criminal underworld who are willing to splash the cash to have some of our tech. Why let it go to waste, aye? What they use it for is up to them, so long as we are not indicated. We work in secret.'

Grey didn't care that what they were doing was wrong; he's done far worse in his relatively short twenty-five years of life.

'But what about Ezra Hawthorne—?' Grey asked.

Adam interrupted. 'Ezra worked for a private military syndicate we had produced for in the past, he was a patient of ours—lost his arms in the 2038 Russian-Egypt war, and we fixed him up good, a new set of robotic arms. Now he's developed an addiction for these Neurons and the abilities that they can provide.'

Grey swung his legs off from the bed so that they fell down to the ground and he sat upright on the edge.

'Abilities?' he asked.

'Yes,' Clare continued, Adam resuming his work on the holo-screen. 'He is a Cybernetic Organism or Cyborg if you want to call it that, just like you. He has augmentations that are intended to enhance human capabilities or to exceed physical human restrictions. Such as the Neuron Kinetic Shockwave he'd let loose on you earlier, or even the Neuron Cannon Blast, and more.'

'Are you saying I'm capable of the same feat?'

She nodded. 'But you'll need Neurons.'

'Neurons?' Then it all came to Grey. This is why the Foxhound Syndicate had them hunting down these specific drugs in secret locations all around London during some of his last jobs. They already had robotics in their ranks and he was feeding their agenda, unbeknownst to him.

'Why? Why help these criminals?'

'We needed the money, we had already invested a lot in the business and when the government shut us down we only had one way to recoup what we had lost and more.' She walked closer to Grey, laid a hand softly on his thigh, squeezing it. He could feel the warmth of her hands even through his cargo pants. It was soothing, reminded him of Bethany's, and he felt the warmness find its way to his blood. 'Besides, what we are doing isn't all bad; we are actually saving lives, prolonging and enhancing it. Human Revolution if you might call it that. We have also stopped aiding criminal organisations, as you can see; we didn't want to give Ezra the Neurons.'

'But it seems the criminals are still finding ways of getting their hands on Neurons.'

'Some of them are getting it imported from other Underground RSCorp from around the world. Ezra's private military and Lucan's Syndicate are the only ones who know of our surviving base here in London. And we want to keep it that way.'

'Lucan? Who's Lucan?'

Adam broke away from his holo-screen and he and Clare exchanged glances.

'He doesn't know,' she said.

'Know what?'

Adam glared at him.

'Lucan Weaver was the man that paid for your operation,' he said. 'His syndicate brought you here after you were in an accident, and we were told to keep you alive by any means necessary.'

'So you were the ones that operated on me and saved my life?'

Adam nodded. 'Yes. But Lucan Weaver was the one who put forward the money in order for us to do so.'

'Where can I find this Lucan Weaver?'

'Don't worry,' Adam said, leaving the holo-screen and walking around toward Grey. 'Before you leave the facility today we'll make sure to tell you where you can find him.'

Grey couldn't believe it, so this Lucan was the one that had saved him and ordered his operation? He'd been in such a rush to leave the facility the first time around that he had not remembered, or maybe he didn't ask? Who knows, he'd just been glad that he was alive, wanted to get home and get back to Bethany as she would've been worried sick. She hadn't seen him for well over a month while he was in the coma. She'd probably felt like he had just up and left her without a word, but when he arrived back at her place and she saw his new mechanical arm, it had been written all over her face—she knew what had happened and welcomed him back with open arms, helping him recuperate, nursing him back to full strength. That woman was a diamond and Grey would love her to his dying breath.

'Now,' Adam said, clasping his hands together and then softly rubbing them. 'How's that Rogue Hand of yours? Anything happened regarding it recently?'

Like you wouldn't believe.

Chapter Fourteen: A Fight with a Ponytailed Monster

Jasper remained suspended in the air—still in the grip of the ponytailed cyborg mercenary known as Ezra Hawthorne. He was all alone, although he'd arrived with Martin; the latter was put out of commission by a stray bullet—from one of Ezra's men—prior, that had lodged in his unprotected leg. He lay unconscious behind one of these pillars of walls, hidden from sight.

Jasper swung his free hands and kicked his legs at Ezra. Ezra laughed, it was in vain. He tried and tried. But still, he wasn't able to break Ezra's hold from around his throat. He was running out of time. He could feel the oxygen in his body not circulating properly, his brain was not getting enough supply, and he felt like he would faint or pass out any moment now.

'This is it, Jasper. This is the end. This will teach you to never cross me again.' Ezra said, his grip getting tighter around Jasper's throat. Jasper's eyes fluttered and he struggled to keep them afloat. 'Killing my men like that, like they were some piece of trash?' he paused, and Jasper felt salvia residue leave Ezra's mouth and land on his face. 'Always trying to get the one up on me, huh?' Then, as if by some miracle, Jasper felt Ezra's grip loosened from around his throat. Jasper's feet touch the ground, and he dropped to the ground, sucking in strong air through his nostrils and mouth. Desperate for air, he sounded like a Grey Seal. Sweat trickled down the back of his neck and his eyes filled with water as they blurred.

He was teary-eyed, and through it, he saw Ezra approach closer to him; Ezra's figure now a black silhouette of a beast.

Ezra crouched in front of him, and Jasper realised how much of a beast this ponytailed man actually was. He was a monster. Not just in height, but in demeanour and presence. He oozed power and something about his aura instilled fear in people. Almost as if he could strike you dead any minute without notice. He gave an air of unpredictability. One minute his stone-cold, aggressive, the next minute he is calm and silent, but his glare was deadly. So were those arms. Regardless of whether he served in the Russian-Egypt war of thirty-eight, those mechanical arms were a mistake. RoyalStarCorp should never have agreed to fit him with it. One was bad enough, to say the least, but two? God, why?

'Jasper,' he said softly, 'I don't want to kill you, you know that, right?'

Jasper raised his hand to his head, trying to stop his vision from swimming.

Ezra continued. 'It's just that when you get involve and disrupt my business and . . . and you kill my men, you leave me no other choice.' He glanced off into the distance, his eyes searching the abandoned building. 'Where's your partner? You didn't do this on your own, did you?'

Jasper quickly came to his senses. 'No, it's just me; I did this on my own.' He wasn't about to let Ezra find the injured Martin, so he lied.

Ezra brought his full gaze back to Jasper, his eyes searching into Jasper's soul to see if he was telling the truth.

'You were never a good liar, Jasper.' He stood back to his feet. 'The REA would never send an agent out into the field alone.' He started toward the wall that housed the injured Martin under its protection.

'No.' Jasper said as he struggled to one knee, clutching his head. His head hammered. How he wished he had a painkiller close at hand. Ezra didn't flinch, continued to walk. Jasper quickly reached inside his weapon belt satchel, and with trembling hands pulled out what last few bullets he had left. He picked up his fallen weapon and snapped opened the bullet chamber, tipping it over and removing the empties and then loaded the new ones. His fingers still trembling as he span the revolving cylinder chamber before he closed it.

He turned and shot at the back of Ezra Hawthorne's head in one fell swoop.

Once. Twice. Three times. Ezra reacted, but he was too slow as all of Jasper's bullets penetrated the area just above his shoulders but below his neck—where flesh was exposed. Ezra wailed, and then he stumbled to one knee. He used his hand to try and hold down the wound as blood gushed out, smearing his mechanical hand in red.

Jasper's eyes widened. He couldn't believe it. He struck the man. He actually did. The beast was down. Now was his chance. He bolted toward Ezra. Ezra without looking raised his other Robotic arm, directed it behind him, toward the oncoming Jasper, and let loose a torrent of fiery energy blasts. Jasper dived to his side, barely escaping, the blasts grazing the barricade he dove behind. Jasper's breath was deep. His heart thumped again, adrenaline running through his vein. He heard Ezra rise to his feet again.

'You son-of-a-bitch, I let you live and this is how you repay me?'

'Yeah. Come and get me!' Jasper yelled from behind cover, trying to draw Ezra away from the injured Martin.

Jasper heard a loud *bang*. He peaked out from behind the cover and saw a large hole had been blown into the side of the building. Debris fell; smoke assimilated, and there was a trail of crimson blood leading out into the streets. The beast had been injured and had retreated back to his cave to recuperate.

Jasper gasped and let out a deep sigh. Relief, he didn't know how much longer he would have lasted. He had done his best against this ponytailed beast that seemed to possess superpowers—the robotic kind. How were they ever going to tame him, and complete their mission before Monday's deadline?

He strode over to Martin. His friend still lay there. He lifted him unto his shoulder; Martin winced as his hands dangled behind Jasper and his legs dangled out in front of him.

Jasper stood for a while with Martin on his shoulder watching the outside world peer in through the hole in the wall, like a long, lost friend you've missed.

The fresh air was welcomed. The air smelt good. He stuck out his tongue. The cold breeze dried the sweat that had accumulated on his forehead.

A Hover car zoomed past as Martin regained consciousness.

Chapter Fifteen: A New Genesis

Grey was still racking his brain trying to comprehend what Adam and Clare had just told him regarding his RHS virus and the voices he'd been hearing inside his head as he headed down the hallways to meet the Biomedical Engineer—Herman Rowntree—in the training gallery.

They'd explained to him that there was a power struggle going on inside his head between his old organic nature and his new robotic one.

A normal brain consists of two hemispheres that communicate with each other via the corpus callosum, but after his accident, he'd had a severe brain injury that required his corpus callosum to be cut to relive his injuries. But now, the RHS virus which had been developed, unfortunately, due to the attachment of the robotic arm, had made its way through the bloodstream and into the right hemisphere of his brain—where the virus has taken root and now resides—and now the two hemispheres of his brain were no longer in cooperation.

The left hemisphere, which controls the right arm and leg, tends to be where language skills reside. The right hemisphere, which controls the left arm and leg, is largely responsible for spatial awareness and recognising patterns. Usually, the more analytical left hemisphere dominates, having the final say in the actions a person performs. However, the right hemisphere (which controls his mechanical arm) wants to have the final say and wants complete control of his mind and body. The right hemisphere feels the left hemisphere can't operate properly, can't think, comprehend, or make the right decision regarding situations well enough, and so the right hemispheres feel it's his place to now help the left hemisphere by taking the dominant role in making all the decisions, hence the frequent rogue outbursts.

They had congratulated him on abstaining from alcohol and experimental drugs as these would have made his symptoms worse. Although he hadn't entirely given up alcohol, he reframed from correcting them and let them have their moment of glory. The medications— Neurazinamide—they had given him to help keep his Rogue Hand in control had worked a treat; Grey hadn't felt so in control of his limbs and clear-headed in such a long while. But how long was it going to last for?

Grey walked through the hallways of the RoyalStarCorp labs. Everywhere he looked there was either a scientist or a doctor busy doing something, intense expressions on their faces as if the entire world dependant on whatever it is they were doing. The same white lab coats on their persons, military-grade robotics beside them. Grey continued to stroll through; just ahead of him was the training gallery. Adam had informed him to meet up with Herman Rowntree in the training gallery before he left so that Herman could teach him about the many capabilities of his mechanical arm.

Grey reached a tall metal door with a small glass window in the centre; he knocked then looked through the window, seeing a really small brown skin man with large rimmed glasses heading toward the door to open it.

The door swung open. 'Hey, you must be Grey Harrow, nice to meet you,' he extended his right hand. Grey shook it, firmly, thinking he seemed like a nice enough fella, even if the poor bastard only reached up to his belly. 'I'm Herman Rowntree, I've been expecting you, come on in, just hang your jacket over there.' He shut the door behind as soon as Grey stepped in.

Grey hung his overcoat on a hook just beside the door and then turned, surveying the room; it was similar to other shooting galleries he had been to in the past, but there were a lot of military-grade robotics and science equipment lying all around. Grey's eyes narrowed at a set of three metallic crystal looking tubes on the table just in front of him—*Neurons*, he thought.

'Right,' Herman said, gesturing with his hands for Grey to follow. 'This way, follow me to a booth. We are going to see what that arm can *really* do.'

Grey followed the short man. Arriving at a booth, he was surprised to see the booth areas were empty, no guns around, not even in the lockers to their side. Why would you bring someone to a shooting gallery and not give him a gun?

'Don't worry, no guns needed,' Herman said as if he could read Grey's mind. 'All we need is that arm and some . . .' he trailed off; walking out behind Grey and over to the table Grey had initially seen the neurons on. He grabbed the three metallic crystal looking tubes and returned promptly. 'This,' he said with satisfaction. 'Now hold out your left wrist.'

Grey stretched forth his hand, and with his mechanical palm exposed and facing upright, Herman used his right index finger and pressed down by Grey's wrist. There was a *click*, and instantly the mechanical parts by of his forearm started to rotate like a Rubik's Cube, expanding slightly, the black and gold of his arm moving all about like the inside mechanism of a clock, tiny blue and white neon-coloured light radiating out, and a small compartment with three empty slots by his forearm opened up.

Herman gently slotted a metallic tube in—in the middle one—it slipped in like a glove, he then rotated it with his fingers and another empty slot beside it became available; he slid in another tube, and then repeated the action once more to put in the final one.

'Ah,' that satisfied tone in his voice again, as if he were Gollum and he'd just found the One Ring. 'That's all of it. The maximum slots available in your arm are three. The neuron in the middle slot is always the active one, and when one neuron empties, it is automatically rotated and is replaced with any of the other two fully charged ones. When all three are empty you can replace it manually.' Herman pressed down again by Grey's wrist.

Grey stared at his arm, his eyes in wonder as the compartment solved its Rubik's Cube puzzle equation and closed shut again with a satisfying mechanical twang—like that of a measuring tap slapping back into place. And so, his mechanical arm had return back to its normal appearance—no more neon blue and white lights, just black with golden mechanical screws and wirings.

'Now, turn and shoot the target.' Herman said.

Grey turned slowly and stretched forth his mechanical hand—open-palmed—out of the booth and aimed for the black and white dummy target in the distance.

'Concentrate, feel the neurons in your arms, inside the compartment, in your bloodstreams, and in your mind, and let it out in the centre of your palm.'

Grey paused, drawing his hand back and then staring at it. He had never noticed it, but there was a small circle in the centre of his palm. *So this is where it comes out from.* He smiled.

Lifting his hand out in front of him again, he concentrated and unleashed a single ball of energy—the size of a tennis ball—out from his mechanical palm, the ball of energy smashed into the black and white dummy target, charring the top right corner, slightly.

'Whoa, no shit, this is awesome.' Grey found himself saying.

Herman smiled; it was an ear-to-ear kind of smile.

'Didn't you know you could do that?' he asked.

Grey let loose another ball of energy. 'No . . . I mean . . . I knew the mechanical arm was strong and durable . . . Heck, I jump out of my five-storey building and this thing gripped to the side of the building helping me to land safely without getting hurt. And then it was able to strangle a six foot four giant of a bouncer—can you believe? And every time I swung a punch I saw it do serious damage. I knew there was something special about it, felt something almost superhuman about it, but this . . . this is amazing.'

Herman pushed his glasses back up the bridge of his nose with his fingers, placed a hand on Grey's shoulder as he let loose another volley of energy, having to stand on his tiptoe to do so. 'And there's still more to learn, my young apprentice.' He said sarcastically, laughing.

Grey stood there, in his zone, mechanical arm still outstretched and palms exposed. A *terrible* thing might have been done to him by the Foxhound Syndicate when he lost his arm and had it replaced with a machine. But now he, too, can be *terrible*, he thought.

Grey flexed his mechanical hand, feeling for the neurons in the compartment of his arms, tried to release another ball of energy, but nothing came out this time.

'Looks like you've drained all three neurons in the arm compartment.' Herman said. 'That's enough for today.'

'Yeah, you're probably right.' Grey said, pressing down on his wrist to open the mechanical compartment in his forearm and removing the empty neurons, placing the empty metallic crystal tubes on the table beside him. He turned to look at Herman. 'Say, you don't have the time by any chance, do you?'

Herman looked down at his watch, '2:34 pm.'

'Thanks, I got to go. Got to pay someone a visit—'

'Lucan Weaver?'

'How did you know?'

Herman didn't reply, but walked over to his desk and grab a tiny black holo-drive, returning to hand it to Grey. 'Adam told me to give you this.'

'What is it?'

'Stick it into your holo-phone. It should give you the details you need to be able to find Lucan Weaver.'

'Thanks.'

As Grey headed for the door, he grabbed his overcoat, put it on, reached inside the pockets, taking out his gloves and wearing them.

As he pulled back the door to open it, turning briefly to gaze at Herman, he said, 'Hey, Herman, have some neurons ready for me when I get back, okay? I have a feeling I'm going to need them. And I'll be ready to pay also; do you have a biometric scanner?'

Herman gestured behind Grey and he saw the little handy machine sitting there on the table, staring back at him with no care in the world, its only worry was feeling the warmth of hands on its body. Even that wasn't a bad thing, after all.

'One more thing, Grey. Adam and Clare have told me of your RHS virus. As you know neurons are experimental drugs, and so can make your Rogue Hand condition worse. Be careful, too much use of neurons can seriously harm your psychic.'

Grey narrowed his eyes at him and nodded.

'And don't forget to take your meds.' He paused. 'Also, you might want to personify that arm of yours, give it a name, make it your own, and own it. That's how you deal with these kinds of things. So, what are you going to call it?'

Grey grinned and said softly, 'I like the name . . . *Genesis*.' And then he left, shutting the door behind him.

Chapter Sixteen: A Whole Different World

Grey arrived outside what looked like an abandoned warehouse in the east of London in Old Street. He stood there in the pouring rain, his face and overcoat soaking wet, the streets, too. He looked down at his holo-phone, the digital map that Herman Rowntree had given to him popping outward like 3D lenses. The map had pointed him to a location where he could find Lucan Weaver, and it had led him here.

He gazed to his left, then to his right. Seeing the coast was clear, he stared back down in front of him to the abandoned building. The building itself was suspect. It looked really old (the irony of its location) and the concrete walls were disintegrating, the colour fading, turning green with mould, the metal rusting away, wooden scraps hung from windows, balconies, and rooftops. An abundance of garbage filled the back end of the building in a ditch that Grey thought looked like it had been dug up fairly recent.

Grey knew these types of building were abandoned and left to rot, and that no government agency or officials cared for it much. He also knew that only the criminal underworld would use such a place as its base of operation. No one would think to look here, but he now knew different having spent the majority of his recovering time in an abandoned hideout in King's Cross. Abandoned buildings and secluded areas like this—far from the main roads and preying eyes—were the Area 51 for the crime bosses, he figured. You come too close without proper authorisation and you are bound to end up six feet under.

'Hello!' he shouted, his voice echoing. No answer. He wanted to step no further, knowing too well he might end up being shot. So, he stood still, waiting, as more and more rain drench his body.

In the far near corner of the building, from one of the windows, he saw a silhouette of a shadow; he squinted, seeing whoever it was readying a weapon and so he quickly raised his arms in the air.

'I'm here to see Lucan Weaver!' he raised his voice.

'Shut up!' the shadow replied. 'Keep your mouth shut. Don't ever say that name out loud again or that will be the last word you ever utter. You hear me?'

Grey didn't know what to do. Is this a trick question? Was he to reply to the shadow? Or keep silent?

Grey breathed a sigh of relief, dropping his hands down when the silhouetted figure stepped out from the shadows of the building and walked toward him. As the silhouetted figure edged closer to him, it slowly took on the form a man before Grey's very eyes; a monster of a man that is, one that was as bald as a cue ball, dark-skinned, with muscle mass on both his arms and thighs, his neck the size of a house. He had a rifle slung over his right shoulder with his right hand holding on to the strap, and Grey guessed he was about six foot six–ish. He was suited in a black t-shirt—a t-shirt that looked two sizes too small due to his mammoth of a size—black cargo pants, and black boots. Grey figured he wasn't cold or too bothered by the rain as the man stopped right in front of him.

'State your purpose here,' the colossus started.

'I'm here to see Lucan Weaver.'

'Why?'

'He saved my life . . . I'm here to thank him in person . . .'

'What's your name?'

'Grey Harrow.'

The man's eyes narrowed as if he didn't believe him. 'Grey Harrow lost an arm, show me yours.'

Grey rolled his eyes and slowly took off his gloves, pulling back his sleeve, and raising *Genesis* to the man's face, stretching the mechanical fingers. 'See, you happy now?'

The man scowled, his face a picture of irritation, but Grey didn't care. Whether the man was irritated by him was none of his business, he was only here to meet Lucan, and get his answers to his questions.

'Follow me,' the man said, turning around and starting, his rifle still held against his shoulders. 'Whatever you do, don't try anything stupid, the folks here don't take to kindly to shit, and won't hesitate to put a few holes in you, cyborg or not.'

Grey put *Genesis* down and followed behind, but not before leaving *Genesis's* mechanical middle finger dangling at the back of the man's head.

Fuck you.

***

Grey arrived inside with the man. *Whoa,* he thought. The inside was the complete polar opposite of the outside. The inside of the building was filled with high-tech computers, gadgetry, machinery, and weaponry, the likes Grey couldn't even imagine. It was like something out of a science fiction movie. It was also filled with a plethora of men and women of different backgrounds and ethnicity, but none of them seemed to be mechanically enhanced. Were his eyes playing tricks on him? All this gadgetry and power, and not one person mechanically enhanced? What's the catch?

It was like a whole different world in there, like he had just stepped through a portal into another dimension. But then it hit him, he wasn't armed; he hadn't any weapon and no neurons inside the compartment in his forearm. If things were to go south, he was in real trouble. After all, who is Lucan Weaver? He may have helped in Grey's survival but can he truly be trusted?

Grey could faintly feel *Genesis* gradually going out of sync with the rest of his body. *Not now,* he thought. The hulking man was oblivious to Grey's mechanical fingers slowly dwindling aimlessly out of his own control, but reaching into his overcoat pocket with his other hand, he took out his Rogue Hand meds and popped two into his mouth, swallowed. *That's one less enemy to fight for the time being.*

They continued and the hulking man took Grey through a narrow corridor when the two emerged out into a wide-open space that smelt of incense and was littered with coils.

The hulking man halted in front of Grey, and without turning around, he reached back and placed a hand on Grey's chest. 'Stop. Wait here.'

Grey did as told. Both men stood. Where they stood was in the centre of what Grey thought looked like a dome-shaped room. Men and women started to pour out from all around, through different side doors, about half a dozen, Grey feeling uneasy and shifting his feet.

'Relax,' the hulking man looked back at Grey from the corner of his eye, his voice but a whisper, his hand still on Grey's chest. 'As I said before, don't do anything stupid.'

Grey rolled his eyes. 'So,' he said. 'What should I call you?'

The hulking man looked at him as if he'd just said something stupid rather than just asked him what his name was. 'My friends call me Behemoth.'

Okay, Behemoth it is.

The men and women that pour out where strapped in body armour from head to toe and looked as hard as nails. He had thought Behemoth was as bad as it got, but he was very wrong. They'd all congregated in an orderly fashion—two groups of three on each side (women on left and men on the right for some strange reason)—in front of a large metallic chair directly situated in front of Grey and Behemoth a few metres ahead. The chair seemed to have someone sitting on it but it was turned so it faced the other way, and Grey couldn't quite make out who it was. Even from this distance, he could see the chair was elevated somehow, maybe on a mound of dirt so that it resembled a high altar.

As the six armoured men and women knelt down beside the throne of their "King", the metallic chair slowly turned. Grey braced himself in anticipation. Was this person sitting on the throne-like chair, Lucan Weaver? Or was he just an imposter? Only one way to find out . . .

He started toward the chair, but Behemoth placed a hand on his shoulder, gripping it. 'Wait,' he said, Grey stopped, feeling every ounce of the man's colossal strength in that grip. 'Lucan is not ready; he'll call you when he is.'

Grey squeezed his eyes shut and set his jaw. He was irritated—a spark had been ignited—and he could feel something akin to fire starting to take hold and rise and burn on the inside of him. But he resisted. Resisted the urge to remove the man's monstrous hand from his shoulder, resisted the urge to cause a commotion. Like Behemoth had told him earlier, he wasn't to do anything stupid. For now, he would comply. At least until his meeting with Lucan was done, he decided.

The chair continued to spin at a snail's pace, finally turning around completely. It revealed a bearded man with a Topknot hairstyle atop it; his index finger across his chin and mouth as if in deep contemplation. The man was black, but unlike Grey and Behemoth, he was very light-skinned, the colour of beach sand, and had a smile plastered on his face; a smile that Grey thought was ominous. He wore workman boots, a large overcoat similar to Grey's that had been button up to his neck, and he also wore gloves, too. What was he hiding?

The light-skinned man signalled with his hands.

'Now,' Behemoth said, letting go of Grey's shoulder. 'Let's go, he's waiting.'

The two walked closer to the other side where the armoured men and women and the man Grey assumed was Lucan Weaver atop the chair were. They halted just in front of the throne. Behemoth knelt, but Grey didn't, choosing to remain standing as Behemoth burned a gaping hole in Grey with his side-eye.

'Well, well, well, who do we have here?' Lucan said, clapping his gloved hands together and then rubbing them off each other.

'Grey Harrow,' he replied. Then, when Behemoth had given him another cold stare that spoke to him telepathically, he just about managed to add another word in quickly. 'Sir.'

Lucan sat up straight, grinning. 'Don't worry about the formalities. I'm Lucan Weaver, but I'm guessing you already knew that.' He paused to adjust his gloves. 'About time you came to us. I was beginning to think all we did to save your life was for nothing.'

'Let's cut to the chase,' Grey said, without wasting any time or beating around the bush. 'Why? Why save me and give me this arm? As far as I know, we are not supposed to like each other.'

Everyone's head rose, Behemoth, the armoured men and women, even Lucan bopped his head back a bit, his face a picture of surprise.

'Really? I thought anyone would be happy to have survived what you did?'

'I didn't ask for it,' Grey's voice, firm and direct. 'What's your game in all this?

'I like you,' Lucan said thinly, 'you don't beat around the bush, and you're direct.'

'Yeah, so I've heard.'

Lucan looked over to Behemoth next to Grey who was looking up at Grey with a frown and when he spotted Lucan's eyes on him he instantly ducked his head back down again.

'Why he asks?' the bearded man looked all around the room, slowly surveying his surroundings before bringing his eyes back to Grey. He stared at him, his eyes not wavering or blinking. 'Because you are too valuable to just let die, Harrow. As much as I hate your guts, I hate the Foxhound Syndicate more.' He pointed his index finger at Grey. 'You may think you're just a brute, but you are more than that, that's why they wanted to kill you. I saw it and gave the go-ahead to keep you alive by any means necessary. We could use someone with your set of expertise, and now more than ever as we plan to take down the Foxhound Syndicate and break their stronghold over this city's underworld.' Lucan interlocked his fingers and crossed his legs. 'Do not diminish yourself, Harrow. If the Foxhound Syndicate wants you dead, then, I want you alive, no matter who you are. You're a skilled ally, and your previous exploits and experience with the Foxhound Syndicate make you invaluable to us.'

'I didn't ask for this . . .'

'You didn't, but it happened. You lost your arm and it was replaced with the highest quality of military-grade robotics. Now you owe me. You owe us.'

'I don't care.'

'Oh, but you should, you are now a wanted man. Words spread like wildfire here in London Town, and it won't be long before the head catches up to the tail that you are still alive and that his foot soldiers have failed in ensuring your death.'

Grey shrugged. He didn't care. They had already tried to get him earlier today and failed, he was up for the struggle. He was up for the fight.

'You still don't care? Listen, I'm not going to sit here and beg you to help me, goddamn it!' Lucan's voice rose an octave, but then he must've realised it because he lowered it again. 'I saved you, gave you back your life, and I can sure as hell take it all away if I wanted to.'

Grey instantly raised *Genesis*, palm exposed, pointing it at Lucan. It was empty, no neurons in the compartment, but they didn't know that, and Grey will try to use it to his advantage, to scare and show Lucan what his newfound arm could do. The armoured men and women as well as Behemoth near Grey instantly drew their guns and pointed it at him. Fourteen-to-one in total and Grey was outnumbered.

Lucan Weaver gestured to the others, and the armoured men and women and Behemoth all holstered their weapons.

'Put that thing away, Harrow.' Lucan said as he slowly stood to his feet and unbuttoned his overcoat, revealing mechanical limbs all around his body. 'You're not the only one with robotics.' He buttoned back up, and Grey slowly dropped *Genesis*. 'But you are one of the only few with it, for now, that is, which makes you important. Heck, it cost a fortune to develop the robotics that fixed you up good. So, it's only right you work to pay me back what you owe. And that can be done by helping to take down the Foxhound Syndicate—your former organisation. The ones that tried to kill you and now will hunt you down. Either way, you need us, Harrow, you'll die out there on your own, and it would be a shame. Do you have a loved one? Someone you're close to, who you wouldn't want any harm coming to? Think about them.'

Agree, Agree . . . Agree to it. Join Lucan and take down the Foxhound, for your arm, for Bethany.

Genesis started up again, and Grey knew it was almost time for his medication.

'Besides, this is bigger than even you.' Lucan continued. 'This war against the Foxhound has been on-going for many years now—oh you didn't know? We've been trying to take them down and recruiting people to our efforts. The Foxhound Syndicate is much bigger than you think. Their stronghold extends to other cities, even almost to the whole country. This is bigger than you and your arm, Harrow, but vengeance can also be served—two birds, one stone.' Lucan got up from his chair and touched ground with his boots.

'Come, let me show you around, if you do decide to join us, I can't have you walking around town alone anymore, you're too important, so ill introduce you to some of the people you'll be working alongside.' Lucan placed a hand on Grey's shoulder and took him for a stroll through his base. They went through a narrow doorway that had white curtains. Drawing the curtains back and easing their tall frame through, they reached another open area, an area that looked like some sort of gym, and where Grey finally saw men and women who had been mechanically enhanced.

'This is Eustace de Maris' Lucan said, pointing at a small but broad man with what looked like a black and silver, robust, mechanical chest. He was working out, lifting weights, and doing pull-ups. He put a thumb up at Grey, and Grey nodded at him.

'That's Elyse Fox', Lucan pointed next at a brown-skinned woman with blonde hair and a single long strand of pink that ran down her wide forehead, running on a treadmill. Grey thought she was rather pretty, but one of her eyes—the right iris—was jet-red like a laser, and Grey gave it another look; narrowing in, saw that it had been mechanically enhanced. She smiled at him and Grey smiled back. 'And that's Gael Cross.'

Gael Cross, who had been stretching, said, 'What's up,' and Grey nodded at him, glancing down at his legs, seeing it, too, had been mechanically enhanced. It was black and silver and corded with wirings and braced with metallic coils.

'This will be your team you'll be working with. These three . . . they are cyborgs, just like you and I.' Lucan paused. 'But on like you, they are in full control of the robotic limbs. We've been told you have a case of RHSV.'

'Yeah, but I'm working to get it under control.'

'You do that, make sure you do, we don't want you going all crazy on us, now.' Lucan walked over to a desk, opened one of the drawers, and took out a case. He flicked open the case in front of Grey, revealing three neuron tubes, and then he flicked it closed again. 'Take these neurons; they should keep you going for a while.' Grey hesitated but then took the case from Lucan, reaching back and placing it inside his overcoat pocket.

'If you have all these mechanically enhanced individuals at your disposal, why do you need me? Why haven't you taken them down already?'

'Because military-grade robotics is not a new thing, although it is now outlawed, private militaries and criminal organisations still have access to them.'

'So, what you're saying is, the Foxhound Syndicate are in possession of military-grade robotics?"

'Of course. You don't run most of the underworld and not have access to a few. You just weren't privy to it, only those who were at the very top were privy to it.'

Grey had already figured it out back at RoyalStarCorp. All this time the Foxhound Syndicate was housing powerful military-grade robotic weaponry and tools, yet Grey and his team were not fully privy to it. They had some inclination, but no proof. What were they to the syndicate? Just some low-level street thugs? Doing mineral errands and expendable? Is that why they thought they could just dispose of him anyway, like common trash? Like he was worthless? Like his life and previous dedication to them were all for nothing? All he had ever wanted was to get out of the game and start a new life with Bethany, but now he was being pulled back in again. He couldn't believe he was actually considering Lucan's proposal. He'd hoped to put his violent past behind him, retire from the dangerous career, but now, after his life was almost ended, he is being pulled back into the fray again to go against his former organisation, the same people that taught him all he'd ever known about the criminal underworld.

'I need your help for something,' Grey started, changing the subject. 'There are four dead bodies in my girlfriend's apartment in Euston.'

'Really?' Lucan raised an eyebrow.

'They tried to kill me last night and this morning they shot my girlfriend. She's in hospital as we speak.'

'Foxhound Members?'

Grey nodded. 'One of them was Hector Foreman . . . a close friend of mine from the organisation. He told me word has got out of my survival and the order was sent to finish the job.'

'Well then, there you have it, you are very important and they know it. Don't worry, I'll send some of my guys to clean up the mess, make the place good as new. Feds won't know a thing. Just give me the address.'

'Appreciate that.'

'Well then, does this mean you're on board?' Lucan Weaver asked.

Just when I thought I was out, they pull me back in, he thought with a shake of his head. 'If you do this, then I'm on board.'

'Good,' Lucan beamed. 'In the meantime stay close to these three here . . .' Lucan pointed to Eustace de Maris, Elyse Fox, and Gael Cross, as they worked out, '. . . at all times and keep your head down, I'll be in touch.' Lucan walked over to another desk, opened another drawer, pulled out a holo-phone and threw it at Grey. 'Throw your other one away; use only this one from now on. The numbers that you need are already saved on it. They were probably able to track you cause of your old one.'

Lucan left the room, drawing back the white doorway curtains and easing his large body through the small doorway as Grey stood staring at his new holo-phone. He then turned to linger his gaze on his newfound colleagues as they continued to work out and stare at him as if he were an alien.

The thought of Bethany's beautiful injured face in the hospital ward flashed through his mind's eye, and then he reached into his coat pocket, drew out his meds, and popped two pills into his mouth.

Chapter Seventeen: A Blast from the Past

When Grey arrived back at Royal Free Hospital he was surprised to see Bethany feeling and looking much better. He'd only been gone a few hours—paying a visit to RoyalStarCorp, then to Lucan Weaver, and on his way back to the hospital he'd stopped by at a local store to pick up a little something for Bethany.

Now, at 4:05 pm, it was getting really dark outside. It was full-blown winter—minus the snow—and in a couple of minutes it will be completely dark, and Grey wanted to get Bethany home as soon as possible. But where was home? Her apartment was a crime scene. And his apartment? Was probably booby-trapped, Foxhound goons probably lying in wait hoping Grey would make a mistake and return to his hideout. No chance. Not happening, mate.

Bethany Rose's face lit up like a Christmas tree when Grey walked into her ward, a bunch of roses in his left hand and a box of chocolate—Ferrero Rocher—in his other. He sat beside her and set the gifts atop her on the bed. She leaned in and smelt the roses, her porcelain-like skin, flushing by her cheeks, and then she proceeded to open the box of chocolate.

'You shouldn't have, Grey,' she said as she pulled apart the plastic covering. They were her favourite; he knew, if anything, Ferrero Rocher would brighten her day. After all, what a day she'd had; she'd been brave, taken a bullet in the shoulder like a true soldier, and she even had a scar to show for it.

'Had to. Saw them on my way back here, reminded me of you.'

She took one of the chocolate balls out, unwrapped the foil covering, popped the entire petit ball in her mouth, devouring it. Bless her.

'Thank you, Hun.' She had a little smudge of chocolate on the corner of her mouth as she spoke.

'You have a little something on the . . .' Grey trailed off, Bethany had a look of confusion on her face, then he leaned in, kissing the side of her mouth and taking with him the smudge of chocolate, licking his lips. 'Never mind,' he said softly, his lips still so near to hers, their mouths partially opened, the only air that hung between them were each other's warm breaths.

He pulled back and she smiled, her cheeks going all rosy again.

'Anyway, are you ready to go? Doctors said you're good to go.'

'Yes,' she paused, 'Oh yeah, those Agents came by to talk to me, told them I wasn't in the right frame of mind to, and so one of them left their card,' she pointed at the small table beside her: a single small white card lay there. Grey picked it up and it read: AGENT JASPER BARNES. ROBOTICS ENFORCEMENT ADMINISTRATION. Tel: 07845673312.

'He told me to call when I'm ready or if I ever need anything.' She went on. 'He seemed like a nice man.'

'They always do,' Grey said, still staring at the card. 'They project themselves as some kind of angel, but in reality, they turn out to be demons.'

'What about my apartment . . . are the bodies . . .' she hesitated, surveying her surroundings; making sure no one was listening. 'Are the bodies still there?'

Grey set the card back down on the table and then turned back to Bethany. 'Listen, Beth, I need to . . . about all this . . . about what's really been going on—'

Grey's holo-phone vibrated in his pocket. It was the old holo-phone, not the new one Lucan had just given him. Damn, he should have discarded it already, just like Lucan had told him to. Especially if what he had said about them being able to track him with it was true.

He took it out, hesitantly, staring at the holo-projected caller I.D—it was an unknown number, and he considered not answering, before picking up and putting the holo-phone to his ear anyway.

'Harrow!' Lucan's voice beamed through the phone. 'Why haven't you discarded this phone yet?' he asked.

'I—erm . . .'

'Listen; are you on your way back to your girlfriend's apartment?'

'Erm. No, not yet, we were—'

'Good, whatever you do don't head back there.' Lucan went on, 'Just got a call from one of my men . . .'

'What's wrong?' Grey looked over to Bethany, her eyes narrowing on him.

'The guys that I sent to clean up the bodies in the apartment said when they'd arrived someone had already been there, that the bodies were gone and the apartment was cleaned, spotless—not even a blemish. They told me that they even doubted whether a highly-skilled forensic scientist could ever find a speck of evidence in this untainted apartment.'

'It must be them . . .' Grey stood up and paced the ward.

'It most certainly was. Trying to cover their asses, leaving nothing behind that could be traced back to them.'

'It's not safe anymore for Bethany to stay there.' He paused, stopping in his pacing, and glared into her crystal blue eyes, wondering how the hell he dragged her into all this mess. 'Lucan, can you help me out? Is there a place she can lay low for a while until I find her a new place?'

'Sure, I know of one. Bring her over to Old Street; I'll have her set up in a nearby flat by our base. And we can keep an eye out for her.'

'Thanks. I owe you one.'

'You owe me a lot more,' he said. 'Now as soon as we're done on this phone, get rid of it, pronto.'

Grey grimaced as he hung up. He looked again at Bethany; he didn't really want to go against his former squad, even if they wanted him dead *and* still want him dead. He didn't mind that to say the least. He was a survivor and he could handle himself. After all, they had already tried to kill him once and he came back from the dead—even so with newfound capabilities. They sent him to hell and he came back with superpowers. Now that's a headline if he did say so himself.

But now that Bethany has been dragged into all this, he is more than willing to cooperate with Lucan Weaver and bring down the Foxhound Syndicate. For Bethany's sake, if anything. He couldn't care less about what happens to him. They had already taken half of him—his arm—and he just wanted her to be safe. If that means destroying his former Syndicate, then so be it, as long as it means she will be safe and free to do whatever it is she wants to do without fear—a fear that was all his own doing. This he wanted to rectify.

His holo-phone vibrated again. The same one he'd been told a thousand times to get rid of, but still was in his bare hand. He looked down at it. This time it had a holo-projected caller I.D and he recognised the number.

It was Brom Ide. Brom Ide was one of his closest brothers that he'd rolled with in the Foxhound Syndicate in the past. They both started in the Syndicate at similar times, and Brom was gutted when he learned Grey was leaving the group, though, they hadn't spoken for a long time, probably because he thought Grey was dead.

He picked up. 'Hello,' he said.

'Grey, Grey, it's me, it's Brom,' he sounded hurried, like he was being chased.

'Brom, what's wrong, brother?'

'They are after me . . . Grey . . . help me . . .' he was breathing heavily.

'Whoa, Whoa, slow down, Brom, tell me, what happened?'

'The Foxhound Syndicate are after me.'

'Why?'

'I don't know Grey,' he said, his voice sounding like he was about to cry. 'I just wanted out, I just wanted to lea—' Grey heard the sound of gunfire in the background, then screaming—the screaming was from Brom.

'Where are you, Brom? Tell me, I'm coming to get you.'

'I'm in Piccadilly Circus, by Baron's Bar, I'm laying low inside, but they are all around, outside. I'm surrounded, even in the alleyway at the back. I see someone—' Brom's connection cut off, and Grey slowly brought the holo-phone down from his ears and stared at it . . .

Then all the lights went out, engulfing the entire hospital in darkness. Grey frowned and stared out the windows. He could see many red laser-sight mounts from guns pointing—in all directions—inside the wards.

Without a second thought, he sprinted toward Bethany's bed, barrelling through a crowd of patients and nurses alike, mind you, and like a desperate fool, he grabbed her, hugging her tight and then rolling under the bed with her as bullets stormed the hospital ward from the outside; glass shattering, wooden frames breaking, walls chipping off, people screaming and collapsing all around, blood spraying about, one woman dropped dead right in front of them and Grey and Bethany from under the protection of the bed could see her lifeless eyes staring at them, accusing them.

Bethany bawled, Grey felt her body tremble, and he held her close, averting her gaze from the woman's corpse, right hand on her back, *Genesis* on her head, like a child hugging its teddy late at night, waiting for the coast to clear.

Chapter Eighteen: A Fox with a Combat Knife

'Ssssh,' Grey whispered to Bethany. She was still in tears, still shaken from the events that had transpired all around her and Grey. Those lifeless eyes were still staring at them—dead in the eyes.

He continued to hold onto her as the bullet storm halted. He heard the last piece of debris fall over, and then nothing. Complete silence. You would think they were in a morgue, what with all the dead bodies, and now, the quietness of the ward. But why was it so quiet? A few minutes ago this ward was bustling, rife with people: doctors, nurses, and patients— could they all be dead?

He didn't want to believe so. It made him sick to his stomach. Who and what? Why? These people had probably done no wrong in their whole entire life. Done nothing wrong to anyone; let alone a fly. But for *him*? He was scum, and Grey knew it. It had to be him. They were after him again, and now more casualties are left in the wake because of him.

Footsteps . . . Grey heard the thumping of boots; he peeked out quietly from under the hospital bed and saw armoured men. He counted roughly six, and as he squinted he could just about make out the insignia on their arm badge: A Fox with a combat knife in its mouth.

It was the Foxhound Syndicate. No doubt about it. No mistaking it. Grey could recognise that insignia a mile away, even if he was doped up high on neurons. He slowly retreated back under the safety of the bed, Bethany still face-down on his chest, but she was no longer crying.

Grey slowly lifted her head from his chest so he could look her in the eye. 'Listen, Beth, we are going to make a run for it,' he said, his voice barely a whisper so as to not alert them to their presence. 'I want you to stay close to me at all times and do exactly as I say, Okay?'

She hesitated. 'Why, what's wrong?' She turned to her side to witness the black boots of the men, and then the flashlights from gun mouths sprawling about the darkness, causing her to squint.

'Those men out there are here for me, Beth. And just like those men back in your apartment, they want to kill me.'

She gasped, and one of the boots turned toward them. Grey held a finger to his mouth, signalling to Beth to remain quiet. The boot edged closer toward them, reaching the side of the bed they were posted under. Grey saw the boot of the man kick over the body of the dead woman that had been staring at them, her body sprawled over to the other side and her eyes were no longing accusing them. Then the boot stopped. Grey knew it was only a matter of time before he saw the face attached to those boots. But he wasn't one for sitting and waiting. He had to go. He had to get Bethany to safety and he had to go and help his friend, Brom.

As the pair of boots creased, suggesting the man attached to the boots was about to bend down and take a peaked under the bed, Grey flung the bed forward, hard, knocking over whoever those boots belong to. The man growled and Grey quickly grabbed Bethany by the arm, 'Go, run down those stairs,' he pointed toward the staircase at the south end of the ward, 'I'll by us some time. Head to the parking lot and wait for me.'

'Parking lot? We didn't bring a car—'

'Just go! I'll meet you there.'

Bethany hesitated, frowning at Grey, and then she turned running down the south end stairs.

After she left, he quickly took out the case Lucan had given him from his overcoat pocket, pressed down by his wrist, opening the small compartment and inserting the neuron tubes—all three—one by one, as fast as he could, but just as he was about to insert the last tube, the man that had been knocked over with the hospital bed, recovered tossing the flimsy bed aside, and Grey hesitated, holding on to the last neuron and shutting the compartment in his arm with only two tubes inserted.

Should still do the job, he thought as pocketed the last neuron and raised *Genesis* directly in front of himself, emitting a soft orange glow, before blasting the man in front of him, sending him sprawling and crashing into a pillar that held part of the ceiling together. Grey heard him wail in pain as that part of the ceiling came crashing down, crushing him.

Grey then turned and headed for the south end stairs, but was stopped by bullets that flew right past him. He ducked for cover, hiding behind a wall, dead bodies of doctors, nurses, and patients were all around him. His heart sank and his belly tightened. This was his fault, he reminded himself. They were collateral damage. Bullets continued to spray toward his direction and he clenched his jaw. He bided his time, waiting behind the wall in the shadows for his opportune time, and when it finally came, he swung out with *Genesis* drawn forward, fingers spread wide apart, letting loose with a succession of small energy blasts. The blasts connected with two of the men, charring and striking them down. Another two came out behind them from the north end side stairs and Grey shot a blast toward the ceiling, causing debris to fall, blocking their passage and stopping them in their tracks. He then ran down the south end to meet up with Bethany.

When he reached the bottom, the hospital had been slowly evacuating its people, and CLP sirens could now be heard in the distance. The cavalry had finally arrived, but Grey was not one to wait around for them to question him, so he bolted toward the parking lot. Bethany should be there waiting for him.

When he got to the parking lot, there were only a few hover cars about. He glanced around; she was nowhere to be seen. *Damn, I told her to stay put here.* Then he heard screaming—from a woman—come from his right. He quickened his steps toward the sound, and when he got there he saw Bethany running, behind her a member of the Foxhound Syndicate pursuing, his gun drawn and aimed at the back of her head.

Grey stretched forth *Genesis* and took aim, 'Bethany, get down, now!' she immediately dropped to the ground, unto all fours, arms raised over her head, and as the neuron metallic tubes in his forearm compartment worked their magic and charged up for usage, Grey's mechanical hand flared up, releasing a large orange ball of energy, it ejected from his palm with such force, staggering him back a bit—and this time the size of a beach ball—grazing a few parked hover cars as it made its way along to its intended target. The Foxhound man halted in his pursuit of Bethany, slowing down just in the nick of time to duck down and slide under Grey's blast. The Foxhound man turned his gaze behind him to watch the energy blast crash into a barrage of parked hover cars, setting them off in a firework display of explosions. Flames poured out of the hover cars and rose—high—into the sky and the smell of oily black smoke filled the atmosphere.

Grey stared down at *Genesis*, then back up at the carnage, open-mouthed, feeling both shock and amazement glinting in his roguish eyes. But there was no time to stand and stare. He glanced over at Bethany; she too was staring in awe, as well as the Foxhound man, who was just behind her. Grey strolled over and took Bethany by the hand, knowing full well that explosion had attracted the attention of the CLP, and it was only a matter of time before they made their way down to the parking lot.

He started with Bethany in his grasp, in the direction of the Foxhound man. As the man turned back his gaze toward them, his face met the powerful left hook of *Genesis*, the flesh on his cheekbone peeling back, the bone caving in with a wet *crunch*, his jaw snapping and dislodging from its hinges, dangling there like a spider on a web, his head twisting, lolling as it landed hard on the concrete floor with a thud. Blood oozed out from beneath the man's head in a single, thick, crooked line. Out of the corner of his eye, Grey saw Bethany grimace at the sight, but Grey didn't care. They had taken the lives of many back at the wards and they'd tried to kill them both. No pity party for them, none whatsoever.

It had taken Grey a couple of seconds to find a hover car that wasn't locked, and just a few more for him to prep the car wires for hotwiring—one of the many perks of being a former member of the Foxhound Syndicate.

'What do you think you're doing?' Bethany asked as he readied the hover car. But what did she think Grey was going to do? There was no backing out now; it was either this or getting arrested by the feds. He was definitely going to take the former.

'Get in, Beth!' he spat. 'There's no choice here.' She hesitated, shifting her feet, took a final glance over her shoulder at the carnage, and then she got in the passenger side, easing her small frame in and slamming the door shut. Grey did likewise.

They zoomed off in a blue hover car, and once they were on the high street, if there had been anyone that had been pursuing them, they seemed to have lost them.

Chapter Nineteen: A Small, Cold, Dead Hand

First thing Grey did before they arrived at RoyalStarCorp was to transfer Brom's number to his new holo-phone and smash up the old one.

'Why?' Bethany asked.

'It's how they managed to track me.' He told her.

'Who?'

'The Foxhound Syndicate.'

She eyed him from the passenger side of the stolen hover car, but said nothing more.

A short while later they had arrived at their destination. Grey had taken them to RoyalStarCorp in Camden Town because he figured that taking Bethany to Old Street and to Lucan's base right now would cause serious problems for them later on. Besides RoyalStarCorp seemed the more feasible option right now. It was faster to get to from where they'd just come from, and RoyalStarCorp was also a secret underground lab where Bethany could be kept safe, hopefully, and it was close enough to Piccadilly Circus so Grey could go and rescue his friend, Brom.

He planned to leave Bethany in the care of Adam, Clare, and Herman, and after a few minutes of pressing on the holo-screen touchscreen and banging at the secret lab front door, the short biomedical engineer appeared. His face looked tired, probably from a lack of sleep, his white clothes dirty with black stains, probably from playing with oily machinery all day long.

'What are doing here, Grey?' Herman Rowntree grunted as he used his right index finger to push his large rimmed glasses up the bridge of his nose. 'Do you know what time it is?'

'Herman, thank God you are still here, I need your help . . .'

'What is it?' Herman glanced to the right, staring at the weary brunette beside Grey. 'Who is she?'

'This is Bethany,' she gave Herman a little raise of the palm, 'I need to leave her in your care, for the time being, I've got someplace I need to be, I will be right back,' he paused. 'Is there anyone else here?'

'No, it's just me; Adam, Clare, and everyone else here at the lab have all gone home,'

Then it hit Grey: Was he really going to leave her in the care of this short man? How could he possibly protect her if it comes down to it? But Herman Rowntree was an intelligent man, he would always have a trick up his sleeves—some type of gadgetry ready at hand—and Grey would do well to leave her with him. After all, the man was one of the people that had crafted the neurons he and many other cyborgs in the city use to power their mechanical limbs.

'Grey,' Bethany started. 'I don't want to leave you, take me wherever you're going. I can help.'

Grey was taken aback at her bravery. He took her hand in his and looked her in the eyes, 'I can't Beth, it's too dangerous, and I'll be back before you know it. Herman here,' he gestured toward him, 'will look after you while I'm gone.'

She stared into his eyes for a long while, frowning, and Grey could see the pain in her eyes, the pain of confusion, of hurt, of abandonment, but also, one of both strength and powerlessness at the same time. Grey knew she wanted to help him—she always did—in any way she could, but she couldn't possibly do that. Not now anyway, and not in the way Grey needed. She wasn't strong enough to take on an army of coldblooded killers, even ones with mechanical enhancements; she simply wasn't built like that. Maybe in time, with practice she could, but not right now. All he wanted was for her to be safe, the only remaining love of his life, the only person that added meaning to his despicable life. Without her, he was a broken mess, a common brute in an endless cycle of nothingness.

She'd come into his life and cleaned him up, triggered a change in his heart, prompting him to want to leave that unproductive life behind. He wasn't about to lose that. Was that selfish of him? So be it. Call it what you want. He was going to do everything in his arsenal to protect the very person that had saved his life—in more ways than one. Plus, she so happened to be very beautiful, and it would sure as hell hurt not to be able to stare into those deep ocean-blue eyes for the rest of his life.

'Alright, Alright, enough of the soppy stuff,' Herman said, gesturing with his hands for Grey to hand Bethany over. 'She can stay the night, don't know what the others will say but whatever,' he moved aside for Bethany to come through the door and, reaching inside his pocket, he produced one shiny metallic tube—a neuron. 'Take this, hope you won't need it. Wherever it is you're going, be safe.'

'Ah, Herman, you're a star!' Grey grabbed it, placed it in his overcoat pocket with the other extra one leftover from Lucan Weaver, making it two he now had in excess. He waved them goodbye and started on his way.

***

Grey reached Piccadilly Circus, hopping out of the blue hover car he and Bethany had stolen earlier at the hospital parking lot. He had parked a few metres away from Baron's bar—where Brom had last said he was—in an alleyway. The strong smell of urine lingered in the air of the alleyway and Grey's nostrils struggled to keep the stench at bay.

From where he was, he could see that the front of the bar was flooded with onlookers and partygoers, so he decided his best bet was to make his way through the back of the bar. He tried Brom's number again. It rang and rang . . . no answer. Grey feared the worst, but he shook the thought away.

When he reached the back of the bar, he could see by the left side of the big building, three men in black metallic armour who looked like they had a similar emblem to the Foxhound on their arms. It looked similar—and he was pretty sure it was them—but from where Grey was standing he couldn't see anything clearly. The dark, night skies had bloomed even darker and swallowed up the area. As he made his way through the right side of the building instead, passing through broken crates and bits of rubbish bins, the stench spewed out from the dumpsters, the grim smell seared his throat. He stopped for a while, crouching and leaning behind a large, rectangular-shaped, metal, trash can—the ones where the smaller rubbish bins get chucked into.

He pressed down on his mechanical wrist, opening the small compartment on his forearm, saw that two tubes were empty and he removed them, replacing them with the two last tubes given to him by Lucan and Herman. He was now fully loaded, more than capable to take them head-on.

He peeked out from behind the rubbish bin; back down to his left where he'd last seen the men in black armour. The vile pollution of the rubbish bin stung at his eyes, tears welling. He squinted, no one was there any longer; all that was left was pitch blackness.

Grey stood, reaching out *Genesis* in the darkness, gritting his teeth and clenching his jaw as he tentatively started toward that area. He reached for his holo-phone with his other hand and tried for Brom's number again—it rang—and Grey heard a phone ring just ahead of him in the same area those men in black metallic armour had just been. He jerked his head, almost like a spasm, both realisation and dread came to him and he quickened his footsteps, *Genesis* still outstretched, the palm glowing a faint orange, ready for any surprise attack that might come his way.

The ringing got louder and more prominent, and finally, he reached the holo-phone, seeing where it resided: in the palm of a small, cold, dead hand.

Grey scrunched his face, he was too late. They had gotten to Brom before him. He lay there not moving, a hole—the size of an old pound sterling coin—indented through the front of his head, blood reeling from the back of his head out to the side, drowning him in a puddle of blood and soaking his clothes with red. His mouth was wide opened, his skin dark and ashen and ghostly.

Then Grey was struck over the head with what felt like a baseball bat. He felt a sharp pain, like a bag of pins and needles had exploded inside his brain, his ears rang, blood trickled down his neck, back, and forehead, and as he fell to the ground, he felt himself fall into an even greater darkness than the one he was already residing in this night. He saw his whole life flash before him; he saw his early days in the Foxhound Syndicate: Brom, Hector, even David, his mother, his adoptive parents, and then finally his reason for being—Bethany Rose. At that moment he hated himself for not coming back to her like he had promised he would. Another explosion to the back of his head and he crashed to the ground, his face hitting the kerb so hard; he felt some bones in his face crack.

With what grace of strength he had left, through glazed over, blurry and bloodied eyes, he looked up to see a shadowy figure of a man, standing and towering over him in the darkness.

Beaten, bruised, and bloodied to almost certain death, Grey reached to plant a soft hand on the man's boot.

The man jerked his boot back and Grey's feeble hand fell to the cold ground and his grey vision gave way to darkness.

Chapter Twenty: A Man Called David

Darkness gave way to black and white, and then it gave way to colour as Grey was abruptly brought back to full consciousness. Strapped to a chair, arms tired around the back of it, and surrounded by three men in what looked like an abandoned warehouse of some sort. The warehouse reeked of sweat and blood. Grey had been drugged, he realised with a start, his vision—foggy, the men moved with swiftness, leaving ghostly trails of their movements in their wake. It was like the feeling of being drunk and oh-so wasted. His vision swam, and Grey could only guess if he'd happen to look upon a mirror right now, his pupils were most probably dilated.

A clenched fist flew toward him, catching him on the left side of his face, on his cheekbone, where the small tattoo of the sign of the cross resided. Grey jerked to side from the impact, his face throbbing, and just when he thought it was over another hand came in again, connecting with his lower jaw this time, near the side of his mouth as he felt blood poured out it like a fountain.

Grey spat out the remaining blood from his mouth. Tired and drowsy, his neck hurt whenever he moved it. But move it, he did, and sluggishly, he turned to look at his punisher.

David Achard's square head with his usual close-cropped skin fade hairstyle and baby-faced, clean-shaven look materialised in front of Grey, a hand towel in his hands, wiping Grey's blood off his hands. Beside him, there were two other men, garbed in typical Foxhound Syndicate armour wear—metallic steel chest plates over black skin-tight under layer and black cargo trousers—but Grey couldn't see their full faces as it was covered from their nose down in a pair of thin balaclavas.

'David,' Grey said softly. 'When I get out of here . . . I'm going to kill you.'

David laughed as if he'd just been told the most hilarious joke he'd ever heard. 'Grey, I forgot how funny you could be.'

'I mean it, David; you better make sure you kill me and I stay dead this time.'

David smiled. 'Ah, the botched assassination attempt on your life.' He walked closer to Grey stretching forth his hand. He wrapped it around Grey's throat, squeezing it tight and looking Grey right in his drugged up eyes. 'Don't worry, when we are finished with you, we'll make sure you stay six feet under this time.' He removed his hand from Grey's throat and Grey gulped in air. He turned away and paced around the room. 'So you killed Hector, huh? Bravo,' David clapped, 'I didn't think you had it in you, Grey. Hector was a fool, anyway. Good riddance. He wasn't worthy. He was always the weakest member of our little group.'

Grey spat. 'He may have been the weakest, but he was more of a brother than you ever were. You're a fucking traitor.'

David halted, turned back to face Grey, glaring, his eyes turning to fire, 'What did you call me?'

'I said,' Grey coughed; spat some more blood, 'You're a fucking T—'

David raced toward him and landed a fury of punches before he could finish his sentence. Grey's head shuddered from side-to-side; a thumping dull pain spread across his features on his face, the sound of a punching bag being hit with full force, echoed in his ears.

Grey's face bloodied, warm blood dripped down it, his nose—broken now, he assumed, leaked blood also, some rolled down to his tongue, the iron-like taste, salty and metallic.

David paused, just glaring down at the bloody, crimson mess that Grey surely was now. 'You see, in my experience and to my understanding,' he started, 'the most memorable thing in a person's life is rarely enjoyable. Pleasure doesn't teach us anything but that pleasure is pleasurable. And what sort of lesson is that?' He turned back to the look at the other two men, 'The nature of learning . . . my brothers?' they said nothing; he turned back to Grey, 'is pain.' And then all hell broke loose again from his fist as he resumed his artistic work on Grey's face.

Grey'd had enough already, his face and body throbbed with pain, but David continued his assault—left and right jabs—his head bouncing back and forth like a basketball, and right then and there, Grey wished he were dead, the pain unbearable, and David unrelenting.

Finally, through bloody, swollen, and bleary eyes, Grey saw the other two men restrain David, grabbing him by the arms and pulling him away, David cursing as they did. Grey breathed a deep sigh of relief; he didn't know how much more he could've withstood. From the ensuing respite, Grey glanced down at himself—the upper part of his body was covered with his own blood, it masked many of his tattoos.

He jerked his hands from behind him on the chair, tried to wriggle free from the strap—it chinked and rattled—but to no avail.

He had put on a brave front, but all of a sudden, Grey felt powerless. He felt weary and alone and wanted to cry, but his pride wouldn't allow him to. Not in front of them. He had been beaten to a bloody pulp by the one man he hated more than anything in this world, the man that has made his life a living hell ever since he decided to leave the Syndicate. That man, David, had now become Grey's primary target. For the pain he had received here today, if anything, he will pay, one way or another.

Grey watched from his bloodied vision as David broke loose from the other two men's vice-grip, 'Get off me, now!' he yelled, walking back down toward Grey, grabbing what looked like an old rusted lead pipe from a table. Grey flinched at the sight, wrinkling his forehead. His throat felt tight like it might collapse in on itself as he imagined the visceral pain he was about to receive. But even he didn't deserve this, did he?

David lifted the rusted lead pipe, pausing, drawing a deep gasp from Grey. 'Anyone the Foxhound Syndicate deems surplus to requirement they get rid of, and you wanting to leave made you just that, it's about protecting the Syndicate's criminal business.' Grey swallowed and David continued with a lower voice, 'And you surviving that "accident"—my kill order—put me in a very bad place with the leaders. You put me in a very bad position, Grey, you just being alive, you just being here.' He teed up the lead pipe like he was about to hit the biggest home run of his career. 'I hope you know why this has to happen? Brom knew the consequences and he paid the price.'

'Put the pipe down, now!' a voice boomed from behind David and the other two men.

The drowsy Grey lifted his head trying to put a face to the voice, but his vision was spinning and he barely saw when David turned and flung the lead pipe in the direction of the voice, the other two men—David's Foxhound goons—drawing for their weapons—a carbine assault rifle and a 9mm pistol, respectively—and firing also in that direction. They retreated to hide behind a wall barricade made up of what looked like old wares and junk.

A battle ensured, bullets flew in both directions, Grey with what strength he had left, pushed himself to the side, tipping the chair he was on over.

He heard one of the other two men shout. 'There's too many of them, let's go!'

'No! We have him! I am not letting him get away again!' David fired back.

'We have too; we do not have the manpower. We are sitting ducks here.'

'Argh,' David stared over at Grey on the ground, still strapped to the chair, their eyes locked over the short distance—in-between the gunfight—hate was rife between them, and Grey knew it. He reckoned David would never let this go, he would die trying, and Grey was ready for it. He wasn't about to let it go, either. David had made his life a living hell, made it personal when he had drawn Bethany into the conflict, and Grey would not forgive him for that. He would have to end it once and for all. And then he would have to take down the whole Foxhound Syndicate with Lucan. If he survives this ambush, that is.

'Let's go,' David said, glaring over at Grey with disdain. Grey could smell and taste his hatred; it was disgusting and it made him sick to his stomach. Then David and his men disappeared through the back of the warehouse and the firing seized.

Before Grey passed out again, he saw two men holster their handguns, a 9mm semi-auto probably, he thought, as they strode toward him, one of them helping to remove the strap from behind him. Grey then felt handcuffs go around his wrists. He was weak, couldn't do or say anything, he had been drugged up so bad, he complied willingly.

'Get the medic ready,' a voice he recognised uttered. He squinted, forming a face to the voice; a square jaw, stubbles, short brown hair. 'Don't worry, we are one of the good guys.' REA Agent Jasper Barnes said.

Chapter Twenty-one: An Interrogation Room

Jasper sat in one of the empty interrogation rooms in the REA office in Knightsbridge. His chair back to front, his arms propped up on the backrest, leaning forward. Grey Harrow, with his head hanging after being tendered to by one of the medics here and wiped clean of his dried blood and stitched of his cuts and bruises, sat opposite him across a large marble table situated between them. He looked weary, like he'd had all the life sucked out of him. His face had been beaten and bruised and swollen. He was barely recognisable, save for the small sign of the cross tattoo on his left cheekbone that Jasper had made a mental note off when they had met earlier in the day at the hospital ward. Grey had his left hand—his Robotic one—handcuff to the marble table, but Jasper decided to have his palm pointed and directed toward his face, in case he got any bright ideas.

Jasper grinned to himself, he had seen with his own two eyes what that Robotic part can do.

After Jasper and Martin's encounter with Ezra Hawthorne and his goons back at the abandoned warehouse, Jasper had taken the injured Martin to Royal Free Hospital so that his wounded leg could be attended to. But it wasn't long after they had arrived that the hospital went all dark—all the lights within the hospital had been turned off, probably by the mains—and all hell broke loose in one of the wards in the Accident and Emergency area.

The Sound of gunfire had ripped through the air, followed by hellish screams from frightened patients, nurses, and doctors alike. Then he had remembered that Bethany Rose girl had been admitted to that ward earlier in the day, for gunshot injuries, and he was fearful for her safety, feared they had come back for her, to finish what they had started.

He had looked around the ward, seeing the perplexed expression on the people's faces as they wondered what in the hell was happening in the other wards. The darkness gave their faces an unusual scary feature, which caused Jasper to jump a little as if he were a little kid that had just watched a horror movie and now can't seem to get the images out of his mind. Nevertheless, he pressed down on the bedridden Martin's chest beside him, and he had whispered to him that he would be right back and then he started toward the other ward, where the gunfire had erupted like a volcano.

And when he had got there, it was silent. No sound, none whatsoever. That ward was a bloodbath, and Jasper felt his stomach turn, he gagged but didn't throw up. Carnage everywhere, and to think this was a place of safety, a safe haven, where people come to heal themselves, but now they suffer the complete opposite. It wasn't fair.

He walked over to the window that peered over the parking lot and made it just in time to witness Grey Harrow—the man with the sign of the cross tattoo on his left cheekbone and Bethany Rose's boyfriend—eject some kind of energy blast from what had looked like a robotic hand. The ball of energy—as large as a beach ball—nearly missed a man and crashed into a couple of parked hover cars, setting them up in flames. That was when Jasper knew he and Martin's earlier hunch about this man were right. He was one of them. He needed to be stopped. Was this massacre all his doing?

From then on that night, Jasper had quietly tailed Grey Harrow, following him to Camden, where Grey Harrow had dropped Bethany Rose off with a small man with large rimmed glasses, then to Piccadilly Circus, where Grey Harrow sneaked around the back of Baron's Bar like a spy. Finally, Jasper witness Grey Harrow attacked by a group of men and taken to another abandoned warehouse where they proceeded to lay into him. One man, in particular, seemed to have a vendetta against him, but even so, Jasper wasn't going to sit back and watch them kill him, even if he deserved it. After all, he was cyborg, and Jasper and Martin's last hope of finding Ezra Hawthorne again and completing their mission before the deadline on Monday.

So Jasper had called in reinforcement from the REA, and they had stormed the warehouse, clearing it of the three men that were laying it hard on Grey Harrow. After a few rounds of gun battle, the men knew they were outnumbered, and they had fled, and Jasper had grabbed Grey Harrow, arresting him with handcuffs and brought him here now, to the REA office in Knightsbridge, where they both currently reside, Jasper preparing Grey for interrogation.

There was a knock on the REA interrogation room.

Jasper brought his head up and turned to the door. 'Come in.'

Agent Alex Wade opened the door and walked in. He stood for a while, saying nothing, just staring at the half-dead Grey Harrow for a long while. Finally, he said, 'Has he spoken yet?' his gaze never leaving Grey.

Jasper brought his gaze back down to Grey Harrow, too. 'No, not a word, he's been badly injured. Those goons, whoever they were, did quite a number on him, I must say.'

'Good,' Alex Wade said. 'These Robotic—Cyborg—peeps think they're above the law—'

'Look,' Jasper chimed in.

Grey Harrow's closed eyelids vibrated and he groaned a little.

He was finally coming back to consciousness. Now was the time to begin.

Jasper stood up from his chair, gently pushed it under the marble table and walked around the side toward Grey Harrow. He sat on top of the table beside Grey, with one of his legs propped higher than the other, one arm resting on the higher leg. 'Mr. Harrow,' Jasper said softly. 'I need to ask you something—'

Another agent bust through the door, it thudded loudly, 'We are under attack!' he shouted and bolted back up the stairs.

'Shit!' Jasper frowned, 'Let's go!' gritting his teeth, he pulled out his Chrome .357 Magnum Revolver, he jumped off the marble table, and he and Alex Wade made their way out of the interrogation room, emerging out into the smell of gunpowder mixed with blood and sweat, leaving the battered and bruised Grey Harrow alone in the interrogation room.

***

Achoo, Grey sneezed as he struggled with *Genesis,* trying to break free from the metallic handcuff strapped to the marble table that Jasper Barnes had used to tie him down, restraining him and rendering him immobile. He found it odd that *Genesis* couldn't break lose despite the shear strength it possessed. Jasper must have used a special REA type handcuff to dampen it, he decided. He noticed the palm of *Genesis* was pointed toward his face and that made him grin. He's neuron compartment was probably empty, anyway, they had most probably removed the two neurons Grey had earlier inserted, and it would be futile for him to try and use it to escape.

Powder, white dust from the ceiling fell onto his face and body. He looked up to the ceiling. Upstairs, just above him, he could hear boots thudding the ground and shouting and gun firing. He wondered what was going on up there. But then he realised he didn't care; he just wanted to escape from the death grip of these metallic handcuffs, leave this place, and get back to Bethany.

Grey stood, pulling back *Genesis,* trying again to break free from the cuffs. Nothing. He tried again. Still, nothing. He furrowed his brow as he looked around the room, searching for something he could use to break the chains and detach himself from the marble table. Meanwhile, the action above him was heating up, shockwaves and aftershocks resonating all around him, knocking him to the ground, the chair he sat on tumbling to the side and out of reach from his free hand. He sat on his butt and grimaced. Frustrated, he was stuck.

There was nothing else he could do but wait. Wait patiently for whatever inevitable fate that was lying in wait for him after the fighting had subsided, and after Jasper—or whoever—had come down to see to him and decide on his fate.

After a few more minutes of sitting on his ass and hearing louder and louder action just above him, he stood and quickly jolted the chains and cuffs once again, this time wildly, like a manic—like a man who's life depended on the chain's and cuff's successful removal. He reached out with his free hand, stretching as far as he could, trying to reach for the fallen chair. He just about got his fingers tips to it, reeling it in. He raised it above his head with just his single hand and crashed it on the marble table, smashing it to many pieces, a long single piece of wood remaining in his hand. He used the wood to dig at the cuffs, back and forth he jabbed with it, connecting with both the cuffs and *Genesis's* metallic mechanical wrist. After a couple of jabs, he halted. What was he doing, trying to dismantle an REA issued robotic handcuffs with a useless piece of wood? It was never going to work, he realised. It was futile.

He paused, looked down at *Genesis*. How he wished he could just remove the arm completely, leave it there in the cuffs, on the marble table, and escape. He studied *Genesis,* glancing up and down, from the fingertips up until his shoulder blade where the mechanical part ended. He began to move his free organic hand toward it, but then he stopped, shaking his head. Even as much as he just wanted to be out of the building, and rid of this terrible nightmare, he knew he couldn't leave *Genesis* behind. It was as much a part of him now, even with his Rogue Hand Syndrome tendencies. Besides, he didn't know what would happen if he was to remove it or lose it. That is if he knew how to detach it. Would he survive the separation? After all the neuroscientists and doctors at RoyalStarCorp—Adam Cardon and Clare Barnes—had said *Genesis* had saved his life and *is* still saving it to this day.

He had closed his eyes, listening to the ensuing gun battle above him, trying to picture what was happening, when he heard boots thudding just outside the interrogation room. His eyes opened again, and his heart raced. He turned to the door, seeing shadowy movements from behind the blurred glass frame of the door. He instantly ducked down, eased his frame under the marble table, but *Genesis* was still attached to the top, sticking out in plain sight. He came back out from under the marble table as the shadowy figures struggled to get the door open and enter the room. Jasper must've secured it before leaving. *Thank God for that,* he thought. He looked up and saw a single light bulb dangling there. It was the only thing giving the rather dull lit room light, and Grey figured if he was to turn it off somehow, whoever was out there trying to get in would not be able to see him, buying him some time.

He reached out to the bulb with his free hand, unscrewing it, it was hot—very hot—but he didn't let it faze him, the matter at hand was pressing. When he unscrewed it completely, the room grew dark, like the skin of a raven bird. The bulb was still hot, and it burned his hand as he juggled it there for a while, before setting it down on the marble table. He figured he could use it as a weapon if it came to it—one drive to the person's head should do the trick, and then the broken shards that would be left behind should serve as a deadly shank.

The door busted opened, and Grey grabbed the now cooled down bulb and dipped down underneath the marble table, *Genesis* still sticking out and lodged in the cuffs.

The door to the interrogation room slowly shut with a thud, closing off the strange heat from the outside that whooshed in, and the scent of blood and gunpowder that Grey could now smell.

Something or someone moved slowly through the darkened room.

Grey waited under the marble table and held the bulb in his free hand, tightly.

He told himself he wasn't afraid, but the slight tremble of his hand told another story.

A single sweat trickled down the back of his neck.

He took a shallow breath.

Chapter Twenty-two: A War at the REA

With *Genesis* still handcuffed to the marble table and his other hand wrapped around the light bulb, Grey waited, patiently.

He heard a flicker of a switch. It must have been the shadowy figure looking to turn on the light. Too bad, there was no light bulb; it now lay in his hands. Grey peeked out the table, the interrogation room was swallowed up in pitch blackness, and he himself could not see a thing. He blinked and strained his eyes, trying to make them become more accustomed to the darkness, just as one would become accustomed to their spouse on their wedding night.

More and more, recently, he'd found himself in a situation of darkness both literally and figuratively. It seemed to follow him around everywhere he went. As if God had cursed him. But here, now, in this mist of blackness, what did this shadowy specimen want with him?

As Grey drew back his head into the cover of the marble table, he felt the back of his head smack off the edge of the table, releasing a thumping sound, which then drew the attention of the shadowy presence. Grey heard him or her or whatever it was cock their weapon—some type of advance pistol by the sound of it—as their footsteps began to be directed toward the sound they had just heard. Grey tensed. There was more thudding, shouting, and gun firing from up above, more ceiling plaster dust falling down on top of him, Grey felt his nose tingle and itch, and he suppressed a sneeze. Thank God for that, he thought.

When the figure finally reached the marble table, and even though Grey couldn't see the person, he could feel their presence, their aura, and it was a huge presence. He or she must be a juggernaut, no doubt, he decided.

As they stood around, Grey reached out with the light bulb in his palm, smashing it against the back of the head of the said person. The bulb shattered into pieces, but only a low groan could be heard from the shadowy figure, and the impact seemed not to have registered any pain whatsoever.

The figure turned around as Grey's eyes became more and more accustomed to the darkness. Grey crouched, running his hand along the ground, feeling about, and then picking up a broken shard of the bulb. He rose back up and thrust it toward the figure, but the figure caught him by the wrist. His heart throbbed a bit faster now, he was trapped—tied to the table—and not able to fight back, death was a certainty now, he decided.

He heard a loud gunshot in the darkness, felt the metallic handcuffs loosened around his wrist, and then *Genesis* was free. He felt light, loose, not over-encumbered anymore. But why was that?

'Stupid, fool.' He heard the figure say. 'Do that to me again and it would surely be the last thing you ever do, regardless of my mission.'

Your mission?—That voice, it came to him, he knew that voice.

As the figure step closer to Grey, his shape grew wide and tall, and Grey knew who it was.

It was Behemoth.

'You're lucky man, Grey, that Lucan Weaver regards you highly. Otherwise, you would have paid for that silly manoeuvre you just pulled.' He kissed his teeth.

Grey let out a deep sigh, relief in its purest form. He was sure he was a dead man. He never thought he would be so glad to see the brute man again, but after the night he'd had— the hospital, Brom's death, David and the Foxhound Syndicate, Jasper and his interrogation— it was a blessing indeed.

Grey squinted in the darkness toward the giant figure and said, 'How did you know I was here? How did you—'

'Listen,' Behemoth cut him off. 'I'm not here to have small talk with you, there's just no time. Some of Lucan's men are upstairs right now, buying us some time, so let's get the hell out of here; I'll fill you in on the way.'

'Right,' Grey nodded, but then he felt kind of stupid, it was dark and Behemoth probably couldn't even see him.

They started to the exit of the interrogation room, Grey following the big shadow in front of him.

When Behemoth opened the door, strong light beamed in into the pitch blackness, causing them both to temporarily go blind. After a few seconds, their vision returned and they quicken up the stairs, two and three at a time. They reached the top of the stairs. The hallways of the REA office was in complete disarray. Walls crumbling, fixtures overturn, and bodies— of both REA and Lucan's men—sprawled all over the rubble. Grey couldn't tell if those bodies were still alive or not. He glanced around, in the distance he could see Jasper Barnes– –his interrogator—taking cover behind an office wall as he and another REA agent took turns in firing at about four or five of Lucan's men who wear clad in special black metallic armour.

Behemoth placed a hand on Grey's shoulder, gripping it tight. 'Come, this way, let's go.' That grip again, Grey loathed it when he did that, it irritated him. Why couldn't he just tell him, why must he grapple with him? *One of these days I'm going to snap that hand of his,* Grey thought. *And then will see what he grips with.*

Nevertheless, Grey followed him as they darted through the hallways, one foot after the other, fast as they could, bullets flew by them, from all directions, Grey and Behemoth sliding down and taking shelter behind a fallen fixture. Their backs pressed to it, Grey's chest rising and falling.

He watched as Behemoth peeked out the corner as a bullet flew by, just nearly missing him by an inch. Behemoth turned, looked Grey in the eyes, and shook his head. Grey knew what that meant. Some of the REA agents saw them duck into cover and knew their

position, they were a sitting duck. As Behemoth slowly pulled out his pistol from its holster

and peeked out again, Grey looked down at *Genesis*, pressed on the mechanical wrist, and the

compartment slowly opened up.

He frowned. It was empty just as he'd assumed. He pressed down again on the wrist

and it closed up. That was it; he couldn't rely on *Genesis*'s abilities now. He was all out of

neurons. He would have to find another way out of this situation.

He turned to Behemoth beside him, who was busy peeking out the corner of the

fixture. 'Hey, you don't happen to have a spare pistol on you do you?'

Behemoth turned, looked at him as if to say: *does it look like I have one?* And then he

turned back, returning to his peeking out the corner. He fired a few shots from his pistol.

'Guess I'll take that as a no, then.' Grey mumbled to himself.

Grey looked around, scanned his surroundings. Out the corner of his eye, he saw an

AK47 lying on the ground just out in front of him a few metres away buried under some

debris. The problem was it was out in the open, no fixture to protect him if he was to go get

it. He laid flat on his belly, stretching forth a hand—his organic one—the AK47 moved,

slightly, his fingers just barely touching it, but that was about it. It was still out of his grasp.

He licked his lips, the taste of dried blood still lingered there—from his beating at the hand of

David and the Foxhound Syndicate, earlier in the night, no doubt.

He continued to stretch forth with his arm trying to reach for the Ak47. Muzzles

flashed, and Bullets rattled into the ground—or more like rubble—near him and surrounding

the weapon. It kicked up small dust, marring the ground with holes, and Grey immediately

pulled his hand back, he wasn't about to lose another hand. But then he reached out with his

other arm—*Genesis*—and when bullets came flying in, it ricochet off it, Grey not feeling any

pain with the impact. He smiled at that and stretched further and further. Bullets kept coming and coming, it bounced off *Genesis*, like water off a duck's back. Every time it did, metallic pockets of sparks danced around *Genesis*. He finally got hold of the AK47, a small joyous smile spread across his lips, and he pulled it back to himself quick, returning back to press his back against the fixture shelter. He flipped open the magazine and slammed it shut immediately when he saw it was loaded.

When Behemoth turned to Grey, he saw what he was holding in his hand. He smiled, nodded, and the two spoke telepathically as they rose up. Grey felt everything move in slow motion from then on, but in reality, it all happened so fast.

They made for the exit of the REA office, bullets came raining down toward them, and they returned fire. Grey with the newly acquired AK47, Behemoth with his pistol. More celling plaster fell around them, fixture crumbled, and debris fell, but they just about made it to the door.

Waiting by the door with his revolver drawn was Jasper Barnes. He had told them to freeze, but before he could finish his sentence, Behemoth had opened fire on him. Grey witnessed a single 9mm bullet penetrate straight through Jasper's right shoulder as his body crashed hard against a wall. Jasper gripped his wound tight with a hand as he slowly slid down the wall, leaving a streak of blood on the wall behind him in its wake, letting out a loud wail. Behemoth readied his gun again, about to let loose once more at the now vulnerable Jasper, finishing him off for good.

Grey threw his shoulder into Behemoth, barging into him, and sending them both sprawling outside, into the frosty, chilled night air, Behemoth's shot going wide of the mark of its intended target.

'What the hell?' Behemoth said as they both stood back to their feet outside, mist emanating from his mouth.

'Forget him,' Grey said, dusting himself off from the debris. 'He's not worth it. Let's go.'

Behemoth gave him a dirty look, kissed his teeth, and bolted toward a hover van packed to the brim with Lucan's men.

Grey followed, his gaze lingering back over his shoulder at the carnage that was now the REA office headquarters.

Chapter Twenty-three: A Fair Warning

After the successful but near-disastrous rescue of Grey from the REA office in Knightsbridge by Behemoth and his goons, they had arrived back at Lucan Weaver's underground base in Old Street.

Lucan Weaver was not too happy about the way things had gone down. Grey had watched the Topknot light-skinned man's face turn solemn as his men reported back to him about the night's events. Grey had guessed he was worried that the unnecessary escalation of what should've been a simple job—get in, get Grey, and get out—could come back and bite him in the ass, and probably before he could have his way in his attempted endeavour to overthrow the Foxhound Syndicate as the powerhouse of the London City's Criminal Underworld.

Grey also knew one thing: he would now be in the crosshairs of the REA after tonight. He would have to put his head down and lay low for a while.

But when all was said and done, he raised his hand; palm exposed and thanked Lucan for the save. Even though he knew, deep down, Lucan Weaver did not do it out of the kindness of his heart. Just like his rescue from certain death at the hands of the Foxhound Syndicate and the attachment of *Genesis* before—Lucan did it because he needed him to fight in his war against the Foxhound Syndicate. A war that Grey, himself, should have every reason to want to fight in, anyway.

A few minutes later Grey's night at the base came to an abrupt end after he'd told Lucan how he had ended up in the custody of the REA agents. He'd told him about the hospital ward and his encounter with some of the Foxhound Syndicate, about his old friend's––Brom's—call, wanting to save him, but ending up captured by David and his gang, and of Jasper Barnes—an REA Agent—who had saved him—for his own gain, just like Lucan. *How everyone loved saving him,* he had thought, *for their own benefit.* But after tonight, after what he'd done for Jasper involving Behemoth, saving his goddam life, Grey decided that they were more than even now.

Lucan had given him a fair warning with a glare that Grey could not mistake; a glare that spoke: this is your last chance, do not make another wrong move.

And that was it, for now. Grey went on his way. He would make his way back to RoyalStarCorp, back to Herman Rowntree, and back to Bethany Rose.

When he reached outside the base building, the freezing cold air burned at the open flesh wound on his face, and he put his hands in his overcoat pocket to keep warm. As he started across the pavement, he felt the holo-phone that Lucan had given him earlier in the day and pulled it out. He stared at it for a long while. *So this is how you were able to find me,* he thought, and then one corner of his mouth lifted upwards. A half-smile. Or a smirk.

He squeezed the side of the holo-phone and the holographic screen popped outward before him like a projectile. He touched the hologram, flicking his index fingers up and down, cycling through until he found Bethany's number. He dialled it. It rung once and then went straight to voicemail. He didn't leave a message, but hung up, putting his holo-phone back in his overcoat pocket. He felt guilty for leaving her at RoyalStarCorp, but he had no other choice. Her apartment was compromised after the rude awakening they'd had, and his apartment was a death-trap lying in wait. It was his fault; he brought her into all of this. Maybe he should let it be and let her go. If he truly loved her, he would. The thought made him sad.

Genesis twitched; slowly he felt de-synchronisation in the movements of his left hand and the thought pattern of his mind. It had been a while since he'd last had his medication. He patted his overcoat pockets, it felt flat, empty. It must've dropped out—what with the night he'd had. Time was running out. He needed more. But where?

He quickened his steps to the Knightsbridge Train Station, hopped on to one of the 24hrs night hover trains, his left hand, contorting aimlessly inside his pocket, bulging outward like a pet hamster who didn't want to be hidden away any longer, wanting to come out and play. Passengers on the train stared at him, weirdly, and he didn't know whether it was the cuts and bruises on his face or the weird hand movements within his inside coat pocket, but he turned away and stared out the window as he slid on the hood of the navy-blue jumper he wore underneath his black overcoat, hoping to God Herman Rowntree would still have some Neurazinamide lying around back at RoyalStarCorp.

Chapter Twenty-four: A Buoyant Promise

Grey, battered and bruised, worn out by the night's events that had transpired, made it back safely to the RoyalStarCorp.

It was almost dawn, and when Herman Rowntree had ushered him in through the metallic front doors, *Genesis* gripped the small man by the throat, instantly raising him up, his legs flailing in the air as his large rimmed glasses fell from his eyes and tumbled to the ground with a cracking sound that suggested it had unfortunately come to its end of it ever being useful again.

'What . . . are . . . you . . . doing?' The now near blind Biomedical Engineer managed to utter as he struggled to fill his lungs with air.

'Sorry,' Grey said, suddenly feeling helpless, unable to bring *Genesis* under his control and help the poor bastard. 'It's not me. It's . . . Have you still got any of the RHSV meds lying around?'

Herman shifted in his grasp, he tried to speak but couldn't. He nodded instead.

Grey used his other hand to try and contain *Genesis*. He pulled and pulled, it didn't relent . . . but then it finally gave way, Herman crashing back down to earth on his rear-end with a thump. He grimaced.

'Hurry, goddammit!' Grey yelled, looking at him, 'and where's Bethany?'

Herman Rowntree scrambled back to his feet, picked up his broken glasses and made haste toward his cubicle.

Grey stood, *Genesis* started; starching his head, touching his face, his chest, stomach, and funnily enough, his ass. He let it. At least it wasn't doing any harm to him or hurting anyone else. But then he could hear the faint voice of *Genesis* slowly creeping back into his head—his mind, whispering its evil suggestions again . . .

Herman returned from his cubicle, a Neurazinamide in one hand, a glass of water in the other.

He opened the med container as Grey stretched forth his hand, dropping two pill sizes in it. Grey threw them back in his mouth and Herman handed him the glass. He swallowed, the water washing down the pill, flushing it down into his nervous system. Grey slowly watched as *Genesis* began to corporate with his normal thought pattern again. He lifted his head and smiled at Herman, who just stood there, a sour look on his face, clearly upset about what had just transpired.

'Where were the RHSV medications you were given earlier?' Herman asked. One of the spectacles on his large rimmed glasses had a deep crooked, cracked line on it.

Grey shrugged, 'I misplaced them.'

'You, what?' Herman looked at him, his eyes unwavering. 'You can't just decide *not* to take your medications, Grey, you are infected with the virus, this is serious.'

Grey lifted a palm to Herman. 'I know, I know, RHSV, Rogue Hand Syndrome, Blah, Blah, Blah.'

Herman's eyes, through one cracked and one un-cracked glass, remained firmly locked at him, boring into him, as if questioning his sanity.

Grey said, 'Listen, I've had a rough night, I was attacked at gunpoint, beaten and tortured, left for dead,' he gestured to the bruises on his face, the broken nose, the cuts to his lip, and the bloody stains on his shirt. 'Can't you see? So don't you give me that look, Herman, not from you, no.' He slowly took off his overcoat and placed it on the coat rack by the entrance. 'I want to be healed, I want to be free from this virus, I want to be fully myself again, more than anyone else could ever know.'

Grey watched the small man's expression change, softer now, a warm smile creasing at the corner of his mouth.

'All right,' Herman said, turning his back to Grey. 'Come with me, I'll take you to the young lady.'

Grey followed Herman, through the corridors of RoyalStarCorp, passing through single cubicles, and many offices, majority of them empty—no doubt every biomedical engineer and neuroscientist were at home getting a well-deserved rest for the night—except one.

Grey turned his head to peer into the office, seeing a woman in her lab coat, working away at something robotic in nature. He turned his head back forward and said, 'Herman, I thought it was only you here tonight?'

Herman didn't turn back to look at him, he just said, 'Oh, that,' as they continued walking forward. 'Clare Barnes came in earlier than expected. She said she needed to work on something, that it was urgent.'

Urgent? Grey thought. What could be so urgent? What was she really up to? After his run-in with her brother earlier in the night, he wanted to speak to her, to clear things up. He wanted to get to the bottom of this brother-sister conundrum, this "on the opposite sides of the spectrum" shenanigans.

But first, he would go to Bethany. He would go and see her and ease any concerns or pain she might have taken upon herself after the past couple of days.

Grey and Herman took a turn and went down a flight of stairs when they reached a narrow metallic-looking door with a holo-screen intercom by its side.

Herman pressed on it and turned to Grey. 'You look terrible—like you've been run over by a hover truck—'

'I feel like it.'

'—twice! I suggest you take a long hot shower. Wash the blood off you and ease those bruises on your face. There are some spare towels and clothes in the room. Feel free to use them.'

The door opened.

'All yours now, mate. I'm heading back up, got some stuff to finish off, let me know if you guys need anything.' He winked at Grey and then gave him that cheeky grin of his, before jolting off and back up the stairs, his little shoes knocking the ground.

Bethany stood by the metallic door in front of him wearing only her black-coloured underwear, one hand rubbing her eyes from her tiredness; he felt at home again, he felt all his worries of the night just fade away. Her body looked so warm, and Grey could smell fresh lilies—whether it was coming from her or the room behind her, he couldn't decide. Either way, the smell was gorgeous and typical of her.

'Grey,' she said through droopy, tired, blue eyes, 'Is that you?' She paused, scanning his face, examining the cuts and bruises, and Grey figured she was probably wondering what in the hell had happened to him. 'What happened?'

Grey forced a smile, his body ached, and all he wanted now was a nice warm shower and an even nicer and warmer cuddle from the warmest heart he knew. 'I'll tell you everything, once I'm inside, and once I've had a shower.'

***

When Grey returned from the bathroom, he sat on the couch and told Bethany everything that had happened to him that night after he'd left her here at RoyalStarCorp. He told her about Brom's death, about David's torture, about Jasper's rescue, and finally about his escape from the REA office. Then, when he spoke of Lucan Weaver's plan to overthrow the Foxhound Syndicate with his help, the expression on her face told him she'd had enough and that she wasn't that surprised anymore about it at all.

'Grey, I'm going back to King's Cross, back to my apartment, as soon as it's morning.' She said as she opened the small fridge in the room, and took out two bottles of water. 'I don't care what's been happening, Grey, it's not stopping me, I've got work to go to tomorrow, and I've got bills to pay.'

Grey looked at her as she strode over to him by the sofa with the two bottles in her hands. She looked so sexy to him. As always, more so because she was in her underwear—her long, pale, toned legs strutting as she walked, her delicate toes arched and bare feet slapping against the marble floor in angelic perfection, one after the other.

When she reached him, she stretched fort one of the bottles, and Grey grabbed it. The bottle felt cold and wet in his hand, condensation taking its root on the face of the bottle as small liquid dripped down off of it.

Bethany eased herself onto the couch next to Grey, her long legs spread across and resting on top of him as she put the bottle to her rosy lips and drank.

Grey caressed her legs with his hand, looked over at her and said, 'Bethany, I understand. You want to get back to work. I want you to, more than anything; I want you to do what makes you happy, but—'

'There's no but, Grey, I'm going home and I'm going to work, and that's that.' She took another sip of water from the bottle. 'If this so-called "Foxhound Syndicate" want me, let them come, I'll show them how brave I can be. They can't stop me from living my life.'

Grey took a swig of his bottle of water. He didn't know what exactly to say to that. She was right, after all, he thought. She was brave; she took a bullet straight through the shoulder, and now she's up and running and in good health. They shouldn't stop her from living her life. But it was risky, and he didn't want her to get caught in the crossfire because of him. Her apartment was compromised and a crime scene, he couldn't let her go back, not yet anyway, not until he's taken out the perpetrators and is done with this life of lawlessness.

'At least come stay at the flat Lucan Weaver has set up for you and me in Old Street.' Grey said, leaning forward, staring into her deep ocean waters. 'You can still go about your normal life, go to work, and see your friends—and do what you normally do.'

She gave that a frown. Then Grey saw that she was contemplating it, her eyes darting all around his face, from his left eye to the right, to the left again, then to the right once more, and then finally to his lips. She held it there. It made Grey lick it, feeling self-conscious. She slowly leaned in and softly pressed her cherry-coloured lips against his, and Grey felt something bubble up in his stomach. Her tongue tasted like heaven—if heaven was a flavour, that is. He pulled away and kissed her neck—her throat so long and slender and inviting. He wanted to grab it, squeeze softly, and as she opens her mouth, breathe deeply, inhaling her sweet, warm breath into his lungs.

She pushed away from him, looked him dead in the eyes and said, 'Okay, I'll stay at the flat in Old Street, but, Grey, when will this stop? When will this all be over? We can't keep living like this, always watching our backs.'

'Soon, Beth,' he said, 'once I help Lucan out with this one last task, I promise it will be all over. No more Foxhound Syndicate, no more Lucan Weaver.' Grey pulled her close by her waist and held her. 'We will even have enough money to start a new life somewhere else if you want—Ibiza, or even the Caribbean Islands.'

She gave that a worried look. She bit into her bottom lip and turned her head to the side, staring off into the distance of the room.

Grey tilted his head. 'What is it?' he asked.

'You said something similar last time,' she said, her head still to the side, 'when you lost your left arm and came back to me half-machine.' She sighed. 'It broke me, Grey, seeing you like that, I don't think I can take it again.'

Grey cupped her cheeks in one human hand and one mechanical hand, and he slowly turned her head toward him. He leaned in close, 'Hey, Hey,' he said softly, his voice warm. Little tears slowly fell from her eyes onto his hands. 'That won't happen again, you hear me? I'll come back to you. I'll come back to you unscathed.'

She looked at him for a long while, her eyes watery, her pale cheeks flushed red and dotted with small freckles, 'Promise?'

'I promise.'

Chapter Twenty-five: A Family Affair

It had been three weeks since the incident at the REA office in Knightsbridge when Jasper had brought in Grey Harrow for questioning regarding his robotic part and the whereabouts of the criminal mastermind Ezra Hawthorne.

It hadn't gone to plan, Jasper had been hoping to kill two birds with one stone, but instead, what he got was: his agency going up in smoke—with many agents dead—a badly injured shoulder, and indefinite suspension.

Jasper trekked through the busy, winter-morning streets of London Bridge, his hands warm inside the pockets of his overcoat. His left shoulder still burned with even the slightest of movement, but after a series of visits to the hospital which cumulated in many stitches and painkillers, his distress had been eased—better than it had been three weeks ago, that's for sure. He'd take that any day. Anything was better than the pain of that day.

He looked up ahead; in the distance, he could see the apartment. He was almost there. Only a few more cold steps—

Someone shouldered him, the force of it taking him by surprise and shifting his whole feet right under him. The man wore a grey suit, held a black briefcase, and was talking really loud into his holo-phone. He turned to regard Jasper, 'Hey, watch where you going . . . fool.' He kissed his teeth and continued on walking.

'Arsehole,' Jasper spat back with a scowl. He was just relieved it was his right shoulder and not his left. The pain would have been unbearable. Maybe in a week or two, the shoulder should be back to working order again, that's if he doesn't aggravate it further.

Jasper reached a crossing and hovering cars shot past him, leaving blue and purple neon-coloured lights in their wake that felt mesmeric to him, almost angelic. He sighed, his breath steaming in the cold. In his current condition, he wasn't able to drive. Instead, he had to settle for public transport and walking in the freezing cold, surrounded by a crowd of arseholes that walk into you without looking where they were going.

When the hover cars halted at the red light, he crossed swiftly and made his way to the tall building on his left. He stood outside it and gazed up it till his eyes found a specific window. *I hope she's in,* he thought. He took out a hand from his overcoat pocket, and with cold, trembling fingers, he reached for the intercom holo-screen touchpad. He typed in the letters: CLARE BARNES and let it ring.

He stood there for a few seconds, waiting in the cold, rubbing his hands together, blowing warm air from his mouth onto them, and then putting his hands back into his overcoat pocket.

After a short while, Clare Barnes holo-face appeared at the intercom holo-screen like an oversized balloon.

'Jasper!' the face said in a robotic voice. 'What's up?'

Jasper rubbed his hands together again, harder. 'Can you let me in? It's fucking cold out here.'

'Oh, of course,' there was a click. 'The doors open, come on up.'

Jasper pushed on the door, and as he entered the hallways, warm heat pressed against the parts of his skin that had not been covered—his face, his necks, and his hands. It felt soothing. He shut the door behind him and was ever grateful for the warmth. Not so much so for the smell of the place, though. The hallways reeked and lingered with the smell of someone that had probably not washed for days on end and of food that had almost certainly passed its sell-by-date by a large margin and that should have probably been thrown out at least twenty years ago.

When Jasper reached Clare's door, she was already standing there waiting, her long pale arms stretched along the door frame, a warm smile plastered on her face. She reached for him; arms stretched, and hugged him.

'Come,' she said with the gestured of her hand.

Jasper followed her in and shut the door behind them. She led him into her living room and Jasper sat on one of the many chairs.

'Coffee?' Clare asked.

'Black, please.'

She snorted. 'Hm, always black with you, okay.'

'What?' Jasper looked at her confused.

She giggled like a schoolgirl. 'Nothing.' Then she went into the far corner of the living room—into the kitchen, and as she did that, Jasper surveyed her apartment.

It was a neat little compact flat. Everything was in close proximity—living room and kitchen synched together like a hybrid, and the bedroom and bathroom together in the next room. Jasper remembered when they were younger how Clare loved her small spaces and how OCD she got when things were out of place. His sister hasn't changed one bit.

Jasper's eyes glanced over many of the accolades and pictures hung up around the living room—accolades of scientific advances in robotics, pictures of bio-medical procedures and achievements—before his eyes landed on a ROYALSTARCORP poster. It was a picture of the first-ever RoyalStarCorp that appeared in the United States.

'So, how's work?' Jasper asked. She was still in the far corner, the sight of boiling water steaming, the sound of water pouring, the echoing of spoon clinking on ceramic wares, and the strong whiff of fresh coffee making its way to his nostril.

The clinking of the spoon abruptly stopped. She seemed to freeze up. 'Oh,' she said, her voice sounding higher than usual. 'Work is fine. You know, still trying to make the next scientific breakthrough with robotics. How are Sarai and little Zack?'

Jasper stared at the back of his sister. He thought it strange that even after robotics had been outlawed in the UK, the remnants of the company are still tasked and allowed to work with robotics. He found it counterproductive giving his job—well, here's to hoping he still has a job after the suspension. But what does he know? Just because the everyday people are forbidden from its dangerous usage, robotics was still a very useful tool for the government and the army in their war efforts.

'They're both great. Your nephew is growing up so fast.'

'I bet he is,' Clare chuckled, 'that little trouble maker.' She picked up the two ceramic mugs and made her way back toward Jasper by the chairs. She took a seat and set the two mugs on a small table between them. One had black coffee, the other mixed with milk.

'Martin and I have been suspended indefinitely pending a decision from our boss.' Jasper blurted out.

'That's horrible, Jasper.' She said, flicking a stray of brown hair away from her face. 'What happened?'

'We were given a deadline and we didn't meet it. And now this attack on the REA office . . .'

'Deadline? For what?'

Jasper reached for the mug filled with black coffee and took a sip from it. 'Walter Marshal tasked me and Martin with apprehending a fugitive robotics arms-dealer. His name is Ezra Hawthorne. He is a very dangerous man with robotic enhancements that is dealing robotic parts to the public.'

147

Clare had her mug close to her mouth ready to take a sweet sip of the coffee, but she stopped when it met her lips, holding it there, her dark eyes widened and she stared at Jasper for a long while.

'I've heard of him,' she said finally, placing a hand on Jasper's hand. 'Jasper, promise me you won't get mad, but there's something I need to tell you.'

'Yeah? About what?'

'About RoyalStarCorp and about Ezra Hawthorne.'

Chapter Twenty-six: A Calm Before . . .

Grey made his way to Lucan's base of operation in Old street late in the cold evening. As he strode through the streets, the sky around him grew dark, the stars came out to play, and half of the moon hung there like a perfectly carved semi-circle.

The journey to Lucan's base today wouldn't be as long for him as it usually was, seeing as he and Bethany had moved into the apartment—in Old Street—that Lucan had set up for them, three weeks ago.

Grey was taken aback when Bethany was actually pleased with the state and design of the apartment. It wasn't too different from her apartment back at Euston. So she felt right at home. The only difference was a state-of-the-art robotic device built into the apartment itself, which could be communicated with and ordered to do things, such as: turning on the heating, turning off the lights, etc.

Grey didn't think much of it at first, but being part machine himself, and knowing how at any time *Genesis* could go rogue; he didn't feel too comfortable leaving Bethany all alone with the strange robotic device. What if it locked her inside and didn't let her out? Or worse, what if it set fire to the apartment? One could never know.

Grey powered his way through the street, the pavement slippery, wet with rain from a few hours ago. After a short while he finally made it to Lucan's base, the old rundown building used as a cover to hide in plain sight stood just before him, dark and mysterious as ever.

Grey sucked in a deep breath and let it out, it steamed in the cold, evening air as he continued to regard the shadowy building with stark apprehension.

He blinked, today; they will attempt to raid one of the Foxhound Syndicate bases. "Attempt" because Grey didn't know what to expect after the day comes to a close. For all he knew he could be dead by the end of the night, lying face down in a ditch somewhere, *Genesis* pulled off his shoulders for equal measures, too.

No one would care as well, after all, they would just chuck it up to petty criminal rival gangs clashing, he figured.

Grey put his hand inside his jacket pocket and felt about, his hand fiddling around inside: A small bottle of Neurazinamide—to keep *Genesis* at bay—and three spare crystal metallic tubes of Neurons (excluding the three already loaded into the compartment in his wrist), all courtesy of Herman Rowntree of RoyalStarCorp.

Grey smiled. *Thank you, friend*, he thought. If he was to survive today, he would owe it all to the biomedical engineer. For sure.

Grey walked to the front entrance of Lucan's Base and pushed on the door and entered.

After walking through the entrance hallways, he entered the main room with all the techno machinery. And as he walked in, he saw Behemoth on his right, sitting on a large metallic-looking machine of some kind; Grey couldn't deduce what it was, but it must have been a sturdy object for it to hold all five-hundred pounds of Behemoth. Behemoth was busy scraping away at a wooden stick with a sharp pen knife with his head down, oblivious to Grey's presence.

After a while—perhaps finally hearing the door creaking shut behind Grey—he jerked his head up from his task and regarded Grey for a long time with a sceptical squint. He remained silent, not saying anything, just staring at him.

Grey shifted in his feet, feeling uncomfortable. Perhaps he is still sour about the incident three weeks ago involving the REA Agent Jasper Barnes. Jasper Barnes had done the same earlier that night, saving him from the dire clutches of David and his Foxhound Syndicate. He wouldn't have been here—standing in front of Behemoth otherwise. He did the only rational thing he knew and returned the favour by not allowing Behemoth to murder Jasper Barnes in cold blood. But was that the only reason he did it? Not out of some unknown loyalty he never knew he had for the REA Agent? Or the fact that his sister was also one of the neuroscientists that had preserved his life, worked tirelessly to bring him out of the coma, and gave his arm a new lease of life?

The two of them continued to eye each other for a long while before the silence was finally broken by a woman who'd just walked in, clothed in black mechanical vest armour. Elyse Fox. The cyborg with the mechanical eye Lucan had introduced him to a few weeks back.

'Grey,' she said, 'you're here; the boss would like a word with you.' She gestured with her hand for Grey to follow. And as he did, he saw out of the corner of his eyes that Behemoth's eyes never stop glaring at him. If eyes could kill, Grey would be dead, several times over.

He followed her; from behind her, he could see she had her long, blonde hair braided into two thick plaits which reached down the small of her back. Her single long strand of pink hair still hung loosely at the front of her broad forehead. Her skin was like brass—dark and smooth and shining, like chocolate.

'Here, just to the left,' she said, pointing down a narrow corridor.

Before they turned the corner, Grey shot one last glance back at Behemoth, he had resumed his scraping, fully giving his attention back to it.

Grey shouldered along behind the armoured women. He could see Lucan's office in the distance, a single mechanical lamp beside his study, shinning bright, his legs propped on his desk.

Grey tightened at the sight of Lucan, swallowed and clenched his jaw. It was finally going to happen. But was he ready? Was he really going to go through with it and attack his former crew? Was he really going to go rogue, so to speak?

There would be no turning back after this.

They reached Lucan's office.

Lucan removed his legs from the table. 'Thank you, Elyse,' he said to the armoured women. 'You can leave us now. Gather everyone; we will be out in a minute.' She nodded, bowed, and left the room, gently shutting the door behind her.

Lucan stared at him. 'I know what you are thinking.' He started. 'The Foxhound Syndicate were family . . . your brothers, blah, blah, blah. But really they are not. Your brothers would not have tried to have you killed . . . twice! Endangering your precious girlfriend in the process.' He stood, placed his hands behind him, crossed by his waist and strode through his wide room. 'They are ruthless and they deserve everything that's coming to them. It's time for a new Syndicate to rule this city's underworld.'

He sat on the edge of the table by Grey, pressed a button on it, and a holographic round image of the city popped up in-between them, spinning in a transparent blue-white glow. He pointed at a particular area on it, his gloved fingers sinking through the holographic image like a ghost.

'There,' he continued. 'Shepherd's Bush. That's where you will be going.' He got up and went back to his chair and sat. 'As the head of this Syndicate, unfortunately, I will not be going with you; I can't be seen in this attack. It's bad for business. I'm leaving this in both yours and Behemoth's hands. I've heard through my informers that they are housing the majority of their illegal high-tech robotics parts, weaponries, and neurons in that warehouse. Recover it all and we will be one step closer to ruling London. Capeesh?'

Grey tilted his head down and closed his eyes. *Just agree to it, Grey,* he thought. *Once this is all done, you will have all the money you ever wanted and you and Bethany can escape and leave this sorry city and its criminal underworld behind.* 'Loud and clear,' he said, raising his head back up, the semblance of a pleasant smile shaping his lips.

Chapter Twenty-seven: . . . A Storm

'This place is heavily guarded,' Gael Cross, one of Lucan's armoured goons with mechanical enhanced legs said, removing what looked like a high-tech, night-vision binoculars from his eyes.

Elyse Fox leaned forward. 'Give it here, Gael, let me have a look.' Crouching, she took the binoculars from Gael and leaned against the parapet, placing the binoculars to her eyes. Grey could hear the sound of her mechanical eye working in tandem with the binoculars, whining and grinding like a not so well oiled machine.

Behind Grey, Behemoth, Eustace de Maris, and one other member of Lucan's Syndicate—whose unremarkable name Grey had already forgotten—stood in a circle, whispering something. Grey couldn't hear what they were saying but he figured it was probably about him. Why else would they be murmuring to one and other like a bunch of little school girls? *Paranoid much, Grey?*

When they were done with their bickering, the three rejoined the rest of them at the foot of the building overlooking the Foxhound Syndicate warehouse.

Grey squinted in the dark night, he could see a lot of movements down below in the distance, flashlight movements—patrols and sentries for the Foxhound Syndicate, no doubt, but he couldn't make them out for certain, he couldn't read their emblem, he needed one of those binoculars in Elyse Fox's hands to confirm it. Though, from his previous time with the Syndicate, he was 99% sure they were.

'So what's it like down there?' Behemoth asked. 'Five? Ten? Twenty?'

Elyse Fox removed the binoculars from her eyes, stood, and turned to face Behemoth.

'I counted around thirty,' she said.

'Thirty?' Behemoth said with a grimace.

'Yes, but I think there is more,' Gael Cross added. 'Hidden in the distance, beyond what we can see.'

Behemoth looked at Grey, his eyes studying him, and then he turned back to the others. 'No matter,' he said, 'whether it is thirty, forty, or even hundred, we will take this place by force.' He turned to the goon whose name Grey still couldn't remember. 'Rollo, are Lucan's reinforcement on standby?'

Rollo reached for what looked like a small gadget-device in his armoured pocket, looked down at it, then nodded. 'Ready to move in when we clear this place out.'

'Good. Alright, let's move out. Eustace de Maris, you stay put and watch over us. When it's time to call in the others you lead them to us. Got it?'

The mute Eustace de Maris nodded wordlessly. He was never one for words.

'This mission, first and foremost, is stealth,' he gave Grey a side-eye, 'so no theatrical tomfooleries.'

***

They were on the ground, crouching, moving along the dark, cold cobblestones, on their toes, careful to not let their boots thud the ground. Grey was surprised that not a sound could be heard from their movements given the amount of armour they were all strapped in. Not even a *clink*.

They reached a darkened alleyway on the left between two tall buildings. All five of them hugged their backs to the cold, bumpy, and uneven wall. It was dark, which was welcomed, Grey thought. The night shadows hid them all well.

Grey, taking point, with a deep breath, curled his head out the corner, slightly. Two Foxhound sentries were fast approaching, almost as if they knew Grey and the others were behind this building, their flashlight muzzle pointed toward him, the glaring bright white light started him as he put his hand to his face and squinted.

Grey pulled back his head behind the wall, blinking in the soft darkness, his eyes still lingering and adjusting to the effect of the flashlight shining in them.

He felt a strong hand on his shoulder. 'What did you see?' Behemoth said.

'Two sentries—heavily armoured—are approaching fast to our position.'

Behemoth turned to Elyse Fox and Gael Cross. 'You two, go around the building and take them out silently.' He gestured with his index finger, pointing upward and drawing an invisible small circle with it.

At once, the two left, moving down along the building side, their palms rubbing off the walls, until they turned to the right and disappeared. Grey hoped everything would go as planned and no other Foxhound member would be alerted. He still had his doubt for the night ahead—

Genesis grabbing hold of his other hand by the wrist brought him out of his thoughts. He tried dislodging the grip, but he should have known better. There was no controlling it in this state.

Behemoth frowned at him in the darkness. 'What is it? What are you doing? You need to remain still and quiet or you'll blow our cover.'

Grey fumbled around with his mechanical hand grasping his other hand as if he were a crazy man who'd lost all his senses, trying to reach inside his overcoat pocket.

'It's . . . it's . . .' back and forth, his two hands moved out of sync as if the two were at war, trying to decide which of the two were the stronger one. Grey already knew the answer to that. He looked over at Rollo beside him, 'Rollo, reach inside my pocket and grab the small bottle for me, please. Quick.' Rollo without saying anything nodded and reached inside Grey's pocket with his hand. After a few seconds of fumbling around in Grey's pocket, Rollo grabbed the bottle of Neurazinamide, popped the lip open with his thumbnail, and Grey threw his head back, and Rollo tilted the bottle in his mouth. 'Two pills,' Grey said. Rollo gently dropped two into his mouth and he swallowed. *That should keep me going for a little while longer,* he thought to himself. 'Thanks, Rollo.' He felt in control of *Genesis* again as he released the grip on the other hand, flexing the mechanical fingers as if testing its functions and blew out a deep sigh. Rollo handed him back the pills and he put them back into his pocket.

'You really need to sort out that hand of yours, Grey.' Behemoth said. 'Get it in check, because one day—it will be your downfall.'

Grey turned to Behemoth, exasperated. 'And how I'm I supposed to do that? You don't think I've tried?

'You could have it . . . you know what, now is not the time. Pop your head out the corner and check on Elyse and Gael.'

Grey did just that. Slowly and quietly he saw that the two sentries were just a couple more stride away from them, their flashlight growing bigger along the dark ground and closer with which step. It ate up the darkness that surrounded Grey, Behemoth, and Rollo.

'They're getting closer,' Grey said, about to step out to their line of sight. 'I need to take them out.'

Behemoth grabbed him by his arm. 'Wait,' he whispered loudly. 'Let Elyse and Gael handle this, trust me.'

Grey looked back at him, in the now brightening darkness—due to the approaching flashlights—and grimaced.

'We need to prolong the *all-out war* for as long as possible. They have the numbers remember.' Behemoth said.

Grey gritted his teeth and then peeked out the corner again. This time he saw two figures approaching the two sentries from behind. Armoured arms stretched forth and wrapped around the sentries' throats in a death chokehold. The sentries struggled, trying to wriggle free from the death hold as their muzzled flashlights beamed in all directions from frightened grasps before leaving their hands and clanking to the ground. Grey could then see that those flashlights were actually attached to military robotics AK47s.

The two sentries, convulsed one last time before slumping to their knees, lifeless, Elyse Fox's and Gael Cross's faces now visible behind them as they let go of the two sentries gently to the ground.

Grey, Behemoth, and Rollo came out of the shadows.

'Quickly,' Behemoth said. 'Bring the bodies. We can hide them behind the building—'

Just as Grey started to lift one of the sentries by the arms, he dropped him back down instantly when he heard the loud clapping of hands. Grey's heart started to race. His throat felt dry. There, they all stood, out in the open, in near darkness, confusion on their faces: Grey, Behemoth, Rollo, Elyse Fox, Gael Cross, trying to deduce where the clapping was coming from.

Grey readied *Genesis* spreading his mechanical fingers wide and stretching it forth, the mechanical palm glowed a warm orange; he spun around, darkness all around him, but no one. The others did the same, readying their respective weapons.

A moment later two large figures strapped to the teeth in mechanical gear that resembled an exo-suit stepped out of the shadows, boots thudding, and armour clanging.

One of them waggled his index finger as they emerged into the dim light. 'Uh-huh, I wouldn't do that if I were you,' he said. 'You are gravely surrounded. Put your weapons down and surrender and maybe, just maybe, we might let you live.' The first figure smiled, and Grey knew exactly who he was—the squared jaw, the hook for a nose, the bravado performance . . .

It was David.

And then Grey's eyes widened with concern as he looked to the larger figure beside David, realisation coming to him.

'Ezra Hawthorne,' he mouthed.

Chapter Twenty-eight: A Sober Lead

'Dad, Dad,' Zack yelled and smiled as he burst through the front door of their home and hugged his father. Sarai followed in behind, Zack's purple-coloured school bag in her hands and the glow of the dark evening skies shimmering bright behind her dark hair and dark skin. There was a chilled breeze that swept in also, Jasper could feel it biting at his bare face and hands and feet, but as she shut the door, it subsided.

'Hey buddy,' Jasper said mussing Zack's coarse afro-hair with his hand. He had earlier sat at the dining table, scanning and fumbling through holo-images and files of REA work, trying his best to find some sort leeway in his case.

'Still working the case?' Sarai asked as she placed Zack's backpack on the tabletop.

Jasper looked at her in her striking, almond-shaped eyes. Zack was still in-between his arms and legs resting his head against his father's chest. He felt warm—his pride and joy. Jasper leaned down and kissed him on the top of his head.

'I have to, Sarai,' he said. 'He's still out there dealing in illegal robotics and spreading what we've been trying very hard to contain.'

'But you're not an REA Agent anymore,' her words stung like a bee. But it was the truth. Why was he still chasing this case? 'You've been suspended, remember?'

Jasper tilted Zack back by the shoulders so that he faced him. 'Zack, son, go to your room and get some of your homework done. I'll come by to help you in a bit, okay buddy?' He nodded and swiftly shot to his room, grabbing his backpack from the tabletop on his way.

Jasper turned back to Sarai—she had already started cooking up something, using the 3D food printing machine.

'What are we having, tonight?' Jasper asked.

'What would you like?' She said with her back to him.

'How about some of those delicious broccoli roast bake you made the other day?'

She turned and gave him a soft, sideways smile, her deep dimples like huge craters of love flashing, melting Jasper's heart again. He would never get tired of seeing it. God, she was beautiful—like one of those ancient African goddesses carved out of stone.

'Broccoli roast bake it is then.' She said and then pressed a few commands on the 3D machine. It was a highly complicated machine that Jasper hadn't learned to use yet, but his wife had.

Just like in the past even when 3D machines didn't exist, women were always the better cook, he thought. It must be their exquisite taste for the finer things in life and their motherly and loving nature. *Something's never change*, he laughed to himself. *Something's are universal.*

A few minutes later the Broccoli roast bake popped out the 3D machine, steaming and smelling like fresh greens mixed with chicken and blue cheese and ranch dressing. Jasper couldn't wait to dig in. After trying it for the first time a few days ago, he'd liked it ever since. It had now become his second favourite dish—after Jollof rice, that is. Jollof rice was a special type of rice that was very popular back in his wife's home country in Africa. She had introduced him to it on their first date back when they were both still at university. After tasting its sultry, succulent, and dancing, spicy flavour on his tongue, he fell in love with it, and then with her, walking down the aisle with her not too long after and never looked back.

Sarai set a plate in front of Jasper, placed one in the empty chair where Zack would sit, and then one before her. She grabbed a jug of orange juice and poured it into three glasses.

'Zack!' she called. 'Dinner's ready, honey.'

Zack's little feet thudded the ground as he ran into the dining room. He hoped on the chair, he struggled at first before eventually sitting atop properly.

She sat and they all dived in—cutleries and plates, clinking and clacking as they tucked in.

Jasper paused looking up at Sarai. 'I'm going to find him, Sarai,' he said. 'I'm going to find him and I'm going to get my job back.'

'How?' Sarai said in-between mouthfuls. 'The REA office is in reconstruction after the attack, and this man you're after is nowhere to seen.'

Jasper took a swig of his orange juice. 'I have a lead.'

'Oh, you do?'

Zack's head went from side-to-side, looking at both parents, clearly confused as to what was actually being spoken, so he lowered his head and dived back into his delightful food, the look of ecstasy on his face as he ate.

'My Sister. She thinks she knows where I can find him.'

'Clare?'

'Yeah.' Jasper used his table knife and fork to slice a large piece of broccoli and chicken in half before dipping them both in the mash potatoes and some ranch dressing sauce and then dropping them in his mouth. He crunched away, it was magnificent. 'She said he attacked the RoyalStarCorp about a month ago. I'm so close, Sarai, I know I am.'

'But, Jasper, you're suspended, your boss will not take to kindly to you disobeying his orders even further—'

'The hell with Walter Marshal!' Some food residue flew out of Jasper's mouth onto the table in his frustration. 'What does the man know? He so up his own ass, all he wants is for everyone to see him and paint him in a good light.'

Sarai remained quiet.

Jasper scraped the last of the mash potatoes and ranch dressing from his plate and ate it and set his cutlery down on the empty plate.

He pushed off the table with his hand and stood. 'Excuse me.'

'Where are you going?' Zack asked.

Jasper mussed his hair again. 'I won't be long, promise. I'll be back to help with your homework and put you to sleep. Daddy's just got to go somewhere real quick.' He kissed him on the forehead and walked over to the other side of the table, leaned in and pressed his lips to Sarai's cheek. She wrapped her arms around his neck.

After a while, he went into his room, put on his body armour, a black t-shirt and navy blue jeans, a pair of workman boots, and his overcoat, grabbed his REA issued Chrome .357 Magnum Revolver and left his home.

***

Jasper stood outside the front door of the Silas home in Brixton. He knocked. A moment later the door creaked opened.

Martin stood on the opposite side of the door, wearing a short-sleeve white shirt, a black pair of jeans, smart shoes, and a bottle of vodka hidden in the bulge of his overcoat pocket—which was plainly evident to Jasper. Jasper smiled and shook his head.

Martin craned his head back into the brightly lit house and shouted. 'Teresa! Honey, Jasper is here. We're going out, we'll be back soon. Love ya.'

Jasper took a step back, and as Martin slowly eased himself through the door, Teresa's voice came blurting back.

'Martin, take it easy with the Alcohol this time,' she yelled. 'The doctors have said, at least till your wound is fully healed, okay? Love you, too. You guys have fun.'

When the door slammed shut behind them, Martin quickly and swiftly took out the bottle he had hidden in his overcoat pocket. He unscrewed the lid, took a swig of it, and then offered Jasper some.

Jasper gestured a "no" with the wave of his hands. Martin looked at him as if he'd just been betrayed. Nevertheless, he shrugged and took another mouthful of it—wrapping his huge lips around the bottle top, tilting his head way back, and emptying the content of the bottle as if it was a competition and the fate of London City depended on it.

As they walked toward his car, Jasper said, 'Remember the promise I made to your wife?'

Martin screwed back on the lid and tucked the bottle back inside his overcoat pocket. He pulled out a pack of cigarettes. 'What promise?'

'The one where I bring you back home sober—that one.'

Martin snorted, reaching into the pack of cigarettes and pinching one out of the pack. He placed it to his lips and lit it with a lighter. He drew on it and blew out smoke.

'She's not the boss of me,' he said. 'I do whatever I want.'

Jasper raised an eyebrow. 'Then why was the vodka bottle hidden in your jacket pocket when you left the house?'

Martin kissed his teeth. 'Anyways, how are you doing, Jasper?'

They reached his car. Jasper hoped into the driver's seat and Martin into the passengers. Jasper pushed on the start button and the hover car sprung to life and took to hovering. He slowly backed out of the driveway, turned the steering wheels, and drove off at a steady speed.

'I'm doing well,' he finally said. 'Holding it together—as best I can. How about you?'

Martin slid the window down and threw his cigarette bud out the window; it fizzed and sparkled off the cobblestone on the roadside. He then slid the window back up, then reached down and pressed the heater button, warming up the car and steaming the windscreens, slightly. He rubbed his hands against one and other intensely. It was still so cold outside—blitzing, now that they had left the large building areas, and are driving in open space, where the biting breeze could flow freely, at its fiercest.

Martin tugged and scratch at his left leg, feeling for the scar, no doubt. Jasper remembered the incident back at the warehouse so vividly. Where the men in Khakis—Ezra Hawthorne's men—had mortally wounded Martin in his leg. They had barely made it out that day, thanks to some quick thinking from Jasper. But Martin had been in the hospital for a long time—almost a month—before he could walk again. So it was good seeing that he was fairing much better.

'Leg's all better now, thank fuck for that,' he said, and then he clenched his fists. 'If I ever get my hands on that Ezra Hawthorne fellow, I'm going to make him wish he was dead——cyborg or not.'

'Take it easy, Martin—'

'Take it easy? We've lost our jobs because of him!' his voice went up an octave.

'Suspended, not redundant.'

'Same thing—it's just a matter of time. Walter Marshal is just going by the books, that cocky, arrogant prick. I swear—'

'Clare has a lead on Ezra . . .' Jasper cut him off just as the hover car came to a stop at a red light.

'What?'

'My sister, Clare, has a lead on Ezra.'

Martin looked at him, his eyes studying him. 'Really?'

The light turned green and Jasper took off again. He took a right down Chalk Farm, before going past Camden High Street, and slowing the hover car to a halt in front of the RoyalStarCorp scientific building, hidden behind two sets of large trees.

Jasper turned off the engine and the hover car slowly descended to the ground, no longer hovering.

'Come, let's go, she's waiting for us inside.'

Chapter Twenty-nine: A Shit Predicament

Grey and Lucan's men were hardly going to surrender. Instead, they took off, trying to find the nearest cover before David, Ezra Hawthorne, and the rest of the Foxhound Syndicate could rain down hell on them.

Grey took cover behind a wall, separated from the others, who had found covers of their own further down to his right. He pressed his back against the cold wall, wondering what on earth Ezra Hawthorne was doing here. It was bad enough to take on David and the Foxhound Syndicate, but Ezra Hawthorne and his gang of green khakis, too?

Grey shook his head, and then he heard David start to speak.

'I'm going to give you guys until the count of three . . . then we will shoot to kill.'

Grey looked over at his squad—Lucan's men—at Behemoth, at Elyse Fox, at Gael Cross, and at Rollo—who had the small gadget-device in his hand, ready to call for reinforcement. But Grey knew now was not the time to call in the cavalry. They would just get them killed. They needed to leave this place—escape somehow—and live to fight another day.

From what Grey knew about Ezra Hawthorne, he knew he was a dangerous man. And he and David—together—would be a deadly combination, one he was not expecting or even ready for. Lying face down, dead, in a ditch somewhere didn't seem far off anymore.

'One . . .' David started counting.

Grey crouched, going prone and, lying on his belly, he rolled across the cold cobblestone in the dim-lit area, hidden from David's glare, finally reaching the others. He squeezed in-between Behemoth and Rollo, reached toward the latter and grabbed the small gadget-device from his grasp, putting it in his pocket. Rollo grimaced at him.

'Two . . .' David continued, his voice echoing around them.

'No,' Grey whispered to Rollo. 'There will be no reinforcement. Not now. What we need to do now is escape this place.' He turned to Behemoth. 'That man counting is David, and the larger man next to him is Ezra Hawthorne.' Behemoth regarded him with an exasperated look as if those two names are meant to mean something to him. Grey had forgotten that he was the only one who knew what those two were really capable of—the others will soon realise.

'Three . . .' David finished. 'Time's up.' Grey peered his head out the cover, saw David turn to his men, 'Flush them out. Shoot to kill.'

Grey ducked back down. He waved Elyse Fox and Gael Cross closer. 'Listen, I'm going to buy you guys some time. The four of you need to make a run for it. Head back to the hover truck as quickly as possible and leave this place. Don't worry about me. Head back to Lucan's base.'

'What the hell are you talking about, Grey?' Behemoth asked, annoyed.

'Do as I say, if you want to survive tonight and not end up face down in a ditch somewhere—'

Footsteps started from behind them. Grey jolted up over the cover, turned, *Genesis* raised in front of him, palms opened, his other hand holding it by the wrist, taking aim. He felt the mental connection with the neuron in the compartment of his mechanical arm and let loose an energy blast—the colour of fire and the size of a small melon.

The energy blast screamed as it flew through the dark alley, lighting the area in a strange orange glow. Grey watched as it crashed into a metal trash container, dissipate, and spread into little flames, causing those Foxhound Syndicate members around it to dive and duck for cover.

Bullets then erupted all around toward their direction.

A stray bullet flew in and struck the unaware Rollo through the skull. It sunk deep into his forehead, and then it exploded in a gush of dark-red as he dropped to the ground with a silent thud among the chorus of bullets.

Elyse Fox grabbed a shocked Behemoth by the arm. 'Come on,' she said to him. 'You heard what Grey said, let's go!'

'Ah, you son-of-a-bitch,' Behemoth grunted, got to his feet and started. 'Lucan's not going to be happy about this.' Gael Cross led the way as they made their way—through a bullet storm—back down the alleyway they had come from. Behemoth turned back and gave Grey one last glare, 'This is on you, Grey. Lucan will not be pleased!'

Grey didn't care. He knew this was the only option. Lucan would have to understand his judgement of the situation. There was no way they could've won here tonight. They were outnumbered and any reinforcement would've just seen certain death.

Grey looked over at the lifeless corpse of Rollo—if anything, Grey had saved Lucan losing more men tonight. But what does that mean for him? Was he going to survive tonight? Was he going to make it home—to the smell of fresh lilies and his warm bed and lie next to Bethany, or end up just like Rollo?

Grey risked another looked over his shoulder—Behemoth, Gael Cross, and Elyse Fox had more or less disappeared into the dark night beyond. He needed to buy them a few more minutes though, so they can get back to the hover truck.

Grey popped out again from the behind the cover, *Genesis* leading, releasing a torrent of energy blast in front of him—one after the other—the bright glare of the energy blasts flashed in his eyes and lit up the alleyway like Christmas.

Men and Women of the Foxhound Syndicate rolled, tossed, ducked, and dove aside to avoid Grey's onslaught. Grey felt his adrenaline kicking in, felt his heart beat faster, and surprising enough, even in the cold weather conditions, he felt tiny droplets of sweat drip down the back of his neck. The heat that flared out of the palm of *Genesis* washed on his face.

He ducked back into cover, and in the distance he could hear the sound of what sounded like a hover truck, kicking into gear and zooming off. He breathed a sigh of relief. It would seem Behemoth, Elyse Fox, and Gael Cross had survived the night and live to fight another day.

Now was the time to escape. There was nothing holding him back now. He'd bought them time and done his part.

Grey popped up from behind the cover—one last time—to weigh his options and plan a route of escape.

As he did, a large hand reached out, he felt it tighten around his throat and then felt his feet lift off the ground. He struggled to breathe; whizzing and gurgling and choking. Through hazy vision, he saw that the hand around his throat was mechanical.

'You again,' the anonymous voice spoke in a thick accent that Grey thought was a cross between English and Russian. 'This time I'll make sure you stay down.'

Chapter Thirty: A Scorching Flame

Grey used whatever strength he had left in his fists to beat down hard on the mechanical hand around his throat. He struggled to break free. But when he felt as if he was about to pass into the next world—most probably hell rather than heaven, he imagined—his fight or flight instinct kicked in.

Using his knee, he raised it high and drove it straight up through the chin of the assailant, staggering him. Grey felt his knee throb with ice-like pain from the connection, but he ignored it. Now was not the time to wallow. Then, placing the palm of *Genesis* on the aggressor's chest, his released an energy blast, sending the attacker—who he could now see was Ezra Hawthorne—crashing back a few metres, which meant Grey dropped to the ground with a painful thud.

Wincing in pain, Grey looked up and squinted in the dark; saw Ezra Hawthorne approaching again, smoke trailing out from his armoured chest where the energy blast had connected.

Ezra raised his hands up, signalling to David, the Foxhound Syndicate, and his gang of Khakis behind him. 'Leave him to me,' he said as he reached Grey and picked him up by the head with his large mechanical hands. Grey grimaced, clenching his teeth and squeezing his eyes shut. 'We have unfinished business.'

Ezra Hawthorne drove his mechanical fist into the sternum of Grey. Grey felt the breath go out of him, his mouth opening wide, and air from his lungs gusting out and steaming in the cold night air. Ezra then got a hold of *Genesis*, restraining it, firmly.

'Who is it?' a deep voice from where the Foxhound Syndicate and Khakis stood— echoed. Grey managed to strain his neck a little, saw that it was David asking the question. 'Who do you have unfinished business with? It's too dark out here, I can't see shit.'

Ezra Hawthorne squeezed tighter around Grey's head. Like a metal or wood caught between a vice-grip, Grey's head felt like it was about to explode.

'Oh . . . just some mechanically enhanced cyborg like myself,' Ezra said, spitting to the ground. 'We met about a month ago—didn't we, Grey?'

How in the hell does he know my name? Grey thought. They had only met for a split second a month ago, back at RoyalStarCorp, before Grey blacked out from his crushing attack, after being sent sprawling into metal crates. Still, it seems something's never change, Grey thought to himself. He was still at the mercy of the same man, once again—

'What?' David's voice boomed in the darkness. 'Wait!' Flashlights pointed toward their direction, and Grey felt Ezra's Hawthorne's grip around his head and *Genesis* loosen as his attention diverted to David's voice and his approaching footsteps.

Grey knew now was he chance—his only chance. He could smell the tension in the air, it was palpable. David wanted him for himself. *He* wanted to be the one to kill Grey, Grey knew this very well.

Grey yanked back his arm, breaking free from Ezra Hawthorne's grip, directed the palm of *Genesis* toward Ezra's Hawthorne's face, and let loose a ferocious energy blast—no, a stream of energy fire—that charred and set ablaze the flesh on the side of Ezra Hawthorne's face. He had just moved at the last second, and that movement had probably just saved his life. He let go of Grey and screamed in pain—a shrill that was bordering on madness, both mechanical hands on his face, writhing and wailing and twisting and thrashing about and slapping his face, trying to put it out.

All the while Grey stared at *Genesis* once more—*I owe you one Herman*, he thought. *Thanks for teaching me and expanding my abilities, needed that one more than ever.*

Grey looked up, saw David approaching, saw him pick up speed, ignoring and brushing past Ezra Hawthorne and his now burning face. *Typical*, Grey thought. The man was a selfish idiot who didn't care much for others as long as he got what he wanted—which at this point in time was Grey, dead or alive.

Grey stood to his feet, smiled, and stretched forth *Genesis*, and fired. Only this time he heard the click in his arm that signalled the emptiness of the neurons in the compartment.

Shit, he thought as he quickly reached into his overcoat pocket, popped opened the compartment.

He dropped two of the three spares he had in his pocket—clinking and clanging on the quiet cobblestone—and being short on time, considering the fast-approaching David with his Exo-suit and machine gun at hand, he loaded the one neuron and closed the compartment in his wrist.

He fired all he had. He lit the dark area up in flames, spreading it along the ground between himself and the others, causing a separation between the two opposing sides.

David as well his men that had been following behind, stood on the other side of flames, unable to cross it as it was still burning bright and most probably extremely hot.

A sullen faced David glared at him from behind the flames, his hidden anger as scorching as the flames themselves.

Grey knew the flames weren't going to last long though, so he did only what he knew would be wise in this kind of situation.

He ran.

Chapter Thirty-one: A Lesser of Two Evils

Jasper and Martin walked through the halls of RoyalStarCorp guided in front by his sister Clare and her Colleague Adam Cardon.

'So you're telling me you guys were robbed by Ezra Hawthorne and his goons and you didn't let us know?' Martin asked as they took a right turn into a wide corridor.

'Yes,' Clare nodded and then glanced back at Martin. 'We didn't think it was necessary—'

'Necessary?' Martin's raised voice cutting her off. 'Of course, it was. If a rogue cyborg is arming himself with powerful robotics and ammunition and then selling it to the highest bidder—I think that it *is* necessary to inform us! Especially when it's someone we've been after for a very long time!'

Jasper placed a hand on the exasperated Martin's shoulders as they passed empty cubicles after cubicles filled with scientific gadgets. 'Easy, Martin,' he said. 'What is done is done. There's nothing we can do now. I'm sure they've learned their lesson and won't be so sluggish about the situation, next time, right?'

Clare said nothing this time, only just faced forward. Adam Cardon, however, turned back to face them, nodded, and smiled. Jasper still didn't trust the man, though. He looked just too . . . clean. Neatly cut hair, a clean-shaven face that exposed a squared jaw, and a clean lab coat that was spotless—a little too perfect. *What dark secrets are you hiding?* Jasper thought to himself.

They reached a metal door with a glass centred middle that enabled one to see inside. A small brown man with large rimmed glasses approached the door and opened it.

'Hey, hey, Clare, Adam, welcome guys,' the small man said, turning and tiptoeing to peer behind them. 'And who are these?' He moved aside, allowing them through into the room.

Adam smiled at him. 'These are Jasper Barnes and Martin Silas.'

The small man's throat swallowed something large. He looked at Jasper with curious eyes. 'Barnes . . . do you mean Clare's brother? The REA agent?'

Jasper strode through the room, Martin beside him, glancing all around at the robotic parts lying around. His eyes landed on the table just to his right, a dozen crystal metallic cylinders perfectly laid out on them.

'That's right,' Jasper finally said without turning to face him. 'And Martin here is also an REA agent, too.'

'Nice to meet you guys,' the small man said quickly, coming up to them to shake their hands. 'I'm Herman Rowntree—scientist and biomedical engineer.' He pushed his spectacles up the bridge of his nose with his index finger. 'Feel free to—' his holo-phone rang and, after raising it to his ear and then lowering it, he said, 'excuse me . . .' and left the room.

Clare and Adam Cardon settled in front of a holo-screen, while Martin fixated himself with some kind robotic part by the shooting gallery, touching and caressing it as if mesmerized by it.

'Come here,' his sister waved him over. 'I got something to show you.'

Jasper went over to her, glanced down at her screen, a holographic image of what looked like some kind of exo-suit orbited.

'What's that,' he asked her. 'It's a suit I've been working on. It's the next generation in robotics, built for the military—for war. Put this on and you become a full machine, not just a cyborg. It's only the prototype but I should be done with it real soon.'

Jasper shook his head. Here: he and Martin and the REA were trying to stop these kinds of things getting into the hands of public and criminals, and here: his sister is freely giving them out, whether she means to or not. He has to stop—

The door to the room creaked open, Jasper turned, and Herman Rowntree stood by the door with . . . Grey Harrow, his head lowered and his arms over the small man's shoulders. His eyes were slightly swollen, his face scratched and bleeding, his armour and clothing stained with red—and looked most likely his.

Jasper didn't know what took over him, but it was probably the image of the REA office going up in smoke and seeing Grey Harrow, the man responsible for its demise.

He walked over to them and, before he could lay a hand on Grey Harrow, Grey Harrow tilted his head up and raised his robotic hand toward Jasper, the tip of the palm glowing, faintly. Jasper could see the orange-red hue of the energy blast that he knew could eject from that palm and disintegrate him, so he stopped, only scowling at him instead.

Clare stood up and got in-between them, her hands spread to either side of her, trying her best to calm them both. 'Stop this, now, the two of you.' She turned to Grey Harrow, 'What are you doing here?'

'Running,' he said, 'running from the Foxhound Syndicate.'

'What?' she said. 'Again? What happened?'

Adam came up behind Jasper and helped Herman get Grey Harrow to one of the chairs. He sat and began to tell of his night and how he ended up here.

'So you saw Ezra Hawthorne with the Foxhound Syndicate?' Martin asked, joining them.

Grey Harrow winced. 'Martin Silas, right? Yes I saw him and I need your help to take him down,' his eyes darted between Jasper's and Martin. 'You get your man, and Lucan Weaver gets what he wants. Everybody wins.'

'Lucan Weaver?' Jasper asked.

'You're crazy,' Martin said.

Jasper said, 'I will not help one criminal organisation overthrow another. What difference does it make? I'll rather take both down.'

'It's the lesser evil—Ezra Hawthorne and your job back. Your sister told me what happened.'

Grey Harrow was most probably right, Jasper thought. Perhaps in the unlikely situation that they agree to it, they could get their man and get their jobs back. But was the lesser evil right, or even worth it? Evil is still evil whichever way you look at it. But Jasper needed to think of his family, of his city, in the bigger scheme of things. He wasn't just living for himself anymore. Gone are his wild bachelor days from university, his got a family to provide for now, and his ambition was always to become Special Agent or Intelligence Analyst, and in capturing their number one target—Ezra Hawthorne—he could very well do so.

'One question, Grey,' Jasper said. 'Why did save my life back at the REA office when that large man had me dead to rights? You could've just left me.'

Grey Harrow shared a quick glance with Clare before turning back to him.

'I didn't do it for you.' He said.

Chapter Thirty-two: A Lucid Dream

Grey Harrow ended up spending the night at RoyalStarCorp along with Jasper Barnes, Martin Silas, Clare Barnes, Adam Cardon, and Herman Rowntree. Clare Barnes had rounded up the rest of the scientists and biomedical engineers and sent them home early, leaving the six of them to their own devices.

Clare ordered the others to get Grey to the medical bay for some treatments. But before they could treat him for his wounds Grey made sure to give Bethany a call to let her know where he was and why he wouldn't be coming home tonight. The last thing he wanted was for her to start to worry again. He had only just begun to alleviate her concerns about him, about the Foxhound Syndicate, about the whole situation.

The second he hung up with Bethany, his phone rang again, this time it was Lucan. Only it wasn't. Behemoth had been using Lucan's phone to call him. The giant man sounded rather formal and stressed out and, after Grey had told him of his escape from the Foxhound Syndicate warehouse and how he was in no condition to go anywhere else tonight, Behemoth told him Lucan would like to meet with them all first thing tomorrow morning, Grey included.

Finally, they carried the injured Grey to the medical bay lab—Jasper Barnes and Martin Silas doing the honours. The lab was a scientist's playground; multi-coloured lines of wires, advanced robotic medical equipment . . . Grey could go on, but some of the things he saw, his unscientific and quite frankly un-interested mind couldn't explain it properly.

They placed him gently down on what Grey thought looked like a translucent curved bench—it had deep circles holes on the headrest and footrest, which held his head and feet in place. It was different from the bed-like thin chair he woke up from a month ago in this same facility after the Ezra Hawthorne's heist incident. While that chair was uncomfortable and small—this bench was big and so much more comfortable, accommodating his body mass, perfectly. He wondered why they hadn't used this bench instead as he was in a worse state then than he was in now.

He glanced up from where he laid, saw a machine hand dangle above him. The machine hand was shaped like a real-life hand—albeit with black and golden mechanical screws—just like *Genesis*. Squinting, his eyes narrowed in on it, and he could now see that the machine hand had a sharp-pointed end that looked like a needle.

He turned his head to the side, everyone was in the room: Jasper and Martin staring at him intensely with their hands folded, Herman holding a tub of medication of some kind, Clare hovering next to him, her hand gently on his shoulder, and just behind her he could see Adam Cardon operating on a holographic keyboard—a 3D hologram of Grey in front of him like a phantom. Grey figured this was some kind of way to measure and to see the full extent of his injuries.

'What's happening—' he started, then slowly he felt metallic straps wrap around his body—two clasp his ankles, two gripped his wrists, and one suppressed his neck. He then saw the machine hand above him open its palm and flash something in his eyes as if someone had just taken a picture of him. The machine hand then narrowed its index finger—the one with the needle-like end—then shot downwards, and Grey grimaced, cringing as he felt the sharp-pointed end of the needle press and pierce deep into his flesh just above his collarbone.

'Take it easy,' Clare's soft voice came calling out to him, soothing him into peaceful oblivion.

***

Grey dreamt. He went in and out of dreams like it was a movie. He dreamt of his early years as an orphan, moving from house to house, from family to family, never really fitting in anywhere. Then he dreamt of his initial inception into the Foxhound Syndicate. Now, those dreams where hazy and fogging—never really taking him back and placing him there completely.

But there was one, one that came to him so vivid like a spectre.

Grey's memories swam as he slept. He remembered that day very vividly. It was a warm night in July, roughly about six months ago. His last job—or so he thought it would be.

'Hurry, Hurry, before we get caught.' David shouted to him. 'The feds are almost here.'

Grey, shovel at hand, penetrating the soil, uprooting dirt, was digging as fast as he could. They were in an abandoned field just on the outskirts of London were their suppliers had buried and stashed their goods in haste. Goods meaning: Neurons and High-tech weaponry. Neurons at the time were a new highly addictive drug the Foxhound Syndicate was purchasing and putting into circulation in London. Their suppliers were an anonymous shadowy organisation abroad. Even the Foxhound Syndicate themselves didn't even know who their suppliers were, and Grey had thought that was quite odd. Despite having control over most of the London Underworld that one information had eluded them.

'You too, Brom and Hector, hurry the fuck up!' David shouted again.

'We're going as fast as we can.' Brom grunted. 'Maybe if you helped—'

'Shut it! And get back to work!' David didn't let Brom finish. 'One of us has to watch out for the feds.'

'Yeah and why does that someone have to be you?' Hector got involved.

David turned and walked slowly over to Hector. He had grabbed him by his shirt collar and pulled him close to his face, the tip of their nose almost touching. 'Because I'm the leader here, out of the four of us, the order has come down to put me in charge, now get back to work.' David shoved him away; Hector stumbled but did not fall, resuming his digging.

Grey watched from the corner of his eye as David went back to the top of the field to resume his watchtower duties.

A few seconds later he came back down and said, 'Alright, that's enough, I think we've got enough, we're done here. Whatever is left, leave it, the feds have arrived. Let's pack what we've managed to remove and head out.'

They moved as quickly as they could, stuffing the Neurons and Weapons in the large duffle bags they each had. When they were done, they headed south, down the back of the fields, back to their hover car packed on the side of the road. Grey glanced over his shoulder as they made their way down the hill and he could now see in the distance the blue and red lights of the police hover car approaching, their sirens ringing.

They quickened their steps, duffle bags full to the brim, weighing heavy on them. They reached the car, and David opened the car boot and stuffed the bags in, one by one, then closed it.

'Get in the car everyone!' he yelled. 'Grey, you're driving!' he threw the keys to him and Grey caught it with shaky hands, not expecting the throw.

They entered the hover car; Brom and Hector sat at the back, David in the passenger's side as Grey started the car, roaring it to life and speeding it off into the dark night.

'*Woof,*' Brom said from behind Grey when they were on their way. 'That was a close one.'

'Yeah, it was,' Hector added. 'Damn shame we couldn't get everything.'

'It's your damn faults,' David turned to look at them from the passenger seat. His eyes were burning with rage. 'Now those Neurons and weapons left behind are for the feds and their evidence locker. What a waste. This is on all your heads.' He gave Grey a quick glance from the side before turning back to face the front. Grey knew that David was partially right; he was the pet of those who were at the top of Foxhound, and if anyone was to get the blame for what went down tonight, David would be the last, even though he was the leader of this group. He was a trusted member of the Foxhound—one of the longest-serving members, his loyalty was unquestionable. Grey, Brom, and Hector, on the other hand, hadn't served as long as David, their loyalties had always been one of great debate among the Syndicate. And as Grey was planning to leave the Syndicate, it would seem the scepticism surrounding his loyalty wouldn't be too far off, after all. Grey hadn't told those at the top himself, per se, that honour he blessed and bestowed upon the leader of their group—David—to do so, but from what David had told him in return, the news hadn't gone down too well with their bosses.

'So,' Grey said, glancing over to his left to look at David. 'Where to?'

David's brow was still furrowed, and he seemed to be in deep contemplation, no doubt still pissed off at what had transpired back at fields.

'To the warehouse in East Finchley,' David said finally after a while without looking at Grey.

David's holo-phone rang; he stared down at the holo-screen for a few seconds, then he answered it.

'Yes . . . got it . . . it shall be done tonight.' David said to whoever was on the other line and then hung up. Grey presumed it to be his wife, but then the seriousness of the expression on his face led him to believe otherwise.

'Who was that?' he asked.

'None of your business. My personal calls have nothing to do with you.' David's eyes still so focused, looking straight up ahead from the passenger's seat.

They reached the warehouse. Grey got out of the car and grabbed one of the duffle bags, the others did the same. They stashed it away in one of the secret compartments of the warehouse, and then the four of them headed for the exit. Grey had been the last to leave the warehouse, and when he got outside he saw David, Brom, and Hector talking to one another.

'Something I should know?' he got involved. 'If not, I'm heading home; this was my last job, after all. I'm now a free man.' He smiled.

At that, David turned and glared at him, almost distastefully, and Grey couldn't understand why, as far as he knew, he had been nothing but a brother to the man. Had it been because he was leaving the Syndicate? Was it so bad that he wanted to turn a new leaf? Change his ways from the life he been forced into since a young boy?

David's distasteful glare turned into a forced smile as Grey approached him, Brom, and Hector.

Brom had been the first to hug Grey, wrapping his arms around him in a death-like bear hug, 'I'm going to miss you brother,' he said, 'take care of yourself.' When Brom pulled his arms back, Hector came closer.

'So I'm I,' Hector embraced his friend. 'It's been a pleasure.' Grey felt uneasy; they were treating him as if he were dying when in actuality he was only leaving the Syndicate. It wasn't like they couldn't still see each other. It had been a weird feeling, and he couldn't quite shake the thought that he was missing something. His fears wouldn't be without some truth, though—he would soon find that out later.

'Alright, alright, enough,' David inserted. 'Let's get going, some of us have a wife to get back to. Grey . . .' he paused for a while, staring his friend in the eyes for a while, and then his voice broke, 'all the best in your new life, send Bethany my love. Tell her . . . I'm sorry.'

Sorry for what? Grey couldn't shake the feeling that he had been missing something again. 'We'll do.' He said.

The four of them then dispersed, each going back to the respective hover cars they had parked by the warehouse before they went on the mission.

And that was it. The last time Grey thought he would ever have to use a gun again or dig up drugs and weapons from dirt.

It wasn't even five minutes into his drive home when his whole world had come plummeting down. He had reached for his holo-phone and was about to click on Bethany's number, and then it happened. The accident that wasn't—he would soon find out. A huge hover truck struck his car, caving in the left side of his car, sending the car spiralling, violently, on its side, first to the side of the road, then into a river, and finally culminating in a fiery explosion, which was instantly subdued due to the water from the river.

All Grey had remembered (and could dream of) from this latter incident during that night was: the white lights of the hover truck, then being dragged out of the river by his right arm as he drifted in and out of consciousness, before finally waking up (from a coma) in RoyalStarCorp a few weeks later with *Genesis* attached to where his organic left arm used to be.

His dream ended and he slowly roused from his heavily sedated sleep.

***

When Grey woke, the straps were gone, and he had never felt better. His jacket and t-shirt had been removed—probably when he was sedated—and only his trousers remained. It would seem they had done some sort of work on him—on *Genesis*—while he was out.

He sat upright, blinking, scanning the medical room, only Jasper remained sitting where Adam Cardon had been seated previously, in front of the 3D hologram image of Grey. No hologram this time, however, just Jasper Barnes staring into nothing, in deep contemplation, one elbow leaning on the desk, hand raised, his chin resting on his fist. Grey wondered what an REA Agent could be thinking of—so much so that it had caused him to stare off intensely into the distance at nothing in particular. Perhaps his family? His wife and kids? His job? What in the hell was troubling the man?

Grey Harrow shifted his legs off the bench so that they dangled off the side of the bench toward the ground, sitting on the edge. He rotated his shoulders, stretched his back, both of those body parts cracking with a satisfying feeling.

Unfortunately, the sound of his shoulders and back cracking brought Jasper out of his stupor, and he turned to regard Grey with those cynical eyes of his. Grey stared back at him wordlessly.

After a while, Grey said, 'What?'

Jasper chuckled. 'Grey Harrow, a former member of the Foxhound Syndicate . . .' he trailed off, looking back off into the distance as if to go back into his deep contemplation again. Then he turned and looked back at Grey again. 'What happened to you? From what Clare and the others have said, you were a big shot back in the days. Why would your own people want you dead?'

'Because I wanted to leave,' Grey said dryly.

'Oh, come on, bullshit,' Jasper raised his hands in the air as if exasperated suddenly, though Grey could tell he wasn't. 'What shit did you pull on them for them to want to put you six feet under? They seem to be staking everything on it, doing everything necessary to get to you, regardless of the public catching wind or not.'

Grey scratched at the back of his head. 'I don't know what you are talking about.'

'If we're going to work together, you are going to have to be honest with me . . .' Jasper stood to his feet and walked closer to Grey. 'I'm putting my life, my family, my job on the line here. I'm risking everything and I'll be damned if I lose any of them trying to help a lying arsehole.'

So Grey Harrow told Jasper Barnes everything. From his initial inception into the Foxhound Syndicate; to their principles regarding members joining, and then finally to the very night he lost his arm in the botched mission gone awry.

185

'So you're telling me they do not allow members to leave the Syndicate?' Jasper Barnes was asking him.

'Uh-huh,' Grey nodded, remembering what had happened to Brom a few weeks back. Brom was Grey's closest friend from the Syndicate. And just like Grey, he had the same idea—he had decided it was time to leave the Syndicate. Grey found his body behind Baron's Bar in Piccadilly Circus after he'd received a call from him to meet him there, and after Brom had realised he was being chased by the Syndicate. Grey was captured and tortured shortly afterward by David and two other members of the Syndicate but was recused from their cold clutches by this very same Agent before him—Jasper Barnes.

Jasper said, 'Why didn't you just go to the police?'

Grey Harrow rolled his eyes, shook his head, and stared at Jasper. 'You and I both know going to the police won't change a damn thing, and if anything it would lead me down to an even deeper rabbit hole.'

'What about your final mission for the Syndicate—the botched mission? Do you think it had anything to do with it?'

It most probably did. But as Grey looked around the medical lab bay, he could see pockets of bright, morning light flooding in through the slits of the windows blinds, and then he remembered he had a more pressing and more urgent matter at hand.

Lucan Weaver.

He would need to attend the meeting Behemoth had told him about last night. The topknot boss was his salvation, and personally, he didn't seem like the kind of guy you'd want to keep waiting.

For what it's worth, Grey would remain on his good side, take all the help he can get, and help him in his war against the Foxhound Syndicate.

Then, and only then, can he and Bethany leave this whole city behind and start anew.

He got off the bench and started walking. 'Where are my clothes?' he asked.

'It's in Herman Rowntree's office,' Jasper said.

Grey nodded and started again, heading for the door, and straight for Herman's office.

Jasper called out after him. 'Where are going? You've just healed up—'

Grey slammed the door to the medical bay behind him as he left, leaving Jasper's question hanging there, suspended in the air, unanswered.

Chapter Thirty-three: A Job Lined Up

Grey Harrow entered Lucan's base strolling in through the feint rundown building past the high-tech computers and gadgetry and machinery and weapons before reaching the narrow corridor hallway that had now been stack and filled with mechanical parts that were either hung up or rested against the metallic walls.

He entered the main hall where he'd first met Lucan about a month ago—the wide-open area still smelt of incense and was still littered with coils. He hadn't been in this part of the building since that faithful day when he first arrived here and when he'd first met Behemoth—the giant muscular man, forever hostile toward him.

Grey glanced around, ahead; Lucan's throne-like chair had been spun around and was occupied, his armoured bodyguards—both men and women—gathered beside and around him, all out in their full force.

Kneeling by the foot of the throne with their heads bowed down were Behemoth, Gael Cross, Eustace de Maris, and Elyse Fox. Grey went to join them at the foot of the throne, grudgingly kneeling before Lucan. He still hated it. Hated the fact he was kneeling for anyone except for God Himself. Was this man a god? But again, he will comply. He was so close to the end, so close to leaving all this behind him. He would lick the ground Lucan walked on if it meant he was done with all of this shit.

The three of them regarded Grey with narrowed side-eyes as if he were an outsider, a blemish in an otherwise spotless piece of armour.

'Raise your heads,' Lucan's deep voice came from up above them.

They all slowly raised their heads toward Lucan. And there he was, sitting like a god, surrounded by his minions, one leg crossed and resting on the knee of the other. He was wearing his favourite attire: a long black trench coat that was buttoned up to his neck, black trousers, and black gloves. No ominous smile this time, however, just concern and confusion in his expression. No doubt wondering what the hell had happened last night. He'd probably thought by the morning he would've been seated on his throne with the Foxhound Syndicate dismantled and full control of their underworld empire in his grasp.

Lucan Weaver's eyes darted from left to right, regarding each and every one of them, his expression pained. Grey could see that the other three couldn't even keep eye contact with him. Whenever Lucan would glare at them, their eyes would drop low, and when Lucan would look away, their eyes would return. Was this man really *that* powerful? Why was everyone so scared of him? He didn't seem that bad of a guy compared with some of the ruthless guys Grey had run into in the past. After all, he'd saved Grey's life and paid for his new arm.

'Behemoth, speak.' Lucan finally spoke.

Behemoth's eyes met Lucan's and he spoke. 'With all due respect, Sir,' he said, pointing toward Grey. 'Our unsuccessful mission was all down to this man.' Grey couldn't believe what he was hearing. How pathetic. Does the man even have a backbone? 'We were ready to move in and claim the fortress but Grey Harrow had other ideas—'

'Sir,' Grey couldn't stand to hear him anymore, so he butted in. 'This man here,' Grey pointed at him with his index finger. 'Was going to get us all killed. I did what I thought was best. And that was to—'

'Sir,' Behemoth cut him off, returning the favour. 'With all due respect, how do we know this man is not working for them? He was once a part of their Syndicate, he could very well be a spy, planted within our ranks, to dismantle us from the inside—'

Lucan Weaver wordlessly raised his palm, and Behemoth stopped talking. He gestured for Grey to carry on.

Grey cleared his throat. 'Sir, if we had called for reinforcement, you would have lost a lot more men. The Foxhound Syndicate has hired mercenaries. A man called Ezra

Hawthorne, who is also mechanically enhanced, is their leader. I have faced off with him before and it didn't end well. So the two groups together would have massacred us.

'And Rollo?' Lucan said softly.

'I . . . I'm sorry, but he didn't make it out.'

Lucan closed his eyes and rubbed his forehead with the thumb and index finger of his gloved hands, his expression turning grave. Despite his position and power, this man really did seem to care about his men. Every last one of them it would seem.

'Where is the device that Rollo had?' he said.

Grey's heart raced. He had left it in the overcoat pocket and had not taken it out since. He quickly reached into his overcoat pocket, searching frantically, hoping no one— particularly Clare or Herman or Adam had removed it from his jacket whilst he had slept.

Relief. He felt the device still in there. He took it out and handed it over to Lucan.

Lucan took the device, held it gently in his gloved hand, and looked at him. 'Grey, as much as I'm grateful for your quick thinking, it was not part of the plan. You should've stuck with the plan, whether or not *you* thought it was going to work or not. It was my order and you do not disobey a direct order.' Grey could see Behemoth smile to himself, pleased, as Lucan spoke. 'This is the second time you've made the wrong move . . .' Lucan trailed off, pausing. 'There will be no third time.'

Lucan stared at Grey with unwavering eyes for a long time; Grey stared back as his jaw tightened. *What does he mean there will be no third time?*

Lucan juggled the device in his hand for a bit, and then looked to the others.

'I need to think about what was said here today,' he said. 'Go, for now, get on with your day, I'll call for you if I need you.'

He dismissed them all.

***

Jasper made his way home in the early hours of the bright but densely cold morning after leaving the RoyalStarCorp, and after he had dropped off Martin at his home. The two of them still without work, suspended.

Luckily enough for them, it was a weekend, and they were not expected to be at work. That didn't matter, however. Jasper still felt like a bum. He felt as if he was wasting away, he needed something to occupy his mind, fuel his mind, and reignite his passion. Being an REA Agent had done that for him. It gave him purpose, made him feel like he was making a difference in the world. He also had plans—ambitions, goals. To work his way up the ladder, so he could provide the very best for his family.

That's all he ever really cared about, after all. Them—Sarai and Zack. It was all for them. A safer London that is free from criminals and their illegal use of Robotics, a roof over their heads, and food on their table.

He'd come from a poor family and from a young age had been determined in his mind to be successful and not repeat the same mistakes as his parents. So he knuckled down, excelled in his studies, and went on to university, achieving a first class with honours.

Jasper walked in through the front door, knowing full well he was about to receive the full brunt of his wife's rage.

'Where the hell have you been, Jasper?' She came blurting out as he entered the kitchen. He hadn't been wrong. 'I called and called and called but no answer. You said you were only going out for a little while and that you would be back to help Zack with his homework.' Oh shit. Zack's homework. He had completely forgotten. 'And look at this Jasper,'—she threw a holographic tablet letters of their many bills on the table—'my income alone is not going to be able to cover it all, Jasp.'

Jasper's eyes narrowed on the holographic tablet letters on the table. Words projected outward from the tablet in holographic style, painting the content of the letters out in blue-white translucent scribes in the open air. He really needed to figure out a way to bring in some income. At least until his suspension (which was without pay, mind you) was over. He could only hope Walter Marshal would take them—he and Martin—back after the thorough inspection and investigation.

That was all he'd trained for all his life. He didn't know anything else. What, could he work as something else? Perhaps in the meantime, he could volunteer as a waiter? Or maybe even a security guard? It was pretty close to the type of work he had already been doing.

'Darling, don't worry,' he finally said, 'you're not in this alone. I have something lined up.' He lied. 'Go to work, don't be late.' He walked over and planted a soft kiss to her forehead, then, planted a barrage of them on her cheeks, her nose, and her lips. She laughed, trying to ward him off, and Jasper could see that heaven-on-earth smile reveal itself on her face again. Her teeth white as snow. Her caramel skin forever glowing. That was his wife. His most prized possession. His treasure.

'Look after Zack, see to it he gets his homework done, okay?' She said.

'Consider it already done.' Jasper winked at her.

Chapter Thirty-four: A Return to the Red-Light District

Grey looked around in the cold, dark evening, to his left and then to his right, his heart beating slightly faster, his mouth steaming with his shallow breaths—in and out—checking to make sure the coast was clear, then he proceeded to climb up the side of the building, using his hands to grip the uneven surfaces of the metallic five-storey building as the chill weather bit at him from all directions.

A few moments later he reached and grabbed onto the windowsill to his old apartment, gaining purchase. The window was still wide open just as he had left it a few weeks back when he had jumped out of it to evade the four Foxhound Syndicate goons in balaclavas.

He slowly manoeuvred his frame over the sill, entered the apartment with a soft press of his boots, and then shut the window behind him. He was now in his bedroom—everything was turned over. His wardrobe tipped over, his nightstand pulled open and the contents emptied out. His king-size bed stripped of the mattress and the wooden frame beneath smashed to pieces. Strangely enough, the room smelt of spirit—alcohol, no doubt someone had lodged in here while he was gone, he guessed—probably a homeless scoundrel or something.

He pressed on toward his now fallen nightstand, around the destruction—the broken pieces of wood and sprawling mess of clothes lying on the floor. He still needed to be as quiet as a mouse. He didn't know if they were still here, or going to come back at any time. He was still a wanted man by the Foxhound Syndicate. For all he knew they could have booby-trapped this place.

He slowly pulled the nightstand upright. Beneath it laid his many packs of cigarettes. He reached down and grabbed a handful of packs—about three—and stuffed them in his overcoat pocket. Not before taking one out the pack, however, and placing it behind his right ear, ready for use later. He did that often. He didn't know why though, just that it felt kind of cool and made life easy for him to have one at the ready without having to dig into his pockets again.

He continued to rummage through the mess, picking out different clothes and shoes and jackets from the chaos and placing them on the nightstand, nicely folded. Finally, when he was done he found one of his old large duffle bags—one of the ones he had used in many of the jobs he had done for the Foxhound Syndicate—and placed them inside. He'd been wearing more or less the same garment, jacket, and boot since he left his apartment in haste all those many weeks ago. So having some change of clothes in his possession now was a breath of fresh air.

Afterward, he slowly twisted the doorknob and made his way out of his bedroom into his living room, his duffle bag—stuffed with his clothes—still in his hand. He glanced around in the pitch darkness, everything was still as he had left it, though his single armchair, situated near the fireplace, had been ripped apart, almost as if someone took a pen-knife to it, slicing and dicing it as if some goldmine hid somewhere inside it. It didn't. It was just a chair. A chair that didn't deserve that kind of abuse.

Nonetheless, Grey Harrow strode over to it and sat in it, placing his duffle bag to the side of it. It felt jagged and the loose parts of the leather chair poked and stung at him—at his bum and arms and back.

He saw his front door still lay on the floor from where they had kicked it in, sending it crashing down. He wasn't too surprised that no one had come to fix it or ransack the place. But then again, Grey didn't have anything of importance that he had left behind. Apart from his clothes, this chair was his most prized possession. Around here in King's Cross, especially within these blocks of apartments, which were heavily rundown anyway, everyone kept to themselves, and anything that didn't concern them, they didn't get involved. And

Grey liked it that way. With all that had happened, he wouldn't want the police to get wind of his lawless endeavours.

He took out the cigarette from behind his ear, lit it, and took a long drag on it, straight into his lungs and, puckering his lips, expelled the smoke into the air, filling the room with the stench of tobacco. He traced with his fingers the scars and marks they had left on his favourite chair, felt the jagged edges, the foamy orange inside of the chair sticking out from the leather.

As he put the cigarette to his lips to take another pull of the cigarette, he heard two distinct footsteps come from the other side of the wall of his old apartment, the sound getting closer and closer.

He furrowed his brow and clenched *Genesis* into a fist. But he wasn't in the mood for a fight right now; he had plans later on, even though he would most probably, seriously, hurt whoever it was on the other side of the wall, vastly approaching his apartment—especially now that he was getting a hang of *Genesis*.

Instead, he got up, grabbed his duffle bag and went back into his old bedroom, treading softly across the marble floor.

He opened the window again, the cold hitting his skin like a hard slap on his face. He slung the duffle bag across his shoulders and chest and climbed back down.

He put his hood up, tucked his cold hands inside his overcoat pockets, breathed out a sigh, and headed toward the Red-light district.

***

Grey Harrow's hair and beard had grown a whole lot since he had last been here. He had stopped grooming—or more precisely hadn't had the time to. The fresh set of afro-black hair that covered his head and lined his jaw was a welcome change. So much so that when Bethany Rose came out to meet him at the front of the Starlight Nightclub to usher him in, the two bouncers by the door—one that Grey acknowledged to be Joe Black—didn't recognise him. The other bouncer was new—a brutish looking white man with a stone-cold bald head and a blond goatee. Tanwar's replacement no doubt. Grey wondered what ever happened to the Asian giant. Word on the streets was that he survived the attack but was forever scarred by the incident that he left the city altogether. So much for strong security guards, eh?

Bethany took him through the dimly lit nightclub—first stopping by the cloakroom to drop off Grey's duffle-bag stuffed with the clothes he had just picked up from his old apartment. She wasn't working tonight and was dressed in a sparkling navy blue dress littered with small diamond-like pebbles. The dress accentuated her figure, it exposed her shoulders and her neck and the top of her chest, her perky bum and toned legs, her heels bringing her up to Grey's level.

He followed behind her, her warm hand lightly holding his as they brushed past people lost in ecstasy, dancing away like there was no tomorrow. It was only his third—or perhaps fourth—time in here, he couldn't remember, but nothing had changed much. The walls to the club were still scrawled with graffiti artistry and markings, neon-lights—purple, green, blue, red, green, and all the other colours of the rainbow—blurted down from up above them in a long stream of beam, alternating colours in a circular motion, hanging by metallic wirings on the ceiling. It was hot inside, despite it being freezing cold just outside where they had come from, and Grey could see sweat dripping off half-naked strippers as they danced away on the raised podium, twirling and sliding on poles. He didn't know whether he found it sexy or revolting. But seeing sweat dripping off those body parts did something to his inside, and so he wetted his lips, averted his gaze and looked up ahead at Bethany instead.

They reached the bar and sat by it on two metallic high stools that Grey thought looked very uncomfortable. As he eased his backside on it, his assumption was right. It was uncomfortable as hell.

After a while, Bethany ordered a few drinks—something light for Grey and something strong for herself—and they both drank and chatted as all around them House music blasted away, causing one of Grey's leg to twitch in tune to the song.

'My back,' Grey said, raising his voice slightly so Bethany could hear him.

'What?' she screamed back at him over the music.

'I said my back!'

'Your back? What about it?'

'It's hurting like a mo-fo, and I think it's because of this stool we're sitting on. No backrest.'

She laughed. 'Silly, it's perfectly fine or else they wouldn't let us sit on it.' She picked up her glass and emptied the remaining of its content in one gulp. Then she pulled his arms as she started. 'Come, let's dance.'

Grey grimaced. He didn't want to. And he knew deep down the reason was that he didn't know how to dance. He didn't want to embarrass himself, especially in front of everyone. But then, the alcohol must've finally hit him because he thought: *fuck it, no one fucking cares; everyone is too busy having the time of their lives to care about if I can dance or not.*

So he let her pull him, pull him toward the centre of the club, near where the half-naked whores danced.

Bethany danced, pulling him close, and then turning around to twist her waist and grind her arse on him. They both moved in tune with the music, lost. Grey felt the world blur out as he moved along with her. The alcohol in his system, the music, the girl—it was all that matter at that moment.

Though the place was filled with sweaty flesh all around them, Grey could distinctive smell Bethany. Breathing her in from behind, so close, he didn't want to let her go, so pure, so clean, he leaned in closer, wrapping his arms around her, he pressed his lips to her neck, to her cheek . . . and then finally to her rosy lips. He felt her lips press back against his, and they lost themselves, even more, going deeper and deeper.

'Grey,' she tapped at his shoulders. 'Stop it.'

Grey looked at her in the dim neon-lit dance floor, confused. 'What?'

She glanced down at her side, Grey followed her gaze, saw that *Genesis* had been groping her, and really hard by the look of the crease in her dress.

'I'm sorry,' he said. 'When I've had a bit to drink it affects my RHSV.'

'RHSV?'

'Rogue Hand Syndrome Virus,' he said.

'Oh,' she said and nodded.

After a while, he managed to remove the hand from her ass. She giggled. And Grey thought that was the most adorable thing he'd seen in a while.

'I guess that's my queue,' he said. 'Excuse me, I won't be long.'

So he made his way through the crowd. Some of the half-naked whores whistled at him from the podiums. Grey didn't even give them as much as an eyeball roll. However some of the other girls in the crowd of people—whores nonetheless, in their tight clothes that didn't leave much to the imaginations, flung themselves at Grey as he made his way to the toilet, pressing themselves up against him in the narrow and packed room.

'Hey, Hunny,' one of them winked.

'Wanna have some fun, handsome?' shouted another, in a really short skirt, which revealed really long legs that were longer than the Tower of London.

Another wetted her lips, stuck her index and middle fingers into her mouth, jerking it in and out mimicking it as if it were a penis.

Grey shook his head and look at the ground to distract himself as he continued onward. The ground—his friend and saviour. The ground was a sight, though, dirty and sticky with Alcohol.

Grey finally reached the toilet and, using his shoulder to open the flap of a door, he entered.

Inside he reached into his pocket and took out his meds. Popped two into his mouth and using the robotic faucet just below him by activating it with the sound of his voice and curling his hand, he drank the water to wash down the tablets. He tilted his head back and swallowed and then stared at his reflection in the mirror in front of him for a while. His hair and beard really had grown, even he couldn't recognise himself anymore, he thought.

Blinking at his reflection, his mind started to wonder why he was still fighting. Still running and still living in fear. He could just get Bethany and leave this city right now, however, he didn't have the money he needed to do that yet, and that would mean they would always live their life looking over their shoulders. And now that Lucan Weaver was involved, it wouldn't just be the Foxhound Syndicate after him. He owed Lucan a debt, a debt he didn't incur himself, but that was shoved upon him when the Foxhound Syndicate betrayed him.

Why I'm I still here? He thought to himself looking down at his gloved mechanical hand. *Just to suffer? I can feel my old arm, even my old fingers, the part of me that I lost, it won't stop hurting, and it's like it's still there, like a ghost. They sent you to hell, remember? But you are going to go even deeper. Take back everything you lost.*

He found himself clenching the ceramic basin, tight—the part that *Genesis* gripped had dented and cracked slightly. He released it and strode out of the toilet, frowning.

Bethany Rose was waiting outside as he exited. Her arms crossed, concern on her face.

'Come,' she said, interlocking her arms through one of his, 'I think we've had enough for one night. Let's go home. I have something in mind that will cheer you up.'

Chapter Thirty-five: A Man That Cannot Provide

So Jasper Barnes took on temporary jobs while he and Martin waited for news regarding their suspension from the REA. First as a waiter at Burger Court in Camden during the day (thanks to his sister), and then as a security guard at a newly opened state-of-the-art strip club in Kings Cross's Red-light district, thanks to Martin's hook-up, and also . . . because of their experience as Agents, obviously.

Jasper preferred the latter job, to tell the truth. Who wouldn't? He'd leave Burger Court when he had finished his shift smelling like grease and fat and when he got home to shower and change for his other job, Sarai would complain. Whining and moaning like she did a lot of the times these days. *You smell like shit*, she would say—thank you captain obvious—and *why can't you find another job? Perhaps something that pays more and is a little more respectable?*

She doesn't understand that a man in desperate need would take whatever comes his way right off the bat. Desperate times called for desperate measures. At least until all the outstanding bills and debts were paid off. Then he can take his time and find something better. For now, this was the best he could do. And do—his best—is what he would do. Besides, surely Walter Marshal will come to his senses and see that the Administration needs them? Even as rookie agents, Jasper and Martin had helped bust some of the hardest Robotics cases this side of London. Don't tell him those three years of blood, sweat, and tears were all for nothing?

Jaspers bounced through the streets of Kings Cross's Red-light district, showered, dressed, and smelling like fresh flowers in the spring. Oh, how he wished it was really spring right now. He was strapped in four layers: his thermals, his white t-shirt, his black cardigan, and his yellow strip Hi-Vis bomber jacket that had SECURITY scrawled in white bold letters on blue on his back.

And still . . . he was *fucking* freezing. Will this winter ever end? Felt as if it had been going on forever. Like Antarctica had swapped its atmosphere with London—minus the snow and ice. Heck, even a bit of snow would be better, he thought. At least then the cold wouldn't be all for show.

Jasper took a left turn into a side road, past the neon-coloured filled hover-train station, past the tall buildings lit up with holographic ads of the latest software and hardware and gadgets and hover cars and the latest futuristic bullshit available that most people couldn't even afford unless you were the people who ran this world or you're willing to put yourself in debt just to appear well off. Stupid.

He quickened toward the side of one particular building, he checked his holo-watch as he did, it was 9:30 pm, he still had time, didn't start work till 10:00 pm. On the side of that particular building—apart from holographic pictures of half-naked whores, with their numbers written below, plastered to the walls in holos *(Those days are over, I'm a married man now)*—there was a biometric scanner.

This one was a sort of ATM where one could check their account balance—only, of course, as cash were no longer in use in this new world.

Jasper remembered the day digital finally took over. He was still in University, and there was this one weirdo of a student who wouldn't shut up about the "digital age takeover", and he would preach to everyone in lectures and seminars—even in dorm rooms and libraries when everyone was just trying to either get some sleep, some sweet time with their boyfriend or girlfriend, or just read in silence.

'The digital age will usher in a new wave and era of robotics like never before.' The weirdo had said. He had then proceeded to demonstrate that through PowerPoint slides, many of which were thesis written on the subject. Oh how the weirdo was right, though, Jasper thought, looking back. What ever happened to him?

Anyways, everything was digital now. Thank the gods for the cyberspace world, he thought as he placed his hand gently on the scanner. Everything was right in the palm of one's hand.

Around his finger, the scanner lit up in many colours, and then it beeped. Jasper felt a slight static shock in the middle of his palm. It didn't hurt. It was a low-level electrical shock, and he had gotten used to it over the years. Most other people, too. It was the cyberspace world doing its business to find a person's data and account information digitally.

His data and account balance popped up on the holographic screen just above the scanner.

He breathed out a deep sigh.

-£13,000 was his balance. How did it get this bad? It was only—

A beefy hand landed on his shoulders, and he quickly removed his hand from the scanner so that whoever was behind him wouldn't see the pathetic state his life was in, turned around so fast he almost stumbled.

Martin stood grinning that smile of his. He too was dressed in his security wear, ready for the nightshift, though, Jasper caught the whiff of Vodka coming out from him.

'Look at us both, eh?' Martin blurted out, and Jasper could tell he was drunk. But not too drunk that he couldn't do his job—just tipsy. 'All kitted out in yellow. Who would have thought we would end up here?'

Jasper grimaced. 'Martin, get it together.'

'What?' he slurred slightly, but then tried to style it out.

'You're drunk. We've work in fifteen minutes. You better sober up.'

Martin waved him off with a flail of his hand as if he was a very posh lady tipping a waiter. 'Silly—'

Jasper grabbed him by the arm, squeezing it tight, and Martin winced. 'Listen, this is only our second day, and you and I know we need this job, so I will not allow you to get us fired—'

Martin shrugged his arm free, his countenance changing from wistful to grave. 'Oh . . . like *you* got us suspended from the REA?'

'Huh?'

A group of girls passed them by, smoking and giggling. Then two hover cars zipped past. The girls turned around as another hover car approached, one of them sticking her hand out and waving it to stop. It was a taxi. They all hoped in, the taxi driver's face a picture of lust. He said something to the girls that Jasper couldn't hear, they said something back, and then the driver titled his funny looking hat and sped off into the night.

'It's your fault we are working this job,' Martin continued. 'I was in hospital, remember? All this happened while I was there, and because I'm your partner, I got the blame also. So don't. And this security gig? If I remember correctly I got it for us.' He was right, and Jasper knew it deep down. It was all *his* fault. Martin was only trying to help. How could he make it right again?

'Martin—' Jasper tried to reach out with a hand but then stop himself mid-air when Martin spoke.

'Don't' he said and started walking. 'Let's go to work.'

***

'Hey, the young lady said no, leave her be, okay?' Jasper said to a short fellow seated by the VIP area in a cream suit, his fingers ringed in gold and silver, a black and gold walking stick in his left hand. He was pulling back one of the stripper girls by her wrist toward him, unwillingly.

'What? You say something, fool?' The man in cream suit furrowed his brow, letting go of the girl. She stumbled a few steps, glanced back, and then walked away. He kissed his lips at her. 'Stupid girl. What do you get paid for, huh? Fucking hoe.'

Jasper's jaw tightened, but he remained silent. He was a security guard, all right, and he had all the right to protect the girls of the club, but this man seemed to be one of the club's most extravagant clients. One of the many reasons he was situated in the VIP section, no doubt, Jasper thought. He wasn't alone either, a group of his friends—more like bodyguards, though, with their blacked-out attire from head-to-toe—swarmed the little man like a murder of crows.

'Watch your tone with the girls,' Jasper spoke slowly, but firmly. 'This may be their jobs, and they may sell their bodies, but respect them, respect their hustle—'

The men all burst out in laughter. The little man in the cream suit held his belly with his ringed fingers, his mouth opened wide, revealing a handful of golden tooth as hysterical rumblings gust out of him. Small tears appeared at the corners of his eyes and he wiped at it.

'Okay, okay,' the man in the cream suit said. 'Here,' he pulled another one of the girls nearby and planted his bare palm on the biometric scanner situated around the belly of the stripper; it beeped, and then withdrew his palm. 'You see, just gave her some money, no strings attached.'

The stripper thank him and walked off somewhere towards the centre of the club.

The cream suited man looked up at Jasper and smiled. 'Shaw,' he said. 'Damien Shaw. And you, my friend, are very funny.' He reached out a hand and Jasper shook it. He didn't seem that bad after all.

Martin rested a hand on his shoulder, signally for them to leave the vicinity and explore other parts of the club for security purposes, and as they did the little Damien Shaw and his men in black giggle like a bunch of school girls again.

'Respect them, respect their hustle . . .' Laughter ensued and they all coughed and hacked at their throats like a smoker.

Jasper and Martin made their way to the back of the club. When they reached there, Jasper noticed that the emergency only exit had been unlocked and left a crack opened. It was only slightly, and only a few people would have noticed it. Jasper and Martin were one of them. Cold breeze blew in through the tiny space, sending chills down Jasper's spine.

A voice came next. Two. Jasper and Martin both heard it, so they nodded at each other and Jasper pushed the door open, wider, but not too much so as to not let whoever was speaking see them.

Jasper peaked through the split between the doors. It was like he was a little kid again, eavesdropping on strangers. He liked it—something exciting to keep this dull job entertaining.

'What do you see? Who is it?' Martin was asking behind him. 'Switch places, let me have look.'

Jasper stepped aside so Martin could peek out. While he did, Jasper turned back to glance around the club, it was still bustling, music blaring. One of strippers was now on the raised pole, half-way up, upside down with her legs spread apart as if to do the split, her chest—bare and dangling, her tongue licking the underside of the pole like candy.

'No shit,' Martin said and Jasper turned back to regard the back of his head.

'What is it?' Jasper asked.

'One of them has robotically enhanced legs. He lifted his trousers to show the other. And he has some kind of duffle bag beside him. Jasper, I think he's dealing in robotics.'

'No shit, this is our chance—our chance to get our jobs back. Let's go.'

Jasper followed behind Martin as he pushed the door wide open. They started straight for the two men, sprinting.

'Which one?' Jasper asked, cold wind gusting in his face as he ran.

'Left,' Martin shouted.

The two men started when they saw Jasper and Martin, security uniform and all. The one on the left picked up the duffle bag, turned, and legged it.

'Get the one on the right, don't let them get away.' Jasper said with deep breaths. 'I got the other one.'

Jasper turned left chasing the one with the duffle bag, while Martin took a right chasing the other. Tonight will be the night they make the first step in returning to the REA. Or so it would seem.

Jasper ran and ran, the fastest he'd ever ran in his life. He would catch this man if it killed him. *Really, Jasper?* Was it that deep? He didn't know, but all he could see as hover cars screamed past and the Red-light district lit up with holograms and neon lights, were: unpaid bills, debts, Sarai and Zack with nothing to eat and no roof over their heads.

'A man is the head of the family,' his religious grandfather had once said to him. 'A man that cannot provide for his family is worse than an unbeliever.'

Jasper's heart raced. His breathing haggard and coming out in loud spurts. He was tiring, his legs of twenty-six years felt like boulders, weighing him down, slowing him down.

The man with the duffle bag just kept on going—must've been those robotic legs Martin had mentioned seeing earlier.

Jasper's breathing stopped, and he collapsed to the hard ground.

***

Jasper came to, Martin's ugly mutt hovering over him.

'Jasp, Jasp, you okay?' he was saying.

He was still lying on the cobblestone pavement where he had fallen. His ribs pained him, his face throbbed, and his legs felt like jelly.

He looked around. 'Did you get him?'

Martin shook his head. 'He got away.'

'Damn. We lost both of them.'

Martin holstered one of Jasper's arms around his shoulders and lifted him up. The two made their way back to the strip club. They worked the remaining of their shift, and when it was over, Damien Shaw invited them over to join them, and they drank and drank . . . and then drank some more. Jasper couldn't remember when it was the last time he had drank this much. And then one of the strippers came over and flattened herself on him, rubbing and twerking against him. Damien Shaw paid for a lap dance for him and the busty, bright-eyed stripper with an arse that wobbled every time she moved just a little inch, took him into one of the private rooms.

Martin just shook his head, laughed and drank so more of his favourite—vodka.

It was just him and the stripper. He vaguely remembered something, someone. He felt as if he should be remembering someone, but he couldn't for the life of him remember who. He was too drunk and horny.

She moved around him, dancing to the tune. Man, she could move her waist. She kissed him all over his head. Her lips plump with red lipstick. He wanted to fuck her, there and there.

But he realised one thing as she grinded on him: he couldn't.

And not because he remembered his wife at that moment, but because he couldn't get hard.

He was all soft and no balls. Thank the gods for that, huh?

So he left the private room, the stripper regarding him with sceptical eyes as if he didn't find her attractive or he swung the other way.

He and Martin made their way home via hover-taxis.

He got home and made his way to his bedroom but then stopped short at the kitchen when he saw that his wife was still up. *Was she making something to eat this late?*

Her arms were crossed, and she leaned against the tabletop.

'What are you still doing up, Sarai?' he slurred his word a bit, tried to control the drunkenness.

She came closer, squinting. She stopped a hair's breadth away, and then pulled back. 'I can't do this again, Jasper.'

'What?' the room span, he needed to sit down.

'These days you come home drunk, and now you're covered in stripper lipstick. Did you fuck her?'

Jasper raised his brow, shocked at the blunt words of his wife. He should've known that those cherry lips of the strippers would leave marks. They were too finely painted not to.

'Babe, Sarai, listen,' he grabbed her by the arms, 'I—'

She forcefully pulled her arm away from his grasp. 'Get off me!'

Jasper instinctively raised his hand and slapped her across the face, her head spinning to the side, hair trailing. 'Stop it; you're going to wake Zack—'

Only then did he realise the magnitude of what he had just done. Sarai held her face with her hand, tears streaming down her bronze cheeks—those cheeks that he saw heaven through whenever she smiled. He'd now made it where he would see flashback of hell through, for however long he would love her.

Jasper turned and saw Zack standing in the dim light by the entrance of the kitchen. His teddy, squashed in his soft hand. It dropped to the ground as he ran toward his mother.

'Mum, mum, mumeee,' he said. 'What's wrong?'

'It's okay, Hunny.' She hugged him. 'Go back to your room and pack some of your favourite clothes, you and mummy are going to take a trip to my sister's tonight, okay?'

Zack nodded his little head, hugged his mum back and kissed her on the cheek that Jasper had so fiercely—in the heat of the moment—slapped. But he couldn't excuse it. Drunk, or tired, or stressed, or angry, or whatever, you never hit a woman—especially a warm-hearted, harmless angel like his wife.

'I'm . . . I'm sorry.'

'Me too,' she said, her eyes losing its glint, her voice gone cold and soft and distant as if something had just died. An invisible cord that held them together had been broken—no, just wounded, Jasper was holding on to the tiniest of hope.

Sarai and Zack left not too long after for her sister's, driving off in the family hover car.

Jasper Barnes, left alone, deflated, with only his—now—sober thoughts for comfort.

Chapter Thirty-six: A Third Member

When Grey Harrow stepped only a few metres from the entrance of Lucan Weaver's secret base in Old street, he heard it then.

The gunshots. The shouts. It sounded like a warzone inside.

Had the REA Agents finally caught up to Lucan?

There was no time to ponder. Reaching inside his jacket pocket, he replaced the empty neuron into his mechanical arm compartment, arming *Genesis* ready. He jerked his arm back and the compartment danced around like a puzzle before slamming shut with a satisfying clap.

He pushed on the entrance door with one hand; loud eruption of bullets from machine guns rang in his ears. The strong smell of gun powder flooded his nostrils.

He quickly walked through the narrow corridors of the base and entered the wide room littered with coils where Lucan Weaver's throne-like chair was situated.

Grey's stomach recoiled slightly, and a sense of dread swarmed him as he saw Lucan's armoured men and women, his bodyguards, the ones he regularly saw protecting Lucan and his throne, sprawled on the ground by his chair, bleeding through their black and silver mechanical armours, lifeless. The chair had been smashed into a million pieces, too. Who? Why? Foxhound? Retaliation?

Grey made his way to Lucan Weaver's office, turning a corner as the gun firing increased and continued. Just ahead of him, Grey could see a group of men—about eight of them—in red metallic armours with an emblem patch of a dog standing on his two feet holding a machine gun in each paw on their shoulders, firing toward Lucan's office. The walls of the room filling with holes, sparks bouncing off them. He didn't recognise any of these guys. They were not Foxhound, nor Ezra Hawthorne's men.

Where is everyone? Grey thought to himself. *Behemoth, Elyse Fox, Gael Cross*. The base was empty, and none of Lucan Weaver's main men seemed to be around. He could only hope Lucan wasn't in his office. Those men were tearing a gaping hole in it. Who were these guys, and what do they want?

Just then, one of the men in the red armour turned around and saw Grey. 'I see one!' he shouted through his metallic helmet. He immediately raised his machine gun and fired at Grey. Grey twisted and flattened his back against a wall beside him as bullets rattled and rang off the walls behind. Sparks flew around him. He scrunched his face, bracing the impact of the vibrations.

More and more bullets flew in his direction, and he figured that the rest of the men— the remaining seven—had all joined to fire toward him.

Shit.

Then, with what sounded like some kind of powerful gust of air blasting and crashing into metal, Grey heard the men howl. One of the men must've taken the full force of whatever that was because he landed directly in front of Grey, stirring. Grey clenched his fist and swiftly knocked him out, pounding through the man's helmet with the fist of *Genesis*, the man's head twisting to the side with a wet crunch.

Grey then turned and peeked out behind him. From out of the carnage of Lucan's office, he saw a large, brown man with a topknot standing there, silhouetting against the fallen ceiling plasters, his clothing ripped to shreds, one hand holding the other arm in discomfort, his overcoat ripped apart exposing mechanical limbs, and his face smeared with blood—most probably his by the look of it as if someone had tried to wipe it off with their hands.

It was Lucan Weaver, and he was injured all right, but a frown of indignation rested upon his face.

Grey studied his appearance. It seemed more than half of Lucan Weaver's body was mechanical and metallic, almost as if he had been sliced in half, at an angle, from his right shoulder blade down to his crotch.

So this was why he wore so many layers, Grey thought. *To hide his appearance? Why though? Why hide it?* He and Grey were not too different after all then.

The remaining armoured men in red around Lucan Weaver, stirred, slowing rousing themselves to their feet. Lucan was in danger, and Grey knew he would have to do something to help the man. He couldn't possibly handle them all on his own. Lucan Weaver may be part machine and a tough son of a bitch, but he couldn't possibly handle them all by himself.

Grey came out from behind the rubble of the wall, sprinting toward Lucan, to join him. Lucan squinted as Grey approached, and the two of them went back-to-back, shoulder-to-shoulder.

'What are you doing here?' Lucan asked from behind him. 'I told you: I'd call you when I've thought things over.'

Grey shook his head. Even in the midst of danger, the man was as stubborn as ever. 'I thought you might need a hand.'

Three of the men in red armour slowly stood up in front of Grey, trying to pick up and ready their weapons, he stretched out the palm of *Genesis*, felt the energy danced around the tip of it, swirling and turning. He connected with the neuron in the compartment of his arm mentally, and then released it in a furious, fire blast of energy—the size of a basketball. The blast left his palm, the force of it jerking him back a bit as it crashed into the three armoured men in red, melting their armour and sending them sprawling backward. The men wailed, crying out for their life.

Grey clenched his jaw, staring at them, wailing and writhing as their life burned away in flames.

Grey then glanced over his shoulder, watching Lucan dispose of the other four men in red armour. One by one he blasted their armoured heads off their body like pinballs with what looked like kinetic energy blasts from both of his mechanical arms that seemed to have morphed itself by the wrist into a cannon shaped hole. The men fell with thuds, like headless chickens.

When he was done, his arms reshaped back to their original aesthetics, and Lucan dropped to his knees, gasping.

'Thank you,' he managed to say to Grey. He looked worn out as if he'd just took a tumble down a very uneven and rough-edged hill filled with pins and needles and shrapnel.

'Who were they?' Grey asked, lending him a hand. 'They weren't Foxhound or Ezra's men or Agents, that's for sure.' Lucan looked at *Genesis*, regarding it for a while before taking it and standing back to his feet.

Lucan looked around at the carnage and death. 'They were another Syndicate: A lower level posse. Not on Foxhound or my Syndicate's level, but they wanted me dead. They call themselves the Dogs of War. They must've found out where my base was and realised that today I would be alone and with less of my main men and women around me, so they struck. Come let's walk.'

'Why?' Grey asked as they started to walk. They strode toward his throne room, where all his armoured men and women lay with bullet holes, bleeding, sprawled on the floor, eyes blank and staring into nothing.

After a while, Lucan said, 'That's how it is, Grey,' he leaned down and closed some of the corpses of his bodyguards' eyes and sighed. 'Have you not learned anything with your time with the Foxhound Syndicate and with me? There will always be those who want to move up the food chain, and those who always want more—me included. It is the way of things and the life we signed up for.'

Grey couldn't believe it. Was he really working with a man who only really wanted to be at the top of the food chain of the London Underworld? How many more will die for his selfish ambition? When will it end? On one hand, he wanted to help Lucan take down the Foxhound Syndicate so he can get payback for their betrayal, the loss of his arm, and for Bethany's injuries, but on the other hand, he was tired of all this bullshit and the criminal wars.

Lucan stood back up, walked over to the broken pieces of his throne-like chair, and sat on the rubble. He stared at Grey, his expression one of deflation.

'I know what you are thinking,' he said. 'I can read you, Grey.'

Grey remained silent.

'This man and his selfish agendas—you see it is not so selfish but more so about social justice.' He kicked some of the broken pieces around his feet. 'You see, I was one of the founding members of the Foxhound Syndicate. Something they never spoke of while you were there.'

Grey was slightly taken aback by the revelation. He had always known the Foxhound Syndicate was founded and run by two men at the very top. But now there was a *third?* It was all starting to make sense.

'They sold me out after I lost my limbs in a raid,' he continued. 'They said I was no longer useful and didn't have the leadership qualities to run a major criminal organisation like this.' He snorted. 'But look; now I run my own criminal empire. Anyways, so I was out on my luck, handicapped and with no money. When the robotics advancements happened, and mechanical enhancement that can improve handicapped life became available, I put myself in debt in order to be fixed. I wanted it. I needed it badly. I wanted my revenge. They thought I wasn't good enough, that I couldn't amount to anything, well, I'm coming back to show them that I can, and take back what was rightfully mine.

'So, I built my new criminal organisation from the ground up, using my new-found mechanical abilities. But then a few years later when the government deemed robotics too dangerous, due to unlawful uses of robotics and the Rogue Hand Syndrome Virus, it became harder, and the REA came down hard on us. We had to go into hiding, not wanting to give up our robotics.'

Grey swallowed, unsure of what to say to this.

Lucan leaned forward, his knees to his chest, his hands down by his side. 'You and I are very similar, Grey. That is why I recruited you. We have both been wronged, betrayed. This is why I want the Foxhound Syndicate. Take back what is rightfully ours. We could rule the London Underworld together—as Kings.'

Grey couldn't care less about running the Foxhound Syndicate, Lucan can have it all. He didn't even want revenge anymore, he decided, he just wanted to be out of it all, once and for all, and if this last mission for Lucan meant that, then so be it.

Boots thudded the ground behind them. Behemoth, Elyse Fox, and Gael Cross appeared and they bent their knees and bowed before Grey and Lucan as he sat on the rubble of his ruined throne-like chair.

'What Happened?' Behemoth raised his head, concern in his eyes. 'Are you alright, Sir?'

Lucan looked at Grey, his eyes lingering for a while, then his eyes flick to Behemoth and he smiled.

'How was the reconnaissance you conducted?' he asked.

Chapter Thirty-seven: A Rogue One

The rain came down fast and furious, the chill midday wind causing it to slap and spray him, leaving him half-deaf and half-blind.

Grey stood at the Barnes's front porch, drenched and soaking wet like a fully aroused woman, neon-coloured lights beaming out behind him, surveying the brown building in front of him and its beautiful surrounding vegetation and flowers. One would think the Barnes's were gardeners with the way their plants and grass were neatly trimmed and tended to. Grey had to admit, it was well kept.

He walked up the metallic stairs, each boot thud kicking up water. When he reached the top step, he almost nearly slipped, grabbing a hold of the banister at the last second to avoid any form of back injury. He wiped his forehead with the back of his human hand in relief. Then, he straightened up, raised the same hand and went in to knock on the front door with his knuckle . . .

He halted mid-way, his eyes narrowed in, and he furrowed his brow, noticing the door was left open a crack, and so he pushed on it, the door creaking open with a whine, wider. He walked in, confusion in his mind, looking around, the house was quiet and dark and it reeked of alcohol. Should he be worried?

'Jasper!' he called out straightaway.

No response. What had happened here?

He shut the door behind him and wiped his shoes on the inside welcome mat as the rain continued outside, rattling the roof like pebbles. His boots knock a beer can. He looked down in the dark, the marble floor littered with beer cans upon beer cans. Grey shook his head. Has Jasper taken up drinking as a hobby or something? Last he heard, his partner— Martin Silas—was the drunkard, not him.

Grey walked over to the blinds, trying his best to avoid the beer cans like some kind of strategic game of chess, and wondering why in the hell the curtains were still drawn close during the middle of the day.

He reached up and drew it back.

'Argh!' a voice came from the vanishing darkness behind him. 'No more, close it, close it!'

Grey turned and saw Jasper—well, a grizzly version of him—laying down on one of those chairs that recline backward so you could sleep on them. The man looked like a shadow of his former self. *What happened to you?* Grey thought. While Grey had grown his hair and beard out of necessity to avoid being recognised and was well kept as best as Bethany could do with a razor, Jasper—now, on the other hand, looked like he was going for something between a hobo and a drag queen. His bushy beard made his lips disappear and his jawline and neck go missing as if the wild forest had decided to come and live on his face. He was almost unrecognisable save for his yellow strip Hi-Vis bomber jacket he'd slept in that had his name badge plastered on the top left corner. If that wasn't there, Grey would have probably had no clue as to who he was. Well, that and the fact it was his home. Still, Grey could've mistaken him for a thief, or a homeless fellow seeking sheltered lodging.

Staring at him now, with Jasper's dirty hand over his face, trying to block out the light from his eyes, he looked pathetic, like dog shit, would probably taste bad, too.

'Jasper?' Grey walked over to him. 'What happened?'

'Who?' Jasper sat up and squinted in his direction. 'Sarai?'

Grey stood over him by the chair. 'No. Grey Harrow.'

Jasper sighed deeply, flattened back on the reclining chair, rolled over to one side, his back to Grey. He was clearly upset about something. His hands were clenched tight. Grey looked down beside his head, on the chair headrest was a white circular patch that stood out against the charcoal coloured chair. It looked as if some kind of liquid had dried on it. Tears maybe?

'Go away, Grey.' Jasper said, still lying to one side, his back still to Grey.

Grey strode over to the other side of the room and sat. He wasn't going to leave until he said what he came here to say.

He leaned back on the chair, ran his hands across his rough beard. 'Your wife left you? What did you do to her, prick?'

'I said; get the fuck out of my house.' He didn't move, remained lying there, his back doing the talking.

'I'm not going anywhere until you tell me what you did.'

Jasper turned and sat upright along the chair, his eyes fixed and staring down at Grey across the room, pain and frustration in them. He blinked. 'I won't say it again . . . '

Grey leaned back further, crossed his legs, got even more comfortable on Jasper's chair.

'I said, get the *fuck* out!' Jasper sprung up his chair, marched toward Grey, the beer cans on the ground rattling and knocking about his feet.

Grey smiled and just stretched forth *Genesis*, felt the palm sizzle. 'Sit your arse down, fool.' Jasper stopped in his stride, Grey saw his jaw move and tighten, even with the jungle that was on his face. 'Tell me what the fuck happened.'

Jasper's head just dropped to the ground, he rubbed his eyes and they went all sad and moist as if he was a helpless child. Then he walked back to his chair and slumped down into it. He reached down toward the ground, sifting his hand through the multitude of cans there, then he clutched one—apparently this one wasn't open yet—he cracked the handle, foam drizzling out the mouth of the can like some kind of volcano. He put the can to his mouth and drank, then placed it back down on the middle table. He looked at Grey.

'So?' *Genesis* still directed at Jasper.

Jasper shook his head. 'I hit her—'

'*Son of a bitch*, I should melt you right now.'

Jasper scratched at his brow. '—and so she took my son and went to her sisters.'

Grey stared at him for a while. He slowly lowered *Genesis*, feeling sympathy for the man. He must really regret what he did, hence all the drinking and lack of hygiene. It was really getting to him. He wanted his family back. And from what Clare had said, Jasper was a real family man, everything he did was for them, and to not have them around kind of left him very vulnerable, like he didn't have anything to live for anymore. Just a walking corpse.

'You're going to get them back,' Grey said, 'don't worry—just give it time.'

Jasper hung his head in his unwashed dirty hands. 'You didn't see her, Grey,' Jasper looked up at him; the alcohol stench emanating from Jasper's breath hit him, even from this distance away, the strong smell almost knocked Grey back on the chair. 'Her eyes, I've never seen them like that before, like disappointment but also like hurt and pain and death.'

Grey didn't know what to say to that. He could only imagine what his wife must have been feeling at that moment in time. What if the roles were reversed and it was Bethany that Grey had hit and she—

He shook his head, didn't want to think about it.

'Listen, you want your old job back, right?'

Jasper looked away toward the blinds. The rain had stopped outside, the faintest of sunshine shun over the horizon in the distance. A hover car blaring loud music zipped past, leaving a trail of purple neon lights in its wake.

Jasper looked back, nodded. 'When?'

Grey stood up. 'Lucan Weaver is planning the final assault on the Foxhound Syndicate this weekend.'

'Is Lucan cool with you working an REA Agent—well a suspended one—anyway?'

'Doesn't matter, we need all the help we can get if we are to be successful against the Foxhound Syndicate and Ezra Hawthorne's men. We do this job, you get your man, Lucan Weaver gets the Foxhound, and I get to go home. Everyone wins.'

Jasper picked up the beer can again from the middle table, downed the last of its content, then crush the empty can in his hand and threw it on the ground, it clanged.

'Let your partner know when the mission is going down . . .' Grey trailed off, staring at the state of the house all around him. 'And clean this shit up. You think your wife, if she does come back, will be happy to see this? Come on Jasper, you're better than this. I thought I was the rogue one.'

Jasper laughed for the first time since Grey had arrived, and then Grey left his house.

Chapter Thirty-eight: A Prototype Suit

'So you're in, Alex?' Jasper spoke to Alex Wade over the phone as he sat in his sister's office at RoyalStarCorp.

'I'm in.'

'Great. Thanks. I knew I could count on you. Remember Walter Marshal must not hear of this until we are successful in apprehending Ezra Hawthorne. It's the only way I can guarantee Martin and I both get our jobs back.'

He hung up the holo-phone and turned back to the hologram in front of him of the new suit of armour his sister had been working on for him. The armour itself was made from the latest tech of robotics—the same tech that powers both the machine parts in Grey Harrow, Ezra Hawthorne, and the rest of the cyborg rogues running around London. It would give him an edge against those criminals, that's for sure. And also, without having to become what he hates most—a machine. It would just be a robotic exo-suit he can don on and don off. Amazing. Impressive.

'So, you're saying this thing will grant me special robotic abilities like those guys out there that are firing energy and kinetic blasts out their arms and hands like cannons?'

Clare nodded, typing away at the holo-keyboard. 'Herman Rowntree will help you get the hang of using it.' Jasper watched the back of her head as it darted back and forth and around the hologram. 'Although,' she continued, 'there have been earlier versions of this particular exo-suit—ones used by the military and some criminal organisations that managed to get their hands on it—this suit is the first of its kind, it's a prototype and it still hasn't been tested before. You'll need to be careful.'

Jasper scratched at his head, then looked at his sister as she continued to type away at the holographic image. So bold, so intelligent, and so hardworking. It's such a shame she wasn't using this talent for something better, he thought. Instead, she used it to aid criminals–

—or "those in need" as she would put it. Clare Barnes, his one and only sister, forever the Good Samaritan.

'Is there one for Martin?'

She shot him a quick glance and then returned back to his holographic image. 'Of course. I can't have one of you running around in one, and not the other. Martin would hate me forever.'

Jasper laughed.

'Besides,' she went on. 'These exo-suit armour are illegal, I don't think the REA would approve of it.'

'Sometimes,' Jasper looked around the lab, 'you have to be willing to go against order and protocols in order to achieve your goal. If that means you have to become the very thing you're trying to stop, then so be it. You've got to do what you've got to do. And this is what I need to do—for me and for my family.

'Just be careful,' she turned and looked him in the eye, stretched and placed a warm hand on top of his. 'The exo-suit is armour, all right, but it doesn't make you invincible. You could still be killed with a great enough force.'

She pulled her hand back and the two remained silent for a while, and then Clare spoke up again.

'Speaking of family, how are Sarai and Zack? Still no word from her?'

Jasper dropped his head low, felt his eyes go all sad, and shook it a "no". Then he raised his head back up.

She moved closer to him, the wheels of the chair squealing against the marble floor as she did, and then she raised her hand, gently laying it on his back. 'It's going to be okay, Jasp. I know you didn't mean to hurt her. I know you, you wouldn't hurt a fly. You love her. It was an accident, I'm not judging you.' She paused, Jasper heard her suck in a deep breathe.

She looked at him point-blank with those imposing dark eyes of hers. 'Just don't ever let it happen again, or else it won't just be Sarai that exits from your life.' She said it very matter-of-fact and Jasper knew that she meant it.

He chuckled on the inside. That was his sister, forever the truth. Her love for her brother was unconditional but even that had its limits.

She patted his hand. 'I'll go see Sarai at her sister's. I'll have a word with her, plead your case for you, and try to convince her to come back home. I feel a girl's night out is thoroughly needed.' She smiled.

Jasper nodded. 'Please do. I miss them. She won't even let me see little Zack.'

'And I understand why.'

Jasper was confused, staring blankly as if he'd missed something. 'What?'

'Look at you,' she scanned him up and down. 'You're a mess . . . and no offense Jasp, you stink.'

Jasper smiled, tell him something he didn't already know. He was a mess, all right, gone weeks without a shave or a shower. All he did—apart from his part-time job flipping burgers at Burger Court and his security post at the strip club in the Red-light district—was drink himself drunk and wallow in self-pity for his sorry life.

'None taken,' he said, standing up to his feet. 'Martin and I will be back on the weekend to pick up the exo-suits. Thanks again, Clare, I owe you one.' He started toward the door of her cubicle.

She called out after him. 'Jasper,' he half turned just as his hand was on the door handle. She stared at him. 'If there's anything that you need—money, food, clean clothes, a roof over your head—you let me know, okay? I can't have my brother bringing shame to the Barnes family.'

Jasper smiled at his sister, grateful for her love, kindness, and support, especially in this difficult time in his life—what with all the REA and Syndicates and his wife and son dramas.

'Thank you,' he said finally, before leaving her lab.

Chapter Thirty-nine: An All-Out War

The day had finally arrived, and Grey felt trepidation eat at him at every corner of his mind. He had arrived on the outskirts of the secret Foxhound Syndicate base in Shepherd Bush, the same spot they had been standing weeks ago when they had first attempted to take the fortress.

Back then they had been greatly outnumbered when Grey realised David and the Foxhound Syndicate had partnered up with Ezra Hawthorne and his Khakis men. That attempt had been one of stealth, where Grey, Behemoth, Gael Cross, Elyse Fox, Eustace de Maris, and Rollo had attempted to sneak their way in at night and narrow the Foxhound number and silently take the place over. A stretch—Grey knew, but it was a shot they were willing to take a gamble on. Besides, they'd had back-up lying in wait, only a button press away. Lucan Weaver had done his homework and was all but prepared. However, he hadn't been prepared for the appearance of Ezra Hawthorne and his men, so Grey decided to think fast and chose to retreat and rethink so they wouldn't lose a lot of men. Alas, they had lost one—Rollo.

Now, standing just outside to the side gates of the secluded Foxhound base, away from the peering eyes of their lookout sentries atop the fortress, late in the cloudless afternoon, Grey glanced around at the people he had arrived with—his comrades, so to speak, for this coup. Coup, because this was a coup after all—one man's selfish goal of taking over an organisation that he feels he so rightfully deserves so he can rule the London Underworld as its majority stakeholder. A really personal motive, if you asked Grey, but he owed Lucan, and he needed the Foxhound Syndicate off his back, so he'd determined that this will be the last time he is ever pulled back into a predicament like this. It ends here, and he would be leaving it all behind him—once and for all.

To his left were Behemoth, Gael Cross, Elyse Fox, Eustace de Maris, and the rest of Lucan's men and women—roughly about 25 of them in total—all clad in metallic looking armour and armed to their teeth with machine guns, pistols, and all manner of Robotic weaponry and gears. Which was rather odd, giving who had just arrived and was situated to Grey's right, he thought.

Jasper Barnes, Martin Silas, and an Agent called Alex Wade—all clad in full REA bulletproof armour and spotting special issued REA weaponry stood to his right, all ready and itching to go. Jasper and Martin, however, seemed to be wearing something extra, a kind of special exo-suit that hugged their bodies like gloves. It was patterned and full of little wiring mechanism like that of Robotics similar to *Genesis*. The silver and black of their metallic chest plates glinted in the bright sky.

Behemoth cocked his head toward them. 'What are they doing here?' he frowned.

'The same reason you're here,' Jasper spoke up. 'To take down the Foxhound Syndicate and dismantle their illegal regime.'

Behemoth looked like he had just been punch by an invisible fist. He left his group and sauntered over toward the Agents. 'You,' he pointed a stiff finger at Jasper. 'You were the Agent back at the REA office standing by the exit when we came to rescue Grey.' He shot Grey a quick glance, letting him know he knew that it was because of him, this man—Jasper—was still alive, here, standing. He looked back at Jasper, who stood there unmoved. 'I should've killed you.'

'Well, yeah, you didn't, so bugger off, fool,' Martin posted up beside Jasper. He pointed toward the Foxhound fortress. 'We've bigger issues at hand, so deal with your daddy and mummy issues later.'

Agent Alex Wade chuckled. Behemoth's eyes seemed to burn deep red, his jaw tightened, and his mouth became a firm line. He started to move closer, and Grey didn't even realise when his whole body moved to step between them.

'Move,' Behemoth said, his voice low and horse. 'You're working with them?'

Grey remained, he shook his head at him. 'Not now, Behemoth. We need them.'

'You think these men like you? These men don't like you. They are only in it for themselves. They will drop in an instance.' Perhaps he was right, Grey thought. And he'd been betrayed one too many times to know this could be true. But right now, they needed all the help they could get. *Isn't everyone for themselves, anyway? Even you, Behemoth?*

Gael Cross and Elyse Fox appeared behind him laying hands on either side of his shoulders.

He pointed that long, stiff finger again, at Grey, the tip of it so close to Grey's forehead, it felt as if he had a laser-point of a gun pointed at him. 'This is on you,' he grunted.

The three of them walked back to his left.

Grey spared a glance to his left and then to right one last time, eyeing both Lucan's men and the REA Agents. He nodded. 'Let's go.'

And so they did. Marching on, boots thudding the muddy ground, armour clanging, weapons clinking, and Grey's heart, deep down, beating fast inside his chest. He felt like a little boy who had just had a gun shoved in his hand and told to go to fight in a war for his country.

He bit down on his lips as they crashed through the front metallic gates and stormed the fortress.

This time it wouldn't be stealth. It would be an all-out assault. An all-out war. Only one Syndicate will be left standing after all is said and done. This was the way he liked it.

This was his final task, after all. His journey from running away from his past, cumulating in him facing it head-on.

It all ends here.

Bullets flew past him, grazing his armour. Gunshots rang all around. Most of Lucan men had taken cover behind large walls or pillars or whatever they could find to use as cover, and as he looked around, he realised that Jasper and the REA Agents had already gone missing in action.

The Foxhound Syndicate, clad in their armours and holding their large weapons, poured out of buildings as the alarm sounded, blaring its foghorn-like horn.

Grey breathed, glancing around in the insuring manic. Men and women on both sides dropped like flies, bullets mowing them down like a bulldozer.

Grey heard someone shouting to his left, turned, levelled *Genesis* out in front of him and fired an energy blast out of its palm, it crashed at a Foxhound assailant who was approaching and readying to shoot him unaware. The assailant dropped to the ground with a thud, his weapon, which looked like a special issue AK-47 dropped beside him, and he was still.

Grey ambled over to him, picked up the weapon, and started firing at whoever he thought was part of the Foxhound Syndicate. He dropped one, then other, and other, until he heard the click of the empty magazine, dropping the gun to the muddy ground. He ran, moving from cover to cover, unsure where to go, or what to do. What was the plan again?

Up ahead of him two Foxhound goons stood shooting at some of Lucan's men. Grey crouched, slowly approaching them from behind, but then he stepped on something—a piece of metal of some kind—and it drew one of their attentions. So he stood back to his feet, put everything he had into his legs and bolted toward the one that had turned, crashing hard against him into a wall before he could fire. Grey felt the bones in the goon's body crack as he slid down. The other turned, and Grey grabbed his weapon by the mouth, yanked the butt up to meet the goon's chin, who stumbled, took the gun from him and fired at him at point-blank, bathing his Foxhound uniform in dark-red.

Grey was breathing deep, hard now. Every breath felt like it was his last. He spat on the ground, swiped at his mouth with the back of his hand. The men of Lucan that he had seemingly helped out, waved at him in the distance, but he looked away, searching.

His leg went out from under him, and his face slammed hard against the muddy earth. He winced, 'Owww,' twisting and writhing. Out of the corner of his eyes, he spotted the goon he had crashed against the wall. He was still alive, but his movement had been subdued, so he crawled instead. Grey lashed out his heel, felt the base of his boot crunch against the goon's head. He lashed it out again and again and again, until the goon's head flopped down, a pool of blood around where his head rested.

Grey slowly pulled himself back to his feet, his face throbbing, and his head spinning. Feeling dizzy and unable to keep his balance he fell to the down again, gasping.

He felt a shadow come over his face, saw a hand dangle above him—a soft, slender, naked bare palm—a female hand, no doubt. He took the hand and whoever it was, was amazingly strong, he thought, because they pulled him up without a struggle.

He stared at Elyse Fox, a single pink strand of hair billowing about her forehead, her mechanical eye winding and expanding, her brown skin still as unblemished and smooth as ever, like butter.

'You, okay?' she asked, and then they had to duck as bullets crashed in their direction. They got on all fours and crawled behind a block of crates, resting their back against it.

'Thanks,' Grey said. 'Where are the others?'

'I'm not sure,' she said, reaching down to her pockets and lifting a cigarette to her lips. 'Maybe we should have thought this over a bit more . . .' she offered one to Grey, he took it and she lit it for both of them.

'Thought what?' Grey asked.

'The plan . . . maybe we should've thought out a better strategy before we came charging in like a horde of elephants.'

'Oh,'

Elyse eyed him. 'Behemoth, Gael Cross, and few others of Lucan's men had gone straight for the main hall.'

'What about the REA Agents? They seem to have gone AWOL.' But then Grey knew the answer to his own question. They had most probably gone after Ezra Hawthrone. That was what they came for, after all.

'Protect the bosses at all cost,' a familiar voice came sounding out from up behind the block of crates where they had been resting. 'Don't let them get to them.'

David, Grey thought. *And these so-called bosses must be the ones that sold Lucan out. And that would be our targets,* he smiled.

'What are you smiling about?' Elyse Fox cocked her head at him. 'In case you haven't seen, the situation doesn't look promising at all.

Grey leaned in closer to her, touching her gently on each shoulder. 'Those two bosses he just mentioned. We get to them, we take this base. Cut off the head of the snake and the body drops and is useless.'

'And how do you suppose we do that—'

A loud bang against the block of crates, it crashed against the back of their heads, disorientating them.

'Grey Harrow!' David's voice came booming out loud. 'I know you are out there, I saw you run into cover, come out!'

Grey shook his head, trying to reorient himself. He reached for Elyse; her hand was on her head, her face scrunched up.

'Come out and fight me!' his boots thudded the ground; his steps were getting closer to their position.

'Stay here, whatever happens.' He said to an injured Elyse Fox and he stood up and walked around the block of crates to face David.

'Ah, there you are . . . the one that got away.' David stood there; standing in what looked like an exo-suit that was similar to the one's Jasper and Martin were wearing. He was fully clad in metallic armour with robotic weaponry strapped to his shoulders and arms, and some kind of jet-pack seemed to be attached to his back. He smiled. 'Why are you doing this?' he asked, slowly taking steps toward Grey. 'Never mind—It was my fault for not killing you earlier. I never should've sent Hector. He did a piss poor job. I'll kill you myself, you fucking traitor.'

All around them there was destruction—dead men and women from both sides covered the ground, and still in the distance they could hear bullet fighting action still taking place, walls shaking, and the ground trembling beneath them.

Still, Grey stood his ground, clenching *Genesis* and regarding David with contempt. He had waited for the day he would see the man who had caused him so much pain again, and hopefully put an end to that suffering, once and for all.

The grim smile on David's face vanished as he stopped just a few metres from Grey, and only what looked like hatred remained there. 'Tell me, have you not forgiven me for your arm? You know un-forgiveness is like drinking poison and expecting the other person to die. Besides, I think your arm looks much better like this.'

They both stretched forth their arms: a huge fire blast left *Genesis's* metallic palm and a huge energy blast left David's armoured gauntlet.

It collided together in the middle of the two of them and exploded as if it were the sun, sending them both crashing back to the ground.

***

Jasper, Martin, and Alex pushed through gunfire, ducking and weaving in and out of cover, as they made their way toward the back-end of the Foxhound Syndicate fortress.

'To the right!' Jasper screamed over the sound of bullets to Martin and Alex on either side of his shoulders. They had earlier seen Ezra Hawthorne retreating toward the far end of the fortress, and so they kept on his pursuit. They will get their man; nothing is going to stop them this time.

They took the right turn, never slowing down their momentum, but instead, shifting their body weight to one side, they managed to curve the turn with relative ease, the exo-suit Clare had designed for Jasper and Martin clinking and clanking as they did. Only a single dilapidated building appeared ahead of them. It stood sombrely on its own before them and nothing else. They halted, scanning the surrounding area.

A group of men in green Khakis armour sprouted out from either side of the building in front of them, their guns pointed.

'Up ahead, find cover!' Jasper shouted again as bullets left the chambers of the guns of the men in green, and he dropped and slid along the muddy ground, dirt smothering his exo-suit and kicking up mud onto his face and mouth. He tasted the muddy earth on his tongue, chalky and slimy, and he spat.

He felt his back hit against a low stone wall, and he let out a sigh. A few moments later Martin and Alex joined him, sliding up beside him. He looked at them, and behind them, bits of the stone wall chipped away as bullets struck it.

'On the count of three,' Jasper said.

Martin and Alex both nodded, jolting their REA issued sub-machine guns against their chest.

'One . . . two . . . three.'

All three of them came out from behind the low stone wall, unloading the sub-machine guns in the men in green's direction. Jasper saw a majority of them get struck on their unarmoured areas: throats, head, forearms, and legs, red blood splurging out like paint as their bodies contorted and jerked with impact. A couple survived and Jasper saw them retreated back into the rundown building behind.

Jasper, Martin, and Alex quickened toward the building, entering it. It was dark; Jasper could barely see anything except for the pockets of light sneaking in through the small bullet-like holes in the building. The air also was damp and stale and smelled of diesel fumes.

Jasper reached down and turned on the flashlight attached to the end of his sub-machine gun, and the others did the same. As he did, the light landed on Martin, saw his friend's body trembling like ripples on water.

'What now,' Martin asked, his body still trembling. Jasper and Alex both studied their friend. They had never seen him like this before. His body seemed to shake and he didn't even notice. What was Martin scared of? His friend was always the brave one, nothing scared him.

'Martin, are you okay?' Jasper asked.

'What? Of course.'

'Then why are you shaking?'

'What?' he looked down at himself, then looked back at them. 'Listen, you guys are not the ones that almost died fighting this Ezra Hawthorne man before, remember?'

A movement to his left, Jasper moved his flash-lighted sub-machinegun toward that direction, something moved in the shadows, so he fired a few rounds, it bounced off the old, worn-out walls, flashes of light coming from the muzzle of his gun. Nothing. No more movement.

He turned back to regard his friend. 'I remember. I was there, Martin. I thought you—

'Down! Jasper! Down!' Martin shouted and so he obeyed, dropping on all fours.

Shots rang out over and behind him. Jasper heard the thudding of bodies dropping.

'All clear,' he heard Alex say.

Jasper stood back to his feet, smoke trailing from the mouth of Martin's gun like some kind of grey snake.

'You were saying?' Martin had a fake, cheeky smile plastered on his face, Jasper could tell, but his body still trembled.

So Jasper forced a smile to his face, trying to ease his friend's burden, trying to understand. Had he been carrying this burden ever since they had first fought with Ezra Hawthorne and his men when he nearly died?

Jasper averted his eyes to the dark and damp patches on the walls, felt a pain in the back of his throat. His chest tightened, he felt guilty. He had no idea what his friend had been going through all this time—the trauma of that fateful day. He had been too busy with his own selfish needs.

'Nothing here, lads, just did a quick sweep, this building is empty.' Alex said, walking back toward them.

Martin said, 'It can't be, we saw Ezra Hawthorne go in this direction.'

Alex only shrugged.

Jasper grimaced, ground his teeth. He needed Ezra Hawthorne, yes, which was the only reason he had signed up for this mission, anyway, going against his own principle. He needed Ezra Hawthorne more than anything so he could get back his life. But his friend wasn't in the right frame of mind, he could tell. 'Alright, let's get out of here, forget Ezra Hawthorne. Martin, you're in no state to carry on. Alex, you just head back to REA office, we're done here.'

'What? Bullshit. Let me have him, I need to make him pay.' Martin walked around them in a circle, still trembling, and now limping. 'You see the limp? Yeah, Ezra Hawthorne needs to pay for this.'

Alex said, 'Let's just get the fuck out of this building; it stinks in here, need a bit of fresh air.'

They made their way out of the dark, dilapidated building, squinting and adjusting their eyes to the bright afternoon light that shone before them, and as they did, an energy blast came scrambling in their direction, it missed Jasper on the left and Alex on the right, but it hit Martin in the middle, crashing against his chest, sending him flying backward into the side of the building and straight into a long pointed piece of sharp metal that Jasper had earlier seen wedging out of the broken-down building.

Martin screamed, but his scream must've got caught in his throat because it came out as a silent, soft thing. The piece of metal seemed to have unfortunately pierced through his friend's heart, protruding out from his left side. He bled out instantly, his head fell limp as he hung there, impaled, unmoving, almost as if he had been crucified on a cross.

Jasper turned wide eyes back to where the blast had come from; Ezra Hawthorne— half burnt on the left side of his face, the flesh sagging—was slowly approaching.

Chapter Forty: A Time of Blood

'I'm going to kill you, Grey.' David said as he stood back to his feet. 'I can't have you still running around like this,' he pointed a finger to his face, 'it makes me look bad—makes me look incompetent, and the bosses look down on me.'

'Then you should've made sure I was dead a long time ago.' Grey said.

David shot directly toward him, his exo-suit's jet-like pack coming to life with a burst of flame, his exo-suit mechanical gauntlet fist leading. Grey swerved last minute, barely missing the gauntlet fist, David trying desperately to regain control of the suit. Grey stretched fort *Genesis* behind the off-balanced David, palms opened, and shot out a few mini blasts from it—the size of oranges. These were not to harm David, but more to disoriented him and buy Grey some time to consider his next strategy.

Grey moved to find cover, pressing his back against a thin wall. He looked down at *Genesis*, pushed down on the compartment, it opened again like clockwork. He saw three neuron metallic tubes still in there, but one had been completely drained; while another was only half full, leaving him with only one maxed out. He will have to be conservative if he is to survive and win this duel.

David came crashing through the thin wall with his exo-suit, the wall crumbling around them like sand, and David grabbing hold of Grey around the waist with his shoulders, led him through the air a short distance before crashing his back against a single metallic pole.

Grey felt his back crack with deep pain, all the breath within his lungs left him. David let go and he slumped down the pole, dropping to the muddy ground and landing on his arse.

He squeezed his eyes shut, shook his head, and winced at the pain. When he opened his eyes, David was already coming at him again, flying like some kind of superman in that exo-suit. Grey, laying there upright on the ground with one hand on his bruised ribs, swung

Genesis outward and shot in rapid succession, David weaving in and out, dodging the blasts, an evil smirk on his face.

A moment later, after dodging all of Grey's blasts, David's knee came down hard and met with Grey's stomach. Spit flew out of Grey's mouth from the impact, and for what felt like a good minute, Grey couldn't breathe. His vision blurred. David stood over him, kneeling to sit atop him. Then he brought his gauntlet fist down on Grey. Not once, not twice, but many, many times. Grey raised his arms to take the brunt of the attack. Back and forth Grey felt his face throbbed with punches from David. Blood smeared across his face, obstructing his view. He couldn't see anything anymore, only red. There goes his promise to Bethany.

And once again, David had him at his mercy. The pain was incredible. He risked it and stretched forth *Genesis*, blinded by his own blood, tried for an energy blast but he must've missed because David was still raining down hell on top of him, screaming like the mad man he was.

A moment later, he heard the sound of gunfire, then felt bullet casings fall down and bounce off him.

The weight of David atop him was no more.

'You stupid bitch,' he heard David say.

'Leave him alone!' a female voice came back.

Elyse Fox, he thought. *No, leave her.*

Still blind, and still in excruciating pain, Grey tried to get back to his feet, but he stumbled and fell face-first back into the mud. More gunfire. More footsteps. He didn't know what was going on. But he knew Elyse was in serious danger. David was a ruthless man. He didn't care who you were, he would brutalise you.

Grey reached up with his human hand, breathing heavily, wiped at his face, trying his best to see again. After a couple of shaky swipes with his hand, he could just about see again, saw David slowly walking toward Elyse Fox, the bullets from her machine gun she was using to rain down bullets on him, doing nothing to his exo-suit but little flashes of sparks.

David reached her, yanked the weapon from her grip, pointed it down toward her legs, shot the left and then the right, she screamed out, falling to her knees.

'Now, beg,' David called out.

'Never,' Elyse responded, tears falling down one side of her face, her other eye—the mechanical one, blinking rapidly—her trousers soaking with blood now.

'Very well,' David raised the machine gun, pressed it to her temple, and pulled the trigger. Her head shifted to the side with force, her human eye rolled to the back of her head, her mouth fell open, and she fell on her side onto the muddy ground with a hard thud.

No!

David dropped the gun beside her and turned, coming back toward Grey.

Grey swallowed. He couldn't move. He was in too much pain. He rolled over on his back as the rain started to pour down. He blinked at it, staring up at the grey clouds above him. Was this it? David's boots came thudding closer and closer. Was this the end? Was he going to die at the hand of this man? Would he never see Bethany again? Her beautiful face flashed before him and he closed his eyes. The rain tapped away at his face, felt some of the mud leave it. Let it wash the pain and memories.

A strong hand wrapped around his throat. David lifted him up, and he felt his airways clog up, he couldn't breathe. He didn't even bother to struggle, just let him do what he had to do. All the while David had a sadistic smile on his face. This man was truly evil, Grey thought; he loved causing pain for people, and to think Grey once called him a friend.

As Grey's vision began to turn to black, he felt David's grip loosen and he fell to the ground.

Looking up with a blurred vision, he couldn't believe what he saw. The monster that was Behemoth had tackle David to the ground and was now unleashing his furry on David, ripping apart his exo-suit piece by piece—starting with his helmet. Gael Cross and Eustace de Maris watched on with their machine gun at hand, ready for back-up.

Behemoth continued to use that hidden beastly strength that Grey knew he had always possessed from the first time they had met back at Lucan's base all those weeks ago. Behemoth interlocked his fists and then brought it down together—again and again—on the now exposed vulnerable parts of David like a hammer to a nail. David whaled and writhed in pain. Behemoth then got hold of David's gauntlet, pulled it off of him, and slotted it on his own arm. He aimed it at David's head.

Grey saw David's face turn pale like a ghost. It was the first time David had gotten a taste of his own medicine. It made Grey jump on the inside. Justice.

Behemoth unleashed a hellish energy blast from that gauntlet. There was a loud bang, and after the smoke cleared, all that remained of David's head was a slush pile of brain residue. David's head had taken the full brunt of that energy blast and was mashed to a pulp.

Grey saw Gael Cross grimace and turn away. Eustace de Maris didn't even flinch one bit. Behemoth stood back to his full height and walked over to where Elyse Fox's dead body was. He knelt by her, gently stroking her corpse, his back toward Grey.

'It's over, we've won,' he said out loud. 'We have the two bosses bound and gagged in the main office. The remaining Foxhound members are subdued by the rest of Lucan's men and have surrendered.'

Grey's head fell back down to the muddy earth with a plop.

'Thank fuck for that,' he said.

***

Shots rang out as Jasper fired from his REA issued Chrome .357 Magnum Revolver and Alex from his REA issued SMG.

Jasper still shell-shocked, his eyes stretched open as far as they possibly could, his mind in disarray. He felt his Revolver jolt as he pulled back the trigger, bullets casings dropping all around him. But still, Ezra Hawthorne continued his trek across the muddy plains toward them, unaffected by the bullets from their guns. He seemed to have upgraded his armour considerably from the last time he and Martin had faced off with him in that abandoned warehouse all those weeks ago.

Speaking of Martin, his friend was dead. Actually dead. Jasper couldn't believe it, didn't want to believe it. He shot a quick glance at his friend, hanging there, limp, like some piece of old furniture, the light gone out from his eyes, blood slowly trickling out and down from where the sharp metal pole had pierced his through to his heart.

Teresa, he thought. *I'm sorry*

Jasper turned back, rage burning on the inside of him, the whole world seemed to fade all around him, turning black as his vision narrowed and only Ezra Hawthorne remained in it. He started to move. Move toward his enemy, toward Ezra Hawthorne, he didn't realise it at the time, but his legs were moving so fast, the fastest they had ever moved in his whole twenty-six years of living.

His Revolver was still outstretched in front—in one hand—the cylinder chambers spinning as he fired more bullets toward the approaching Ezra . . . until it became empty.

Jasper wasn't thinking straight, still so consumed with rage regarding Martin's death, that when he heard the empty clip sound, he looked down at his gun with disbelieving eyes, and then flung it in Ezra Hawthorne's direction, the gun crashing against Ezra Hawthorne's metallic armour like a feather to a stone wall, fell back down to the muddy puddle with a plop.

Ezra grinned. Alex Wade was still firing at him with his SMG, stopping from time to time to reload.

Jasper continued on, and, increasing his speed, used the momentum to leap up, ever so slightly, hurtling back down with a thump, his arse taking the small pain from the impact, and then he slid along the wet earth past Ezra Hawthorne. He promptly sprung back up behind Ezra, his hand balled into a fist, pulled back, clenched, charged for a powerful gauntlet punch. He swung the hand, but it met the robotic palm of Ezra Hawthorne. Jasper's fist burned with righteous vigour, but still, it was of no use. It was not enough. It would never be enough. Not with this cyborg.

Ezra Hawthorne hadn't even turned around, only reacted on reflex to Jasper's attack.

He finally turned around slowly, Jasper's fist still in the palm of his robotic hand.

Jasper could hear Alex Wade reloading his SMG.

'Jasper Barnes,' Ezra Hawthorne's eyes were cold and he grinned malevolently, the corners of his mouth wrinkling. 'We meet again.' He looked over at Martin's corpse hanging in front of the old building. Jasper felt Ezra Hawthorne's grip tighten hard around his fist, and despite himself, he let out a loud cry. 'A shame we can't say the same for your partner over there.' He gestured with his chin. 'About time he met his end, don't you think?' Jasper swung his free hand in another outburst of rage; Ezra Hawthorne caught that one also, effortlessly. He let out a yawn—a mock more than anything, Jasper knew. 'You two have been a pain in my arse for far too long. It is because of you, because of what you did to me last time we met at that abandoned warehouse I had to upgrade my armour and robotics.' He leaned closer to the smaller Jasper, his face close to him. His garlic-like infested breath wafted in Jasper's face and he shuddered. 'So I thank you, I thank you for letting me know my weakness.'

Ezra Hawthorne then squeezed and twisted Jasper's right hand, harder and harder, Jasper cried out more, until Jasper heard cracks, and then felt his hand lose all strength in them.

Bullets from Alex Wade's SMG came in their direction, and Ezra Hawthorne—turning his attention to the shooter, Alex—released Jasper from his grip. Jasper thumped to his knee, the muddy ground softening the impact.

Ezra walked back toward Alex Wade, calmly, through the storm of bullets that was soaring in his direction, none of it affecting him, only grazing him, scratching his armour, setting off little sparks.

Alex Wade, backpedalling now, was frantically trying his best, reloading just as quickly as he fired, his hand were trembling, unsure of what to do to bring down this seemingly invincible fucking Cyborg.

'Jasper!' Alex shouted, reaching down with one hand to pull out an REA issued combat knife from the sheath beside his side pocket. 'What should I do?'

Run, you fool, run, Jasper thought but didn't say. He couldn't say much. He was in a hell of pain himself. He looked down at his right hand, crushed and mangled. His fingers looked like tangled roots.

When he looked back up, Alex's skeleton-handled blade was now in the clutches of Ezra, the seven-inch mini-sword reflected in the daylight, shinning bright into Jasper's eyes. He blinked, and Ezra Hawthorne swiped at the neck of the frightened and helpless Alex, pools of blood gushed out of a thin line across his apple's apple as he fell first to his knees, his hands flailing up to try and contain the exposed wound on his neck. Blood swallowed his hands.

Ezra Hawthorne watched on, bloodied knife in his hand as Alex Wade struggled for his life.

There was a wet gurgle—the sound of someone gargling water—and then Alex's bloodied hands fell down from his neck to his side, dangling there like two lifeless ropes.

He fell face first, his face slamming hard to the muddy earth, it splashed, dark-red mixing in with the brown.

Jasper closed his eyelids, squeezing them tight. Another Agent had fallen, and all because of him. What has he gone and done? He's led them to their own death.

Ezra Hawthorne came back to him and stood over him, Alex's REA combat knife still in his hand, his shadow falling over Jasper.

Before Ezra Hawthorne could even say a word, Jasper moved quickly to dig *his* REA issued combat knife into the Achilles Tendon—one of two exposed and vulnerable areas on Ezra Hawthorne's armour that Jasper had only just noticed.

Ezra Hawthorne writhed in pain, and instantly fell to the ground with a thud, the wet earth slushing as he thrashed about, slowly bleeding out. Without wasting a moment, Jasper rose and jumped at the fallen Ezra, his REA issued knife—in his good hand—leading. He jammed it into the second vulnerable area—Ezra's shoulder blade. The knife lodged in without resistance, biting into the flesh like a soft pillow.

Alex Wade's REA issued knife dropped from Ezra's grip, and Jasper moved to grab it, quickly digging it, too, into the other exposed shoulder blade, pinning him down for good.

Ezra Hawthorne cried out, tears actually falling from his eyes.

But there was no sympathy for him, none whatsoever.

'Kill me then, you son of a bitch.' Ezra screamed.

Jasper reached down and removed Ezra's protective helmet. Ezra spat at him. Jasper punched him with his good hand, knocking him out cold, and a small lump could now be seen just below the eye and above the cheekbone of Ezra Hawthorne's face.

Jasper stood and towered over him. The rain came down hard now. Jasper's hair wet and matted against his face. 'As much I want to kill you—especial for Martin and Alex—I can't. That would be too easy.' Jasper reached into his side pocket, pulled out two REA issued handcuffs, slapped one against Ezra Hawthorne's wrist, the other on to his ankles. He would not be getting away this time.

Jasper walked over to where Martin's corpse hung. He swallowed, but his throat felt raw and dry, and no amount of swallowing seemed to help. With a little struggle, he pulled Martin's body off the sharp metal pole, carried him, and then laid him down beside Alex Wade's corpse.

He had done it. He had apprehended that slippery bastard. But at what cost?

His friends were now dead. Even if he got his job back, it wouldn't make up for the emptiness and frustration that tugged at his heart.

Time to get these bodies and Ezra Hawthorne and get the hell out of here.

All around him, it was quiet, the gunshots, the fighting, it had all died down, and it had for a while now, Jasper realised. Well, at least since they had started the confrontation with Ezra Hawthorne. Had Lucan's men done the deed? Had they won? He wasn't sticking around to find out. He didn't care much for their rivalries and war. He had only come here for one thing, and that one thing was lying handcuffed to the wet earth, ready to be carried and handed over to the REA.

In the distance, up on top of one of those buildings, in the centre of the Foxhound Syndicate base, Jasper could see Behemoth, frowning and staring coldly—with disdain, like Jasper was a piece of gum or dirt stuck to his boots.

Jasper shook his head, sighed, ignored the man, and started to move.

Chapter Forty-one: A Promise Kept

Bethany Rose came out of the bathroom holding something behind her back that Grey couldn't see, her eyes were wide, fuller, sharper, lit with something that had entered the world centuries before robotic things. She fixed her gaze on Grey.

'It's positive!' she shrilled, pulling out what looked like a small white, plastic stick— a pregnancy test, Grey realised with a shock—from behind her back, jumping up and down, arms flailing in the air, just like a little baby herself.

Grey didn't even know how to feel, how to take it. He just lay there on their bed, duvet cover over himself, weary from the events that had transpired the last couple of days.

After they had succeeded in taking over the Foxhound Syndicate base from the grasp of the two leading men that ran it, Lucan had driven in to assume full control of the now-defunct criminal organisation. On his way to the throne, he had finally gotten revenge on the two men (the leaders of the Foxhound Syndicate) he deemed to have betrayed him. He had them executed right in front of Grey, and Grey could actually taste the sweat that dripped from their fearful foreheads, their bulging eyes and purple faces as they hanged from nooses in the main office of the Foxhound Syndicate base.

Just as he felt now, he didn't know how to feel about that whole situation. Even David—his archenemy—was dead, killed by the savage hands of Lucan's second in command: Behemoth. He didn't even get to exact his own *vengeance* on David. Perhaps Behemoth had done him a favour; a man so consumed by vengeance could just as likely end up as . . . well . . . Lucan Weaver—where one would spend half their entire life seeking unforgiving justice, which would no doubt lead one to their downfall, one way or another.

Bethany sauntered over to the bed, climbing on, shaking the bed and snapping Grey out of his head and back into reality.

'Mr. Grey Harrow,' she said laying her head down beside him, her eyes sparkling. 'We are going to be parents.' The thought frightened him, he wasn't going to lie. He was scared shitless. Him—a father? Incredulous! He didn't know the last thing about being a father. Even he himself didn't have a father growing up; he hadn't been fathered, unless you count his brief spell with his foster father, Rasheed. But still, he wouldn't know the first thing about being one.

He had grown up with only his mother (God rest her soul), up until he was seven, or eight, he couldn't remember, but then he was sent into foster care, going in and out of families like a prostitute allows her clients to do to her every other night.

He laid a hand on her and just smiled, putting her at ease, if anything. 'That's amazing; you'll make a great mother.' He leaned in and kissed her forehead, she closed her eyes, and Grey could see that warm smile of hers. That peaceful bliss. That feeling of his world making sense again, that right here, with Bethany, is where purpose and meaning resides. His life made sense whenever he was near her, even if all around him there was only chaos, trauma, and pain.

Grey leaned back on the bed, laid his head against the soft pillow. He turned his head and stared out the window, small breeze flew in through the open slit.

Outside, night had come on as the city partied on. Police sirens and loud chatters and music and hover car engines played on from down below their apartment. Typical, Old Street was no different from King Cross—or any other area in London for that matter. London was the city that never sleeps. Period.

Grey motioned for the state-of-the-art robotic device built into their apartment, telling it to turn off the lights and turn on some white noise to drown out the sounds of the outside world. It obeyed with a mechanical-twang sounding noise, like that of a radio being tuned to find a station.

Bethany rolled over, mumbling something, 'Raheem . . . or Elena.' She said.

'What?' Grey cocked his head at her.

'Baby names, I like those names. Raheem—if it's a boy, and Elena—if it's a girl.'

'Oh,' Grey chuckled. 'Nice. Well, hopefully, he fits in well . . .' he trailed off. '. . . In Ibiza. We leave in a week's time.'

She sat up, bolt up-right. 'Awesome, you really came through, Grey, you said you would and you kept your word.' She leaned in, her warmth smelling natural aroma, dangling in the air between them. Grey loved that smell. He lived for that smell. He worshipped that smell. She kissed him, lightly on his lips, then after a couple of seconds pulled back and smacked him on the arm.

'You said *he*,' she said.

'I guess I'm slightly hoping for a little boy.' When he saw Beth's expression change, he said. 'But I would just as much love a little baby girl.'

She shook her head and smiled, wrapped her arms around him, snuggling close to him, her embrace, warm and beautiful. They lay back and fell asleep, the white noise the robotic device of their apartment was playing, soothing and calmly, and the stars that hung and splayed across the night skies just outside their window—like otherworldly beings— sending them into blissful slumber.

Chapter Forty-two: A Special Agent

Jasper Barnes strode through the newly reconstructed REA office in Knightsbridge, his fractured right hand in a white cast that allowed for only his index finger and thumb to freely move about whichever way they pleased.

Eyes stared at him from all directions as he trudged through the office corridors. Some were filled with sorrow, some pain, some pity, and surprisingly, given what had happened recently, some were filled with adulation.

Jasper was on his way to meet with Walter Marshal. This will be the first time since his suspension that he would be meeting with his manager. He didn't know what to expect. He was certain that Walter Marshal was aware of the apprehension of Ezra Hawthorne as well as the deaths of Martin Silas and Alex Wade.

But what did he think of the whole situation? Was he going to blame him for their deaths? Was he going to fire him for definite this time? The thoughts killed him. His throat felt raw, his mouth dry, and his uninjured hand, twitched involuntarily, something he couldn't quite understand as to why.

He reached the front door of his manager's office. He rapped his knuckle on the door, twice, and then lifted his hand to the door handle; it hovered above there for a while, sweat starting to trickle down the back of his neck, his face felt hot, and the heat quickly spread down his body.

Finally, he wet his lips, swallowed, shifted his feet, turned the handle, and opened the door.

Walter Marshal was seated; his feet stretched out and crossed at his ankle on his desk. He was scrolling through a hologram of something, deeply immersed in whatever it was.

When he noticed Jasper, he gestured for him to come closer, and then gestured again for him to sit on a chair that was situated opposite him.

Jasper did as he suggested, calmly easing his frame onto the chair opposite Walter Marshal.

Walter Marshal swiped at the hologram in front of him, clearing the image, then he pressed down on a button on his desk, and the hologram shut off completely.

He looked at Jasper for a long while, not saying anything, hands under his chin as if Jasper was a subject and he were studying him.

Jasper remained silent, his palms were sweaty, but he put on his best smile, waiting for his opportunity to speak, to plead his case if necessary. He needed his job back, now more than ever. Not just for his family, but for Martin and Alex, to honour them in their deaths and clean this city up.

'I'm revoking your suspension,' Walter Marshal took his feet off his desk and sat back in his chair. 'And I'm now promoting you to Special Agent.'

Jasper's heart froze. Then it started to pound again, his skin tingled for some strange reason.

'Sorry?' he said.

'That's right,' Walter Marshal said. 'You heard me, you've got your job back and I'm promoting you to Special Agent.'

Jasper couldn't believe it. He was stunned and speechless. He just stared at Walter Marshal blankly; his mouth opened slightly, his breathing deepening. He had thought that when he was told he had a meeting with his manager that he would be pleading his case and giving Walter Marshal a theatrical performance for the many reasons why he should have his job back, but none of that was needed, the man wanted him back, and he had promoted him to Special Agent. For however long Jasper had known he wanted to be REA Agent—his second year at university—Special Agent or Intelligence Analyst had always been the goal. Not only for the financial stability it brought, but for the power and autonomy it brought with it. Jasper would now be able to command and lead a group of agents of his own as their boss, almost like Walter Marshal himself.

'Thank . . .' Jasper faltered. 'Thank . . .' and again. 'Thank you,' he finally finished.

Walter Marshal said, 'No, thank you.' He stood to his feet and walked around his desk toward Jasper. He held out a hand. 'You finally apprehended a dangerous robotics criminal that we have been chasing and trying to catch for a very long time.'

Jasper stood, mouth still slightly opened, lost in wonder, and he shook Walter Marshal's hand with his uninjured but weaker left hand.

The man's grip was firm and strong and Jasper realised Walter Marshal was probably left-handed.

Then Walter Marshal's face turned sad and he grimaced. 'I'm sorry about your partners—Martin Silas, and Alex Wade. They were good men. I feel I'm partly to blame. If I had known what you guys were going through we could have probably done more to help.'

'Thank you.' The funeral took place last week, and the majority of the team and agents had come to pay their respect. Teresa took it the worse, Martin's wife balling her eyes out throughout the service, unable to control herself, and Jasper felt her eyes burning into him, blaming him—she was not going to forgive him, that he could feel. But he prayed a silent prayer that she would somehow find it in her heart to forgive him eventually.

Oddly enough, even that lawless cyborg, Grey Harrow, came to pay some respect, however much it was. Still, he was grateful for it, it was the thought that counted, and it would seem Grey Harrow, deep down, seemed to possess some kind of semblance of a decent man.

'Go home, Special Agent Jasper Barnes,' Walter Marshal said. The title had a nice ring to it; Jasper had to admit with glee. 'Spend the rest of the day and the weekend with your wife and son, and come back to work first thing Monday morning,' his manager's smile was broad; Jasper hadn't seen him smile like that in a long while. 'We've got work to do.'

Jasper nodded. 'Yes, sir.'

And he was on his way out Walter Marshal's office when he remembered what his manager had just said about spending the rest of the day with his wife and son.

He sighed.

He hadn't seen them since that very night he hit her.

Chapter Forty-three: A Cruel, Cruel World

Bethany awoke to the smell of smoke and burning plastic. It brought her out of her stupor immediately and she sat bolt upright and her vision was clouded by greyish smoke. They obstructed her view, she couldn't see anything, and then she found herself coughing, the smoke was making it hard for her to breathe, finding its way in through her airways—her mouth and nose—and filling up her lungs with its blackness. She could taste the muskiness.

What the hell was happening?

She jumped off the bed and started to move toward the front door, through the clouded room, when the plastered ceiling above her fell down. She jolted back in time to avoid it collapsing on her. She exhaled a sigh of relief, but the path to the front door was now blocked. She breathed in deep as best she could, given the air that was all around her.

She raised her arm across her face, her light pyjama's sleeves doing their best to protect her from inhaling too much of the smoke. Her heart thumped in her chest, the heat all around her beat down on her skin, made her sweat.

Then, seeing the red and orange flames rising behind the thick cloud of smoke, she finally realised. It hit her like a fist to the gut. Their apartment was on fire.

She quickly called out for the state-of-the-art robotic device, but there was no response. And with Grey out, she was all alone. A cold chill crawled down her spine and she shivered, felt goose pimples grow on the skin of her arms. She was scared, scared for the life of her unborn child. She had only just found out two days ago that she had been with child. Although it had been unexpected and definitely unplanned, she and Grey had come to accept it and had only just begun to prepare and welcome the idea of a child between them. She placed a hand on her belly, stood to her feet, and made for the windowsill.

She quickly pulled back the blinds and shoved the window open with trembling hands as the fire rage wilder behind her, the heat engulfing her as if she were in a sauna.

She screamed out the five-storey window, 'HELP!' the sound of her voice frightened even her.

She knew their apartment was too high up for her to climb down through the window. She was trapped. Her only hope was to shout until her lungs collapsed. 'Help!'

She could now see a few people congregate down below.

They coiled their hands around their mouth like cones and shouted back at her. 'Hang in there; the fire brigade are on their way!'

Some more ceiling plaster fell. The fire was spreading, coming closer to her now; she would have to move away from the window and toward the bathroom where the fire hadn't reached as of yet.

Her eyes were burning up from the heat and smoke, it felt watery, made her squint and blink fervently. She wiped at her forehead with her hand, it was wet with sweat. She coughed, the smoke choking the life from her.

Grey, baby, she thought. Tears fell from her eyes, she looked left and right, up and down, lost, confused, unsure of what to do.

She felt lightheaded, the room span, the fire danced, the smoke swirled, the heat stabbed, and she collapsed to the ground on her back. Her body hit the floor with a thud, her head bounced off it, and she cried out in pain. She could faintly hear others in the next room screeching. It seemed she wasn't the only one affected by the fire. *Was the fire spreading to the other apartments?* She thought. *What happened? How did it start?* So many questions she realised she may never get an answer to.

Bethany felt her airways clog and she coughed a few more times, staring off into the distance, watching the flames get wilder and wilder, engulfing their bed, swallowing their nightstand, melting their walls, and she felt another tear roll down her cheek. Her lips trembled. She held her belly and got into a fetal position. *Please no, please, someone. Not my baby, no. Please, God.*

The ceiling directly above her came down in a loud crash.

She was covered in rubble and could no longer feel any of her limbs.

The fire came closer and fiercer and licked at her skin, blackish smoke filled her lungs, choked her like black hands around her throat.

And Bethany Rose couldn't breathe.

***

Just as he sooner arrived out of Old Street station, Grey Harrow's mouth fell wide open as his eyes landed on the tower of inferno that was his apartment.

Bethany. He swallowed and immediately felt hot. Ignoring all the mixed feelings that were currently rising on the inside of him: trepidation, confusion, anger—Grey sprinted toward his apartment building.

The area around him swam with many on-lookers, huddled together, some holding one and other in embraces with concern on their faces, many of them were his neighbours, Grey noticed, but a few others were just curious spectators he hadn't seen around the apartment blocks before.

Three fire brigade hover vans zipped on ahead past him on the road to his left as he ran, heading straight for the burning apartments. *Please be okay, Beth.* Grey's stomach twisted and turn, and he resisted the urge to be sick. He prayed Bethany was okay, that she had managed to get out in time. He blamed himself—for leaving her all alone, for leaving her all alone with only that stupid state-of-the-art robotic device for her only protection.

As he edged closer to the apartment, the night air all around him became thick with the smell of smoke, and he could now see a single shadowy figure—who clearly wasn't looking where they were going, but instead craning their neck behind them—sprinting away from the inferno in the opposite direction toward him.

Grey slowed, squinted, shifted to one side so the person running wouldn't barge into him, and as he did, the figure's face became evident to him.

'Behemoth,' Grey said with surprise, tilting his head to the side.

Behemoth halted in the dark night, turned back to regard Grey, his eyes were wide like he'd just seen a ghost from his very evil past.

'Grey . . .' he said softly, almost a whisper. 'What are doing here?' his voice was shaky, and he stared back and forth between the burning apartments and Grey. 'You should be in there.'

Grey furrowed his brows, narrowed his eyes, suspicious, 'What have you done, Behemoth?' he asked. 'Bethany is in there!'

Grey turned to look at the burning building, and when he turned back, Behemoth was already stomping down the street, disappearing into the night shadows.

He grimaced and ground his teeth, realisation hitting him, he wanted to chase after Behemoth so he could get some answers, but Bethany's safety was all that concerned him right now, and so instead he started and continued the short distance to the front entrance of the apartment building.

When he reached there, men and women of the fire bridged—in their yellow and blue attire and helmet—were trying the best to keep the crowd as far back as possible. Water gushed out from hoses, splashing the side of the building, but not doing much to douse the flame out quickly. It still raged on, strips of red flames and thick grey smoke lifting up toward the skies like horns on the buildings.

Grey shouldered through the first flew fire-fighters closest to him—two of them—and made his way straight for the front entrance of the apartment building. He was grabbed by someone, but he easily shrugged them off, knocking whoever it was to the ground behind him.

'Bethany!' he shouted as the heat of the inferno washed over him like paint. He felt the metallic parts of *Genesis* heat up as he got closer to the fire. 'Beth!' he looked around at the stunned and confused looking fire-fighters, some still with hoses in their hands, water still pouring out in streams.

He looked up the side of the building, trying to spot their windowsill, but then he felt huge arms wrap around his body, tackling him to the ground and pinning him there. He realised he had been tackled to the ground by two fire-fighters. They were strong. Grey felt subdued, unable to move.

'She's pregnant! Do something!' Grey cried out in their firm grips.

'Relax,' one of them said, 'we are doing our best. My men are doing their best.'

He didn't believe them; they were not doing their best. He looked around and half of them were just standing around doing nothing but spectating, no one was brave enough to run into the blaze and rescue her.

One side of the building collapsed in on itself, pieces of debris falling and crashing down beside Grey and the fire-fighters. They flinched, and that was all Grey needed, an inch, a second, and he was gone, he shrugged them both off him, both fire-fighter falling like trees to either side of him. He yanked one of the helmet face masks off the fire-fighter, shoved it down on his head and over his face and he entered the blazing fire.

He didn't care that the flame would burn at his skin, char his face, mar his features; he just needed to get to her. He made his way through the flames, through the heat, ducking and weaving, crawling and climbing, his skin sweating profusely, felt as if he were taking a shower as liquid dripped off his skin. He held the mask tight to his face, taking the path of least resistance.

When he reached the front door to their apartment and he tried to open it, it felt wedged, barred by something on the other side of it. Red flames surrounded him, grew fiercer and fiercer, his skin burning, his eyes stinging from the sweat that was dripping down into them from his forehead. His mask was steaming up, his vision blurred.

Regardless, he swung *Genesis* out in front of him, placed the mechanical palm against the flaming door. The door flung open with a loud *crash* as he levelled it with an energy blast from the palm of his hand, then there was a loud *bang* as the door and whatever debris had been behind it came slamming back down to earth.

The path was clear, but thick smoke obstructed his view. He ambled on, slowly, squinting, made his way toward their bed; he felt for the bed, it had been chewed up in the flame, nothing but hard and burnt rubble now.

He craned his neck back, searching the room, breathing through his mask frantically . . .

Beth, where are you? He thought, his heart raced, panic was engulfing his every fibre and he thought the worse.

Then he saw her, laying there, near the windowsill, her normally white pyjamas, now black.

Grey went over to her. He placed his hands beneath her body and cradled her in his arms, her skin had been covered in dust and her usually rosy skin now looked pale, and her eyes were closed as if she were in a peaceful sleep.

He stretched forth *Genesis* again, Bethany still in his arms, and blasted open the glass window with another energy blast, it shattered outward, screeching—the sound of glass breaking—the glass debris falling like crystallised rain down below.

Grey used his hand to grip the side of the building—a pole like pipe—and started to climb down, slowly, with Bethany cradled to his chest in his other arm. He could hear murmuring down below as he descended, the fire-fighters still shouting and ordering people back.

When Grey landed, he lay Bethany down on the cold ground. Looked at her, then grabbed her again, pulling her close and hugging her tight, the corner of his eyes wet with tears.

The fire-fighters gave him a wide berth as the ambulance brought out a stretcher. But he knew it wouldn't be needed. Not anymore.

He couldn't feel a pulse.

He held her some more, squeezing her pale face to his, sobbing. 'You're the very best part of me,' he whispered into her ears as if she could still hear him in whatever realm she now resided in. 'Bethany, I'm a better . . . human . . . machine . . . just because I've loved you.' He closed his eyes. 'I'm so sorry.'

He traced his fingers down her cold, soft body and touched her belly. Thought of their unborn child, and his heart sank. It had happened all over again. Just like a month ago at her apartment in Euston when she had been shot in the shoulder by Hector and his balaclava Foxhound goons. Just one more week and they would've been out of this city—out of this hellhole. Off to start a new life.

But now, he knew, he'd been pulled right back in . . . again.

An image of Behemoth's smug face flashed before him and he punched down hard on the cobblestone with *Genesis*; a mini crater appeared around where the fist had landed.

It pained him.

He'd lost her, and now there was nothing left.

A man with nothing to lose.

As they lay her onto the stretcher, zipped her up in a black bag, and took her away, he felt his eyes burn with rage. Like laser beams, they seemed to penetrate wherever they went, wherever he looked. All he'd ever know now . . . was hatred. Hatred for Behemoth. Hatred

for the world. And hatred for any god out there that would let this happen to the only thing he

had ever truly cared for in this cruel, *cruel* world—his beloved—Bethany Rose.

Chapter Forty-four: A Struggle for Redemption

When Jasper stepped through his sister-in-law's wooden front door, the smell immediately hit him.

Sarai's smell.

That velvety, fresh aroma of hers had taken over even her sister's home. It followed her wherever she went. The smell of peace, and it made him sad, he missed her. Just like a toddler yearned for its mother, Jasper yearned for her peace again. And peace is what he would get, no matter what. After all, that's why he had come here today, right? Not for war—he had had enough of that in his life in the last couple of weeks involving the Foxhound Syndicate and Ezra Hawthorne—but for reconciliation.

Debbie, Sarai's younger sister, shut the front door behind him. Jasper turned to regard her; she was wearing a green blouse with black trousers and slippers, her long, black dreads draping down past her shoulders, the tips of which were wrapped in little gold beads. Her features were strikingly similar to Sarai, he remembered—same shiny brown skin that looked like clear marble. It was so clear and glowed that one could see their reflection in it.

Debbie leaned against the front door with her back; her arms were folded and she stared at him with narrowed, slit eyes, looking him up and down, like he was trash, and Jasper knew she, too, had a bone to pick with him. The last time he had seen her was about six months ago at Zack's birthday party. Back then she still looked up to Jasper, the man that had swept her sister of her feet and looked after her for as long as she could remember, loving and caring for her with unwavering affection, but now, she was staring at the man—the monster—that dared lay a hand on her precious sister.

'Why, Jasper?' She finally spoke. 'How could you?'

Jasper said nothing, turned away from her, and studied his surrounding—her home.

The house was relatively big and spacious and it had African tapestries along the walls, floors, and ceilings, no doubt paying homage to Debbie and Sarai's heritage. With four rooms including the one he was standing in right now—the living room—Sarai and Zack would've had no problem staying here. Each would have had their own room to sleep in. And with no grumpy old man to raise a hand to them, why would they ever want to leave?

Jasper made his way to the couch in the middle of the room, and as he did, he heard the floorboard up above him creak, movement, feet thudding the ground.

He sat; Debbie remained by the door, arms still crossed.

'I'm speaking to you,' Debbie spoke again, her voice sounding frustrated. 'Are you just going to ignore me?' That was what he was going to do. He hadn't come for her; he had come to speak with his wife and owed Debbie nothing.

Jasper said, 'Could you please tell Sarai that I'm down here.'

Debbie sighed, pushed herself off the door, and started. 'You do it yourself, you piece of shit.' She left the living room, and Jasper could hear her footsteps as she climbed up the stairs.

He breathed, calming himself. He held his hand to his temple and shook his head.

A few minutes later, little Zack came hurtling down the stairs and into the living room, screaming.

'Dad, dad,' he shouted and ran to hug Jasper, innocent.

'Hey, Zack,' Jasper said, embracing his son, squeezing him tight, inhaling him. After a while, he gently pushed him back, held him by the shoulders. 'How have you been, boy?'

The boy didn't look his father in the eye; instead, he looked to the ground, shifting from one leg to the other, his face saddened, he reached up with a hand and rubbed one of his cheeks with the back of it. His bottom lip stuck out and was turned upside down.

'Mum said you were gone, that you were not coming back—'

'What?'

Zack nodded his little head, and Jasper's heart sank. How could she? Jasper was his father, and he would not abandon his family. Not ever.

He leaned in. 'Listen to me, son, I'll never leave you, okay? Know that,' Jasper tapped his index finger to Zack's temple, 'Your father will never leave you, nor forsake you.'

Zack said, 'Okay,' and nodded his little head again, he smiled, hugging his father again, Jasper leaning his head down and kissing him atop his head.

Zack pulled back, 'When are we going back home, dad?'

Jasper slowly raised his head and there was Sarai, standing there, silent like a thief by the entrance to the living room, wearing a white blouse and a black shirt that revealed those long, toned, brown legs that Jasper adored so much. Regardless of what had happened between them, she still looked so good to him, ever beautiful, like he was seeing her for the very first time again. His eyes darted around her face and then fell still on her full lips, he remembered the taste of her mouth, and he could almost taste it again.

He pulled Zack back and Zack turned his head to see his mother. 'Hey buddy, your mum and I need to speak, run up to your auntie, and pack you things, we will be leaving soon, okay?'

Zack nodded and then his little legs thudded the ground as he ran past his mother and up the stairs.

Sarai came closer. 'Pack your things? We will be leaving soon? Really?' She giggled mockingly. 'Your audacity knows no bound.'

'Sarai . . .' Jasper started and stood to his feet. 'This is not our home, we need to go back home. Be a family again.'

'And if we don't go, what then? Are you going to hit me again? Maybe you'll punch me this time.'

Jasper ground his teeth and grimaced. Was he ever going to be forgiven? Was there ever going to be any sort of redemption for him? Yes, he was in the wrong. Yes, he was a bad guy. Yes, there was no excuse, but was there not a way back for him? Could he not be redeemed?

He took a couple of steps closer to Sarai. She took a couple of steps back, and so Jasper stopped.

'Stay back, Jasper, don't come any closer.' Her voice sounding frightened. Oh God, what had he done? She was now afraid of him.

'I'm not going to hurt you,' Jasper's voice caught in his throat, choked him, he was trying his best to reassure her. 'I'm exhausted, Sarai, of us, going back and forth, kicking and scratching and wailing at one and other,' he stretched forth his hands, palm showing. 'I surrender, you win. I am a bad guy, I know this, and I've been going over this in my head—over and over again. It's killing me on the inside.'

'So you sent your sister to me instead?'

'I didn't know what to do, I was lost, and you made it perfectly clear that you didn't want to see me again, and Clare offered to come. You know her, stubborn as hell, I couldn't stop her. But again, Sarai, not seeing you for the past couple of weeks has destroyed me on the inside. Ask anyone, I was a total mess.'

'Good,' she said studying him with her eyes, glinting like glass. 'What happened to your hand?'

Jasper looked down at his broken right hand—the one Ezra Hawthorne had maimed. 'Work injury, long story.'

Upstairs, in-between the wide berth between them, the floorboards groaned again, movements from Debbie and Zack, probably playing a game of some sort, Jasper imagined.

'Jasper, you broke my heart,' she said and her face scrunched up and some tears rolled down her cheeks. Jasper wished he could catch them before they could fall. Seeing her like this was like a stab to the heart. 'You broke my trust, I . . . even if I forgive you, I don't know if I can ever forget.'

Jasper took a cautious step toward her, she didn't move back this time, and then Jasper took another, edging closer to her. 'That's okay, love, it's a start. Trust me; I never wanted to hurt you. Every single thing I did and everything I'm doing now—is for us and Zack. You have to believe me. I'm so sorry. As God is my witness, I will never lay a hand on you again.' And that was the god honest truth, pure and naked.

Jasper was now within a hair's breadth away from her.

He leaned in and gently wrapped his strong arms around her slender waist, and she reached up and slowly wrapped her soft arms around his neck.

They clasped, snug as a glove, and they both sobbed into each other, bodies vibrating and trembling with tears.

Chapter Forty-five: A Man Apart

'Don't let anybody make you cruel; no matter how badly you want to give the world a taste of its own medicine, it is never worth losing yourself.' Clare Barnes said to Grey as she held his arm at the funeral service.

Grey bent down and snatched some dirt from the soil onto his hand. It was warm to the touch and soft. The gradually scorching summer had arrived and was doing its work on dear mother earth.

He stood back up with a closed fist, and then opened his palm slightly, letting the dirt drizzle out like water onto the closed coffin of Bethany Rose, silently praying a prayer for her soul.

A single tear fell from his eye, dropped onto the dirt.

After the funeral service was over—a service that was attended by many of Bethany Rose's close friends and family, including those at RoyalStarCorp (Herman Rowntree, Adam Cardon, and Clare Barnes), REA Agent Jasper Barnes, and New Foxhound Syndicate Leader Lucan Weaver—Grey went back to the beginning. All the way back. Back to his old apartment in the Red-light district area of Kings Cross, and now that his nemesis, David, was dead and the Foxhound Syndicate were no longer after him, he was safe—a free man.

Or was he? He was free, all right, but at what cost? His reason for breathing was no longer here, and he seemed to no longer care what happened to him.

Behemoth had not been seen since the night of the fire. No one seemed to know his whereabouts, and Lucan Weaver had assured Grey that if he was to ever show his face again, he'll be dealt with accordingly. According to what? Hanging from the ceiling and dying from asphyxiation like the two former leaders of the Foxhound Syndicate?

Not good enough. Grey needed answers. He will be the first one to find him. That much was for certain.

As he lay his head on his pillow in his apartment, Grey felt *Genesis* twitch—a slight movement of the hand that he was unable to control. It had been a while since he'd taken his pills. About five days now, he surmised. Ever since Bethany Rose passed over onto the other side, he'd stop taking it.

What was the point? He thought himself. *Nothing matters anymore.*

Exactly, another voice in his head said. *Let me be free.*

Grey scrunched his face, raised both his hands to his head.

Embrace the pain, embrace me, embrace us, together will get Bethany's killer.

Grey rose and sat on the edge of his bed, legs dangling, his face still scrunched up, his heart racing now, and he felt hot.

Genesis came to life right before his very eyes, for the first time since their first failed assault on the Foxhound Syndicate base last month, it fully thrust itself up from his side and wrapped its cold mechanical fingers around Grey's throat like a lock.

Grey struggled, air was not leaving or coming in, and he felt his eyes bulge in their sockets.

Stop it, stop it.

He was thrust backward through the air, crashing through the wall of his bedroom into the main living area with a loud *thump*. He slumped to the ground, he back screamed, his spine wined, his ears rang, and he saw that everything in the room had a twin of itself.

He slowly stood back to his feet—sweating now and boiling hot as ever—and as he did, out of his control as if possessed by a demon of some sort, *Genesis* pointed its mechanical palm straight back into his bedroom, through the gaping hole that now resided where Grey had been sent careening through, and levelled it at his nightstand. The energy blast left his palm like a ball of fire—unbeknownst to him—and exploded as it blew up the nightstand, shattering the wooden bedside table, splitters flying everywhere, and disintegrating the contents inside.

Neuranzinmide, Grey realised. The last of his RHSV medications.

'What are you doing?' Grey found himself saying out loud, talking to himself again.

Trying to help you, the voice of *Genesis* said. *You need me; we will get revenge for Bethany Rose. I, too, loved her, just as you did.*

Grey, still standing, confused as fuck, stared around him at the mess—the carnage this rogue part of himself had wroth. He'd just managed to get the apartment back to respectable living standards, and now *it* (*Genesis* or whatever it likes to be called) had gone and undone all the hard work. Fucking hell.

Now get your phone and call Gael Cross, Genesis came again. *Elyse Fox is dead and he is the only living close friend that would know where Behemoth is—where he is hiding.*

Regardless of the manner in which *Genesis* was getting things done, it was right, Gael cross would—should—know where to find Behemoth.

Grey patted himself, dusting off the wall plaster that engulfed his black t-shirt and black combat trousers, reached into his pocket, pulled out his holo-phone. He decided he would use a private number to call him just in case.

He thumbed through the holo-screen, dialled the number, and it rang.

'Yo,' came a deep, rough, Behemoth-like voice on the other side. 'Who this?' the voice came again. Grey remained silent. 'Oi, Gael, come get your phone, whoever it is that is on the line isn't saying shit.' The phone made a swishing, windy, sound as if it were being thrown across the room, then a *pap* as it landed on what sounded like a hand or a chair.

'Hello,' came Gael Cross's meek voice.

Grey hung up.

He went back into his room, shrugged on his overcoat, grabbed two metallic tubes of neurons and a pack of cigarettes from his wardrobe, shoving them down into his overcoat pockets, and then left his apartment.

***

Grey Harrow stood across the street from Gael Cross's house, watching and waiting, doing his best to look in through the tinted windows.

Tinted windows for a home? What are you hiding? Stupid fool is bound to raise suspicion from every agent and police alike from all around London. Still, Grey couldn't see shit. He needed to get closer.

Hover cars hummed past him, gusting strong wind in his direction in the process, their neon-coloured base, lighting and painting the road—as well as the sidewalk—in all the colours of the rainbow.

It was late now; he looked down at his watch—10:45 pm.

He pushed himself off the railing he'd been leaning against, stretched himself out, his whole body crackled and a yawn left his now elongated mouth. He looked around the area, in the distance he could see only one robotic camera, it faced toward the main road. Good. There will be no disturbance for what he was about to do.

He made his way across the road, the point of his boots knocking about small stray stones, careful to cross safely while avoiding being spotted by Gael Cross himself. He wanted to surprise him; silly fucker had lied to him about not knowing where Behemoth was. But the private number phone call he'd sprung on Gael Cross told him otherwise.

Tonight both will get their comeuppance.

Grey tugged at *Genesis* as he walked along the road, pulling up his sleeves. He clicked on the mechanical compartment; it slid open, took out the empties, and place two full metallic tubes of Neurons, and closed it.

He rolled down his sleeves, sunk behind a tall bush round the back of Gael Cross's home, and watched on again.

Nothing.

No movement . . . but the lights were on.

Then he saw him, Gael Cross appearing in the slit through one of those shoddy looking tinted windows that had been left open ever so slightly. He had something in his hands that Grey couldn't see, and he seemed to be doing something with it.

Now is your opportunity. Whether it was the mind of *Genesis* or just his, he didn't know, but he knew this *was* his opportunity—they were in agreement on that—and so he started, slowly.

He reached the front door, sucked in a deep breath, counted to three. He then leaned back, spreading and shifting his legs. The used the mechanical part of his left shoulder to lunge into the front door, smashing it wide open, the door dislodging from its hinges like a broken tooth.

Soon as he entered, he immediately raised *Genesis* in front of him, the tip of which, glowing a bright orange.

Two little girls that looked about nine or ten years jolted up from the ground in front of him, scuttling away from him like rats toward the back of the room where Gael Cross stood with what looked like a round bowl and wooden spoon in his hands, white powder marred his skin and attire. The girls seemed to have been playing a board game of some sort. As he edged forward, accidentally, he trampled on it, and the dice rolled away as if making an escape of its own.

The bowl that Gael Cross held in his hands dropped from his grasp with a clang, creamy and powdery liquid splashing everywhere. He grabbed hold of the two little girls in a soft embrace as they buried their faces into his midriff, scared for their life.

'Hey, it's okay,' Gael Cross said to them in a quiet, assuring voice, 'Daddy's here, okay?'

He looked back up and squinted. Grey still had *Genesis* stretched forth; flame still dancing at the tip, itching to burn a whole in the lying man.

Gael Cross positioned the two girls behind him, raised his hands out in front of him, then took a few tentative steps toward Grey as if pushing an invisible block of crates. 'Grey,' Gael Cross said, squinting, unsure. Where Grey was standing was dark, after all. 'What are you doing here? And why are you pointing that *hand* in this direction—at my kids?'

'Shut up!' Grey found himself saying, very loud, very angrily. 'Where is Behemoth? And don't lie to me—for your children's sake—I know he is here.'

'What?'

'I heard his voice on the phone.'

'What do you want with Behemoth—?'

Grey took a few determined steps toward Gael Cross. 'Don't fucking play with me, I have no time for games,' he snapped and grabbed Gael Cross by his collar with his other hand and shoved *Genesis* right in front of his face, letting him see the inferno that burned within the circle-centred palm of the mechanical limb.

The two girls scattered around them and screamed, *'Dad!'* it was a piercing sound, like a needle through the ear drum.

But Gael Cross reassured them again, he looked back at them as they congregated near the table top and said, 'It's okay, girls, Grey Harrow here is an old friend of your father,' he forced himself to smile at them, but to Grey, it came out more as a grimace.

Just killed this fool and search the damn house. 'I won't say it again: where is Behemoth?' Out of his control again, *Genesis* wrenched the mechanical arm away from the face of Gael Cross and pointed it at the two little girls, who stood huddled together, watching with fearful eyes.

Genesis let loose a controlled fire blast . . . but it crashed inches away from them into the kitchen's table top, crushing into it, nothing but rubble remaining of that section of the kitchen.

'Okay, okay,' Gael Cross said, exasperated, looking incredulous.

Fuck, who asked you to do that? And you had to use the fire blast—energy, no?

Grey let go of his collar. Gael Cross's jaw worked like a meat grinder and he scampered over on his one human leg and one mechanical leg to his daughters and wrapped them in his arms again, glaring back at Grey with disdain.

'I don't want to do this, but I will if you do not tell me where the fuck Behemoth is.'

'Listen, Grey, I won't try to talk you out of what you want to do to him—even though Behemoth is my best friend—but in all my time with Lucan's Syndicate, I've never as much seen any profit in revenge. Nothing good comes out of it.'

'I won't ask again.'

'He didn't kill Bethany, he wanted to kill you.' Gael Cross took off his shirt and flung it over his daughters.

'What?'

'He wasn't trying to kill you; he didn't think Bethany was inside when he started the fire.'

Grey ground his teeth, his jaw worked and worked, clenched and clenched, his eyes burned, his heart thumped, every limb in his body—except the mechanical parts—clamped tight.

Rage.

He found himself sprinting at full pace toward Gael Cross and his daughters. All he saw was red. He would kill them all.

A black giant appeared in his peripheral from the left, out of the darkness below—from the basement, no doubt—and that giant caught him with its large shoulders, as big as a castle, straight through the chest.

Grey heard something crack, felt pain shoot up his body like a burst of cold water on the skin on a freezing morning.

Grey found himself flying and crashing through wooden fixtures around Gael Cross's home. It *snapped* and *crunched* all around them. He was dragged and smashed through numerous objects that were too much to count and difficult to describe—giving his current predicament and limited view of things.

His vision blurred, tasted blood on his tongue, and he could now smell whatever it was Gael Cross had been trying to make before he had so rudely interrupted him.

Grey lay there, looking up at his attacker, about to bring down a big boot on his face.

He did . . . and again. Grey's face throbbed with sharp pin-point pain.

He saw the giant retreat toward Gael Cross—his daughters still in his firm clutches like some sort of guardian angel—he reached into one of the drawers in the kitchen, cutleries and wares, rattling and clinking, reverberating its metallic twang. The giant pulled out a sharp butcher's knife that was so sharp, Grey could've sworn it winked at him, glinting, shining.

Grey swallowed. He couldn't move. Too much pain. Fatigued.

'No one's good, no one's bad. Everyone's just trying to make their own way.' Behemoth's dark face became evident as he ambled over to Grey, butcher's knife big in his hand, wrapped around those gigantic fingers, itching to be slid into his heart.

'She was my world, and you took her from me.' Grey managed.

Behemoth stood over him and raised the knife above him. In the distance, Grey could see Gael Cross shield his daughters' eyes with his body from the gruesome scene that was about to take place.

Behemoth thrust downward, and Grey flinched as the blade dug deep into his right thigh. The pain was unbearable, piercing, one of the worse, the worse of the worse; Grey would not wish it on anyone. Not even his worst enemy. He cried out.

'Slowly,' Behemoth breathed. 'Suffer,' he pulled out the blade as Grey's blood splattered out in little rivulets of bubble around the mortal wound. Dark red dripped off the blade.

Grey wanted to utter something but it came out as a whisper. Behemoth smiled and leaned in close to try and hear better.

'Why?' Grey said. 'Why?' And then he planted *Genesis* on the face of Behemoth with a sound that resembled a clap, covering all of the meathead with its mechanical palm.

The flame that came out of the palm was like a flamethrower, it melted Behemoth's head clean off like an ice-cream left out in the heat, or a paper set alight.

Behemoth roared in agony. His face faded away and what was left of him slumped, first to his knees, and when they gave way to the weight of the man, his body collapsed backward in a heap.

At the same time, *Genesis* fell to the ground beside him with a thud, his body groaning with pain.

A few minutes later, as he still lay there in all kinds of pain and tired as hell, a shadow fell across his face.

'What happened to Bethany wasn't fair.' Gael Cross said holding some kind of robotic weaponry. 'But what's fair in this world?'

He pulled the trigger.

Chapter Forty-six: A Walking Dead

When Grey Harrow was younger, about eight-years-old, he learned how to survive on his own, how to be strong alone.

He'd lost his mother to a hit and run, and—having no father—became an orphan. He went into foster care and moved from family to family, not really forming any kind of bond with any of them. But there was one—a stoic black man named Rasheed Guthrie, a retired boxer, who with his wife (who wasn't able to conceive), took him in, and taught him most of everything he'd come to learn.

Patience. Empathy. Strong-will. Bravery. And Forgiveness.

One day he came back from school and told his foster father how there was this one kid—a hulk of a boy—in his school called Khalid that bullied him to no end. He was the tallest and biggest of their age and so no one could touch him. Grey was not his first or only victim, but Grey seemed to be the one the hulking boy enjoyed to torture the most.

Some days Grey would come home to Rasheed and his clothes would be ripped apart and he would have a bruised eye or streaks of bloodied scars across his arms and legs.

Rasheed had told him to talk with the bully to find common ground, and if he didn't listen, he would teach Grey to fight back, so Khalid would never touch him again.

When Khalid would not listen and continued his torturing of Grey, Rasheed taught Grey some of his moves and techniques he'd learned over the years during his time as a boxer so that Grey could use them to take down the oversized school bully.

Looking back at this, it wasn't really the right way to go about dealing with a bully, but it worked.

Grey fought with the bully on a raining wet day, fighting with the will of his surrogate father, using the ex-boxer's punching, parrying, and dodging techniques to tumble over the giant Khalid onto the muddy wet ground of the playground.

Everyone saw it, and as Grey went to finish off the shitfaced bully and humiliate him further, he stopped, taking in what Rasheed had taught him about mercy—even for those that do not deserve it.

Khalid never bullied him again, nor anyone else for that matter, for the remainder of their school time there. They even became friends through their teenage years, before Khalid was murdered in a gang-related squabble regarding stolen drugs and unpaid money.

Grey left Rasheed's care when he was about sixteen, able to now do as he pleased, and he fell into the wrong crowd, joining the Foxhound Syndicate.

And now, when he came to, by the window of some sort of warehouse, the sun shone into his irises, and he blinked.

Groggy, his head ached as if someone took a drill and was drilling into his brain. He felt for his arms—which were angled behind him—and he realised it was tied by chains to a metallic crossbar.

He looked down and saw that he was on his knees, and when he looked back up saw that he was surrounded by men and women with a plethora of robotic guns in their hands or in their holsters by their hips, the symbol of the Foxhound Syndicate on the shoulders of their armours.

He looked at them, trying to spot anyone he'd recognise.

A large metal-like hand flattened on the back of his head, clenched on his hair, grabbing a handful of his now fully grown afro, and tugged him back.

Lucan Weaver's upside-down face laboured over him. His topknot hairstyle still immaculately cut and styled. He grinned and then let go of Grey's hair, Grey's head lurched forward instinctively as he did, jarring his neck. He winced.

Lucan Weaver walked around him, stepping in front of the glaring sun that came in through the window, bathing Grey in his shadow.

'Gael told me what happened,' he said. 'He told me you went to his and found Behemoth there and you killed him.' Lucan Weaver spat, wiped at his mouth with the back of his metallic hand. 'And so he knocked you out and brought you here for judgement.' Lucan Weaver clapped, and Grey searched the crowd of men and women until his eyes found Gael Cross, looking all proud with himself, like he was a hero or something. Grey's eyes felt like daggers as he stared down Gael Cross.

Gael Cross looked back at him, his arms crossed. Grey couldn't believe him—after he had spared him and his daughter's life even though he'd been lying to him.

Grey's thigh still hurt, it throbbed, and there was now a bandaged on the wound where Behemoth had stabbed through.

At least the son of a bitch was honourable in treating my injury, Grey thought. *I'll remember that one when I kill him.*

Lucan Weaver said, 'Come here, Gael,' and the son of a bitch did. He stood beside Lucan, and Lucan placed a hand on his shoulders.

Grey said, 'Why have you got me tied up Lucan, I've done nothing wrong. I got the man that murdered Bethany.' He still felt groggy, but he was slowly coming back to himself.

Lucan Weaver smiled. 'Behemoth didn't kill Bethany . . . you did.'

'What?' Grey was baffled. But to a certain extent, he could understand how that was true.

Lucan Weaver let go of Gael Cross's shoulders and stood side-by-side with him, both looking over at the restrained Grey.

Lucan closed his eyes and rubbed his forehead with his fingers. 'You betrayed me, Harrow; you went against my orders and worked with those REA rats.'

Grey couldn't believe it. What was Lucan trying to say?

'I clearly remember telling you how I despise them, hate them, think they are the scum of the earth, and now you go and bring them here—to my base of operations? Now they have Intel and know where to find us. We will have to find a new base. Damn it.' He stamped with one of his boots, the ground vibrating below where Grey's knees lay. Some of the men and women of the Foxhound Syndicate around him flinched at that and murmured something between themselves that Grey couldn't hear.

'It was my plan to have Behemoth set fire to your flat—the flat *I* gave you, mind you. But instead, an innocent woman dies.' He started to pace the warehouse, but then he stopped and stood beside Gael Cross again, laying a hand on his Boy Scout's shoulders. 'I too had been looking for Behemoth . . .' Gael Cross's eyes seemed to grow larger and his body seemed to flinch. Lucan's eyes were still directed toward Grey, but his grip on Gael's shoulder was still firm. 'Even good leaders make bad choices. The best of them take responsibility for them.' Instantly, without looking, his eyes still focused on Grey, Lucan reached around with one of his mechanical hands and planted it on Gael Cross's chest. The wrist and hand area transformed itself into a cannon-shaped hole. He blasted the poor bastard with a kinetic blast so large; it ripped open his chest armour and he flew backward from the impact, crashing through the warehouse window and straight through into the deep black river that waited outside the warehouse. The river was black because it was swarming with all manner of filth and waste from all parts of London.

Gael cross *splashed*—once in it, then slowly sank into the deep black, swallowing and drinking in the filthy water into his lungs until they explode. Large bubbles lay around the area where he sank.

Grey's body tingled with electricity, felt so bad for Gael Cross, regardless of if he deserved it or not. He had daughters waiting for him to come back home. Now they would never see him again. Orphaned. Another generational curse.

None of the men and women moved, none went to fetch Gael Cross's corpse, just let him sink to the bottom of the black river. They stood and maintained their position, watching on as their leader did his thing.

Still, Lucan stared at him, unconcerned about Gael Cross. His cannon-shaped arm reforming back to its original form, his features neutral to it all: a man who felt everything he did was warranted and justified.

'I'm sorry about Bethany, I truly am—her death still haunts me.'

Grey jerked his hands wrapped in the chains behind him, it rattled. 'She was pregnant, you son-of-a-bitch.'

That finally brought a reaction from the statues that surround Lucan, his men and women drawing up their special robotic guns, pointing it toward Grey. Lucan raised a hand, prompting them to lower their weapons.

Grey caught an unpleasant whiff of something, like stale fish, or rotten cheese, but he couldn't guess where it came from. He wrinkled his nose.

Lucan said, 'That's where it hurts. So I'll give you a chance to settle the scores if you think you can take it,' his hand still in the air. 'I'll give you a one-on-one duel with me—to the death. And I'll tell you what, if you win, the entire Foxhound Syndicate is at your beck and call—all yours—to do as you please.' He lowered his hand and turned to regard his men and women. 'Did you hear that? If this man beats me in a one-on-one duel to the death—he's now your boss. Yes?' They all looked at one and other, confused, but nodded in chorus, nonetheless. Lucan turned back to face Grey, gave him sad eyes as if he really cared or something. 'Life, my good man, means competition. The best man wins.'

He couldn't be serious, could he?

'Release him,' Lucan Weaver said.

Was he just going to release him and both of them fight to the death like dogs?

The chains loosened around Grey's wrist and then unclasped. His arms slumped down beside him and he gently rubbed his wrists, soothing the area where the chains had previously been clamped tight.

Well, that answers the question. They *were* going to fight like dogs—to the death.

Lucan Weaver slowly took off his overcoat, handing it over to one of his men, his robotic limbs shiny an opaque black in the sunlight through the window.

Grey didn't think, must've been *Genesis* because he suddenly stretched forth his mechanical hand with the intention of blasting Lucan Weaver to smithereens. When he did, he heard the *click* of an empty neuron compartment, and he sighed in disbelieve.

Lucan Weaver must have heard the *click*, too, because he looked back at him, kissing his teeth. 'Do you think I would be that stupid to leave neurons in that arm of yours? Silly, boy.'

Grey stood to his feet, following Lucan Weaver's actions in removing his black t-shirt—bare-chested now—but leaving his black combat trouser on.

'This will be a good old fashion fight, man-to-man, fist-to-fist, cyborg-to-cyborg,' Lucan Weaver said as reached up a hand to his hair and removed the small band that held his topknot in place, the silky, relaxed, black hair untangling and falling down to his ears like dreads. He turned to level himself with Grey and raised his mechanical fists to his face in a boxing-like stance. 'Just so you know, I wouldn't suggest a fight if I thought you had a chance in hell. I like competing, but I don't like losing.'

'I've noticed.' Grey did the same as Lucan, getting into a boxing stance, remembering watching his ex-boxer foster father on TV as a young boy. 'But you've got neurons in your robotic arms? How's that fair?'

Lucan Weaver grinned ever so slightly; it must have been the first time Grey saw the man actually smile, sincerely, if ever, revealing a set of teeth that were not yellow but also not white—an off coloured yellow/white then. 'You never learn, do you? What is fair in this world? But if I must . . .' He reached into the compartments in both his arms and pulled out his neurons and handed it to one of his men. Grey narrowed his eyes at the man, he remembered him. It was Eustace de Maris, the man with the black and silver mechanical chest. 'Now fight me.'

Lucan Weaver didn't need to tell him twice, Grey wanted to take his head off—clean––from his shoulders for what he had set in motion that led to Bethany's death. But he didn't know what angle Lucan Weaver was playing at, where he was actually going with this, putting what he had worked so hard—and sacrificed—for most of his life, on the line. Why?

Lucan swung a fist at the left of Grey's jaw. Grey ducked at the last second, the fist barely missing. Grey swung back a fist of his own, and Lucan dodged, seemingly effortlessly. They both shuffled back, giving one and other a wide berth as they circled each other, like a predator stalking its prey.

Grey studied Lucan's movement, watching his leg movement, body tilts, and hand movements. He was looking for an opening. His breathing increased, adrenaline kicking in— fight or flight.

He pushed off the ground, sprinting toward Lucan, the fist of *Genesis* leading, but Lucan ducked and brought his left mechanical fist straight into the gut of Grey, spit flew out his mouth, sending him staggering backward until he flattened on a pile of wood and metal.

It felt as if someone had turned his stomach inside out. His breath came out of his mouth in haggard bursts, almost as if he were breathing through a straw.

Lucan was tough, no doubt. He hadn't gotten to where he was now by chance, not at all.

'Is that all, Harrow?' Lucan hollered. 'Bethany would be turning in her grave right about now.'

And that set him off. He pushed himself off the pile of wood and metal and ambled over toward Lucan.

Round 2.

The two jostled again, mechanical hands dancing back-and-forth, judging one and other's movement.

There, Grey saw an opening. His foster father had taught him how to spot an opponent's weakness by watching what part of the body he or she protects the most. For his childhood bully—Khalid—it was his jelly body, and Grey had exploited that when he took the giant child down.

For Lucan, it was his head. The man was more or less machine parts save for his neck and head.

Grey stood still and waited. Lucan came closer, planted a foot forward, and swung wildly at Grey. Grey took the full force of the punch in the forearm of *Genesis*, not feeling much pain, but a dull thump, and then instinctively returning a vicious punch of his own, straight for Lucan's head. The man staggered back, shaking his head, and panting like a wild animal.

It seemed to have riled him. He came back swinging wildly, Grey doing his best to duck and weave them. A few connected with Grey's body, but he firmed it, trying his best to not think of the throbbing pain.

Lucan continued to swing, left and right hooks—Grey remembered Rasheed telling him which was which—and Grey was on the defensive, the man screaming like a beast as he landed some of his punches on the wooden fixtures behind Grey, causing them to *crunch* all around them, like a mouth filled with biscuits.

Grey bent down, then jumped up, his right leg leading, landing a firm roundhouse kick on the small of Lucan's neck, Lucan's body twisting as he crashed to the ground with a groaning thud.

Grey, too, fell back down on his behind, his right thigh now paining him; having aggravated the injury Behemoth had dealt him with the butcher's knife. He looked down at it, touched it, blood soaking around the bandaged now.

When he looked back up, Lucan Weaver was coming at him, roaring.

Grey tried to get to his feet, but couldn't, his right thigh hurt like a motherf—

Lucan Weaver picked him up, like a rag doll—the man was beast—and threw him back onto the pile of wood and metal.

Grey crashed down, woods snapping, metals clanging.

Despite the pain, Grey managed to get back to his feet, hoping on his one good leg, before Lucan speared him with his shoulders through the warehouse walls as they landed outside, near the black river. Gael Cross, coming to his mind for a split second, before he had to roll to the side to dodge a pummel of interlocked hands from Lucan. The earth beside him dug in deep from where Lucan had smashed it.

Grey rolled and rolled and rolled away, then finally stood back up.

The black river stood behind him.

He was trapped.

He looked down at *Genesis*, saw that it was almost dislodging from it hinges by his shoulder blade. It no longer seemed to respond to his movement, the connection must have been severed. It was no longer useful, Grey thought.

Lucan Weaver walked closer.

Grey reached up with his other hand and pulled. He clenched his jaw and breathed out through gritted teeth. The mechanical arm dislodged further, and when it finally came apart, it tore a piece of flesh by his shoulder. Little sprinkles of blood fell to the earth like rain.

Genesis was no more.

Lucan watched him, confused.

Grey smiled despite the pain that was currently making him feel hot. His stomach twisted and twisted, like some kind of tangled wire.

He held the whole mechanical arm of *Genesis* in his other hand. It was surprisingly light for the amount of power it packed.

He edged toward Lucan with it in his hand—some kind of one arm soldier walking to his death, striving to make one last impact to turn the tide of war.

He swung it at Lucan's head, he dodged, but then he swung it again, judging where Lucan's next move was going and connecting with his head as he stumbled to the ground. Grey brought it down on Lucan's head again . . . and again. Lucan brought his arm up to try and protect himself. Grey continued, like a mad man, driving it down on him, loud raging roars as he did.

Shots lined the ground around him, and Grey stopped, rising and taking a step back.

Eustace de Maris stood by the warehouse, his weapon draw and pointing, his finger on the trigger, itching.

Lucan groaned, eased himself up from the ground.

Grey dropped his detached mechanical arm, it crashed with a clang unto the earth, lying there, like an arm gone rogue.

He dropped to his knees, bloodied, tired, hungry, with only one arm, and surprisingly he didn't care what would happen to him next.

Lucan signalled to Eustace de Maris for his neurons; the mechanical-chested man came and handed it over, Lucan placing them back into his arm compartments. He starred at his hands, flexing them both as if he were playing with invisible stress balls.

'Any last word, Harrow?' Lucan said stretching both his hands forward, transforming them into the cannon-shaped aesthetics, the circular holes dancing with flames. Grey stared at them, wondering if heaven was still a possibility despite all his short comings. 'Again, I'm sorry about Bethany; this was between us. I didn't want her to be involv—'

A bullet came in and penetrated the only un-machine part of Lucan—his head, cutting him off before he could finish. His brain sprayed the riverside, painted the ground, and he fell earthbound, silent and still. His eyes lay open, staring back into the soul of Grey—a soul that he probably felt was as black and evil as the river he stood in-front of.

Lucan Weaver's men and women turned to return fire, but when they heard, 'Freeze, lower your weapons, this is the REA, and you are greatly outnumbered,' they didn't.

The REA swarmed the scene; arresting the Foxhound Syndicate members and seizing the many robotic types of weaponry that were housed in this headquarter.

It seemed, to Grey, that this would be the day the Foxhound Syndicate fell and disbanded, for good.

They, he hoped, would be no more.

But how glad was he to see Jasper Barnes's arrogant mutt staring down at him now, wearing that mechanical exoskeleton suit his sister had so gracefully made for him. Looking like some kind of superhero straight out of the comics.

'Need help?' Jasper smiled—that cocky, sure of himself kind-of smile—extending a hand to Grey's now only good one, helping him to his feet.

Chapter Forty-seven: A Way Out

Jasper pushed the top button on the holo-touchpad and then placed his palm on the biometric scanner beside the vending machine.

A snickers bar—his favourite—dropped out from the bottom, and then a bottle of chilled water followed. The satisfying rumbling sound of both items dropping pleased his ears. He reached down and grabbed them, the bottle of water cold to the touch. Jasper twisted the cap, lifted it to his lips and downed the content, the water washing down his throat, refreshing him on this baking, hot summer's day in London. It was also a welcome change for him—the water. He'd cut back on his drinking habits that he had picked up from his late friend, Martin Silas, and that had drastically increased when he and Sarai had their falling out. But they were back together now . . . and expecting their second child—a baby girl—and Jasper needed all the level-headedness he could muster. He wasn't going to lose her again. After all, this was his last chance, one more stunt like the one he pulled before and he would lose Sarai and Zack forever.

Jasper put the snicker bar to his mouth as he walked, making his way to the meeting area of the Grange prison. When he pushed on the door and entered, the smell of the place hit him like a right jab to his gut. It reeked of really bad body odour and it penetrated his nostrils and seared his throat. It was almost as if the inmates weren't allowed to take a shower or perhaps scared to, Jasper thought. Maybe they figured they would get raped up the bum or something if they dropped the soap, so it was better to stink like hell than lose their bum hole to another man.

As Jasper looked around him, he saw many inmates of the Grange prison in green attire (shirt and trousers), armed police standing by, and prison guards with enormous batons at their hips, watching on with a keen eye, ready to pounce on any drama that, being a prison that housed many of the worst this society has to offer, could quite possibly occur. This particular visiting area was moderately compact though, Jasper thought, with roughly about forty chairs and twenty tables. So that's two chairs per table.

Jasper sat down on one of the chairs by a table he was led to by one of the prison guards, arms and legs crossed, and he waited.

A couple of minutes later, Jasper raised his head and saw a visibly fatigued Ezra Hawthrone—dressed in his green prison garment—bounced along into the room, tugged tightly on the only arm he now had by a muscular prisoner guard. The arm itself wasn't even his, still, it was an unremarkable prosthetic made of plastic that couldn't even hurt a fly (Only afforded to him so he could still function as a semi-normal human being). His eyes were ringed with dark hollows from lack of sleep, and his ponytailed hair had been cut off, and he looked like everyone else now, nothing special, nothing distinctive, just a pitiful handicapped man—a shadow of his former self.

The prison guard let go of him when they reached Jasper's table and walked back to the entrance of the room, posting up alongside the other guards, like mannequins, leaving Jasper and Ezra alone.

Ezra Hawthorne said nothing, just sat down and stared daggers at Jasper. Jasper could see that one side of his face was still badly burnt, not fully healed yet. Black and red and fleshly and hard, the skin looked like candle wax dried up on the edge of a candle, all bumpy and ragged.

The eye on that side of the face rolled in Jasper's direction. Jasper winced on the inside. It was a scary thing to look upon. He almost felt bad for the poor bastard, but then he thought of what he did to Martin and Alex and he fought back those feelings, suppressed them. No sympathy for him, none whatsoever.

'What do you want?' Ezra Hawthorne finally said, his voice sounding all bitter and angry. 'You disturbed my game of cards. And I was winning.'

'Really?' Jasper grinned at him.

'Yes. Do you know how hard it is to get a pack of cigarettes in here?' Jasper didn't know, but he guessed quite hard.

'Shut up and listen, Ezra.' Jasper leaned forward, interlocking his fingers on the table between them. Ezra leaned away in the opposite direction, his eyes narrowing in on Jasper. 'I didn't come here out of the good of my heart, or to be all *paly paly* with you, so you can tell me about your time here, your card games, or how hard it is to get cigarettes. I don't care. I came here for business.'

Ezra Hawthorne hissed and pushed air out of his mouth through his teeth. 'That figures. What do you want?'

'Your help.' Jasper said point-blank.

'My help? For what?' Ezra Hawthorne looked around the room, first at the prison guards by the entrance door, then at the other inmates talking with their visitors, some of them family, no doubt, while he was stuck with only Jasper Barnes, REA Agent, the man that put him in here in the first place. Jasper wondered if Ezra actually had any family.

'I can't say now,' Jasper told him.

Ezra Hawthorne crossed his one prosthetic arm out in front of him, over the table, thinking. 'In exchange for what?'

'Your freedom.'

'I'm not exactly in the right shape to help anyone,' Ezra looked down at his left arm, where there was nothing there from the top of his elbow down—just a stump.

'Don't worry; you'll get your robotic arms back.'

At that, Ezra's countenance changed and he grinned cheekily. 'Then I'm in. When do I get out and when do we start?'

Jasper checked his surrounding, reach into his jacket pocket, pulled out a brand new pack of cigarettes—about four stacked together back-to-back, and then slid it across the table, covering it with his hands, before Ezra did the same with his prosthetic hand, stuffing it into his prison underwear or whatever he wore underneath those green wreckage.

Jasper stood and nodded. 'I'll be in touch.'

***

When Grey woke up in RoyalStarCorp, he was surrounded by Clare Barnes, Herman Rowntree, and Adam Cardon. His body throbbed still from all that he'd been through at the hands of Lucan Weaver, but he felt much better than yesterday. Yesterday was the day he lost *Genesis*, his arm . . . again, while fighting with Lucan Weaver and his goons.

'How are you feeling, Grey?' Clare Barnes stared at him, biting her lower lips.

'Like I've been run over by a hover truck—the truck stopping then reversing back on me again.' He coughed.

Herman Rowntree patted his one good shoulder. 'Typical, Grey Harrow,' he said, shaking his head. 'Always finding himself in the worse of situations. Why, my friend?'

'You're lucky, Jasper Barnes brought you here, and not a second later, your vitals were critical.' Adam Cordon said as he stepped into the light, a hologram in front of him as he typed away.

Clare Barnes said, 'It's not the first time he has been in this state, Adam, he will be fine,' she waved him off.

Herman hovered around Grey like a little child as he lay still on the bench, connected to all manners of wires, but as Grey looked down, saw that he was still missing his left arm. It was like an apparition, he clenched where the arm would be and felt movement, felt pain, but it wasn't there, like a ghost, a phantom pain.

He didn't know how to feel: should he be glad that he no longer had to deal with the voice in his head or the uncontrollable advances of *Genesis*?

But before he could process the thought, Clare Bares said, 'I can make you a new arm, one without a defect, one without the Rouge Hand Syndrome, hopefully, we will do our best, Grey.'

Grey turned on the bench, looked at her. 'Thank you,' he said. 'But I think I'll go on living without one. I'm done with mechanical limbs for now.'

She nodded, and he continued to stare at her, almost unconsciously and something about her reminded him of his love, of Bethany Rose—maybe it was her milky skin, or her caring heart, or her fierce determination, or strong will to accomplish things. Whatever it was, it brought back memories and it pained him. His heart broke, again and again, ripping it into a million pieces. He missed her. Wished to smell her again, hold her in his embrace, feeling her warm, soft touch on his skin.

The four of them remained in silence for a while.

Then Herman—always Herman Rowntree, forever the class clown—broke the silence with a joke that Grey couldn't remember, but found himself laughing hard at. Weird. But the glasses-wearing short man had a way like that.

'Hey, why don't we all head out for dinner once we patch Grey up?' Herman suggested.

'Sounds like a plan,' Adam agreed. 'I'm kind of famished.'

'I'd like that.' Clare nodded.

Grey winked at him. 'Can I get a cigarette, bud?'

Herman reached into his lab coat pocket and pulled out a pack of twenty. He opened it and handed one over to Grey's good hand, then lit it for him.

'One more thing,' Herman said boldly. 'Grey, you and Clare here would make a great couple if I do say so myself. You're both single, and I'm sure Jasper would give his blessing.'

Clare seemed to blush at that as she tampered with the medical wiring attached to Grey's body, her pale cheeks going all red and rose-coloured. Just like how Bethany's used to go when she was embarrassed or uncomfortable.

Grey Harrow gently lay his head back on the bench, stuck the cigarette between his lips, closed his eyes, and smiled.

The End

Printed in Great Britain
by Amazon